Dead Mule Swamp
Druggist

an Anastasia Raven mystery
Joan H. Young

Copyright © 2014 Joan H. Young
Published by Books Leaving Footprints

ISBN: 0-9908172-5-3

ISBN-13: 978-0-9908172-5-3

DEDICATION

TO:
Nancy Lynn Miller
and the Shagway Arts Barn
for a summer of expanded possibilities

Ana's Notes

I'm loving my new life here in Dead Mule Swamp and the surrounding area. Most of the people are so good to me and kind and honest in their dealings with our neighbors. Of course, there are always a few who don't follow the rules. This case— yes, there's a reason I'm using this more official word now— seemed to wander all over the place. There were so many leads to follow without knowing where they might end. A lot of people, too many dogs, an unlabeled key, love letters... Was there one murder or four? Or none? But in the end, all those bunny trails led to... oh! Better find out for yourself.

1

Colin Mueller was dead. Isabel Adams was dead. Ham Nelson was dead. Milo Sendak was dead.

Even in a small town like Cherry Hill, in the middle of rural Forest County, people die. There were obits in the paper every week. I'd read them faithfully for over a year at my new home of choice in the Northwoods, after leaving the suburbs of Chicago and a husband who had chosen someone named Brian as his new life partner. I'd changed my surname to Raven, in hopes of remaining semi-anonymous. All water under the bridge, as they say— changes and death. But I mention these four deaths in particular.

Colin Mueller had died in his sleep in late March. He was eighty-five.

Isabel Adams was only thirty-two. She was found dead in her garden where she had been raking dry leaves from the beds in April, a victim of anaphylactic shock, stung by a bee. Her epi pen was in the house.

Hamilton Nelson was killed in August, in a car crash. He'd failed to stop at a railroad crossing, and well... he'd died instantly. Few people mourned Ham. He was fifty-six, mentally challenged, and did odd jobs on various farms. It wasn't his handicaps that put people off; it was his aversion to showers that was the real issue.

Milo Sendak took an overdose of oxycodone and went to bed. He called no one. His was not a cry for help, but apparently a well-executed suicide. The problem was he had no reason to kill himself. His first grandchild had been born on September twelfth, and his daughter and son-in-law were bringing the baby to meet her grandpa. They had found him cold and still.

The cause of Milo's death was not obvious. He'd had back

trouble for years, but apart from that he was a healthy, energetic fifty-five-year-old tennis-playing businessman. An autopsy revealed the overdose of painkiller.

However, an enigma presented itself since he'd just refilled his prescription the day before, and only one pill was missing from the new bottle. How had one pill flooded his system with the drug? Had he been hoarding capsules?

When officials checked Cherry Hill Pharmacy's records for Milo's oxycodone purchases, they discovered that Colin Mueller, Isabel Adams, and Ham Nelson had also filled prescriptions for the same potent drug just days before their deaths.

The druggist, Charlie Dixon, was sweating bullets.

2

Charlie sat in a hard straight chair by the front window of the unimaginatively named Cherry Hill Pharmacy, a beam of September sun piercing the window and spotlighting his bald head. Emotionally, he probably was sweating bullets, but beads of real perspiration rolled off his pate and dripped from his ears, nose, and the fringes of hair at the back of his head. The shoulders of his blue pharmacist's jacket were actually dappled with wet spots.

I know this, because I was there when our young Police Chief, Tracy Jarvi, came to the store with Officer Kyle Appledorn to question Charlie. I happened to be purchasing toiletries, which I usually put off even longer than buying groceries. My over-the-arm red shopping basket was filled with toothpaste, deodorant, shampoo, band-aids, burn cream, and other sundries. The hard plastic handle dug into my flesh as the weight increased with each addition. But there was no way I was leaving until I saw how this turned out. I pulled some paper napkins, orange with white ghosts, from the shelf nearest me.

I worked my way slowly along the few aisles, keeping my ears open and peeking at Charlie as I reached the end of each row. I'm not a gossip hound like my friend Adele Volger, but there was no use passing up a real opportunity to get local news firsthand.

Charlie shifted his padded, past-middle-aged frame on the narrow chair and asked if he could get a towel from the restroom. Tracy raised her head. She was studying computer records behind the counter but now looked at Kyle and jerked her head in the direction of the rear of the store. The slim officer stopped watching Charlie but gave him a sideways glance as he walked away as if afraid the man might bolt. He returned a moment later with a small terrycloth rectangle.

The nervous owner of the drugstore wiped his forehead. Suddenly a panic attack took him, and he gulped deep mouthfuls of air, unable to catch his breath. He began to hiccup and then to sob.

"I don't know what you are looking for," he objected. "My records are in order. I'm very careful. I had nothing to do with those unfortunate deaths. My God! I would be out of business in a heartbeat if I weren't meticulous."

Perhaps realizing he might soon be out of business anyway when news of this catastrophe got out, Charlie broke off and shut his mouth with a snap, giving his shining head another swipe with the towel.

Tracy came and put her hand on the man's shoulder. "Charlie, calm down. No one is accusing you of killing Milo. But you need to tell us what you know about his prescription. The others too, if you can remember."

"OK. Yes. Milo has some back issues. He's got a bad disk, but he likes to play tennis, so his doctor prescribes him the pain meds because he won't quit the game. He's been taking them for, oh, maybe five years. Never abuses them, just fills the scrip every so often."

"Why did he get his medication here? He lives in Emily City. That seems odd," Tracy noted.

"How should I know? We're small. Maybe he appreciates the service. I've known him all my life. I'm not going to tell a customer to shop closer to home if he wants to give me his money," Charlie said.

"Was there anything unusual about the last time he picked up pills?"

"Nothing at all. He came in on Saturday morning. He was talking about his daughter coming for the week and bringing the new baby. Said they would get here Sunday afternoon."

"That agrees with the records. The Saturday morning part," Kyle called from behind the counter, where he'd begun studying the digital data.

"All right, Charlie," Tracy continued in a soothing tone, "what can you recall about the other prescriptions?"

Charlie put his head in his hands and waggled it from side to side. "I don't know. I don't know. I'll have to get into the computer." He looked up and cocked his head toward Kyle. "We fill hundreds of prescriptions here. You can't expect me to remember every transaction. I probably can't even guess the right months without looking."

"You should be able to do that much, Charlie. They all died the same month they filled their prescriptions."

Charlie gulped again and wrung his hands. That's when he caught sight of me. "What's she doing here?" he demanded.

Tracy turned and saw me. A look of annoyance crossed her face. "Ana. I didn't realize anyone was in the store."

"Just doing some shopping," I explained, trying not to sound sheepish.

"Well, you'll have to finish another time," Tracy said, lifting the basket from my arm and placing it on the floor. "Off you go."

She escorted me to the front door and nearly pushed me out. As I turned toward the sidewalk I saw the card in the window flip to "CLOSED."

3

"Druggist Questioned in Four Deaths." The headline of Wednesday's Cherry Hill Herald screamed the biggest news to hit our small town in months.

One of my best friends, Adele Volger, and I sat on the couch in her cozy front room with the weekly paper spread out on the coffee table. Adele will always tell you she doesn't poke her nose where it doesn't belong, but what you might not understand is that she hasn't really found any place that doesn't fit the criteria for belonging. Occasionally, if she is miffed at someone, she'll refuse to tell you what she knows. But she knows.

Charlie the druggist's picture was the largest, but small headshots of Milo, Ham, Isabel and Colin were featured as well.

"Charlie's owned that drugstore for over thirty years," Adele said. "Thirty-three, if I'm remembering my dates correctly. No one else has the fortitude to keep a store like that going in such a small town."

"It seems unusual to me," I admitted. "It's nice to be able to get toothpaste, and ointment and stuff, without driving all the way to Emily City, but I can't imagine how he does enough business to stay open."

"He can afford to get by without a large profit because his wife was heir to Thorpe Metalworks."

"The company that made cow stanchions? There was real money in that?" I had learned about this long-defunct local company from my other good friend, Cora Baker Caulfield, the local historian.

"Oh, for sure," Adele said. "They made all sorts of metal farm equipment for decades. Faye is the only descendant of Granville Anderson. He ran the company. Granville had enough sense to quit before the demand for his products petered out."

"Faye? That's Charlie's wife?" I asked. Everyone knew Charlie, but I couldn't recall ever meeting Faye.

"Yes. She's Shashawqua Township Treasurer, too. That doesn't pay enough to live on, but added to the inheritance and the drugstore receipts, she and Charlie do all right. No kids to support."

"They never had any?"

"Nope. Charlie was adopted, and he told everyone he was afraid to pass on some awful syndrome. Maybe his genetics carried some unknown problem. Let me get us some fresh tea," Adele added, pushing her ample bulk up from the mossy green vintage cushions. A light groan escaped her lips with the effort. She collected our cups and headed toward the back of the house.

I stayed where I was and studied the pictures in the paper. Charlie and Colin were both bald old men. Colin was older, of course, and I had never met him. Ham was gaunt and thin and wore a sort of lost expression. It was a good picture, though. I'd seen him a few times when he was alive, and I knew he probably had mild cerebral palsy in addition to his mental difficulties. Seen in person, his body had been obviously asymmetrical. I had also met Isabel Adams before she died. She was an artsy-craftsy person known for her showcase flowerbeds and hand-dyed yarns. I'd gone on the county garden tour both summers I'd lived here. Hers was included the previous year. Of course, she was dead before the current tour. Milo, the most recent to die, was pictured in a formal business portrait. Suit coat, tie, neatly-combed shortish hair, pasted-on smile. Very much the professional. I hadn't known or even heard of him.

"Adele! Where did Milo Sendak work?" I called.

"He's a CPA with Accounting Plus," she yelled back from the kitchen. "Well, he was. They're over in Emily City." She came through the doorway carrying fresh cups of tea and a plate of homemade gingersnaps. "A dull job to my way of thinking, but I'm glad some people can do it."

"That kind of work might be stressful. Maybe he really did have some reason to kill himself, something we don't know about," I suggested.

"Here, have a cookie." Adele set the plate in front of me, and the spicy, sugary aroma grabbed my immediate attention.

Adele clicked the television on to catch the closest thing we had to local news. The nearest station was located about seventy miles away. Only really big stories from Forest County ever made it to the broadcast. In my continuing effort to preserve a low-tech lifestyle, I still didn't own a TV but visited friends often enough to be aware of what channels were available.

"I try to catch the evening news," Adele said, settling down beside me again.

The anchorwoman spoke in serious tones. "Our lead story tonight once again focuses on the events unfolding in the village of Cherry Hill, seat of Forest County. Bringing you the latest updates, we go now to M. Jack Smith, on location. M. Jack?"

On screen, the formidable gray stone walls of our Courthouse filled the background, while a young man in khakis and a blue shirt smiled with the delight of a news-hound snapping up a juicy tidbit.

He began, "Today, Forest County Prosecutor, F. B. Thomas, has ordered exhumation of the bodies of three additional local citizens known to have died within days of filling a prescription for the powerful painkiller, oxycodone. The most recent death in what may be a related series was that of Milo Sendak, which occurred on Friday."

"That only makes sense," Adele snorted. "They call this news?"

"...the pharmacist who filled the prescriptions is currently not being charged with any crime, pending further investigation. The three doctors who wrote the prescriptions are also being questioned in the case. Their names..."

"Do they really think we've got a serial poisoner on the loose?" I asked of no one in particular. "That would be pretty ridiculous."

M. Jack pointed at an upper window, and the camera panned to take in the blank pane. "F.B. Thomas speculated earlier today, in his office, that although unlikely, the possibility of a serial killer operating in this rural county is very real, but no motive has yet been suggested. Nothing specific apparently links any of the four victims."

The reporter recounted information we already knew, and Adele turned the volume lower, although she clearly didn't want to miss any other segments that might be of interest before the national news began.

"Well, I can certainly think of some links between the victims," Adele said with more force than I thought the situation warranted.

"Really?"

"Of course. There are always connections. The question is whether they mean anything. Isabel and Colin went to the same doctor, Don Smith..."

I interrupted. "Smith? Wasn't that the name of the boy who was just on the TV?"

"It's a very common name, of course. Dr. Smith is an allergy specialist. I really don't know all the Emily City doctors, but my grandson has some issues with certain kinds of mold, so Marissa has taken him to Dr. Smith several times. You met my daughter—last summer at the parade."

"Yes, I remember," I commented, but Adele forged ahead as if I'd not spoken.

"Ham did odd jobs for Colin Mueller. Well, he did odd jobs for a lot of people, but it is a connection. Milo's daughter and Isabel were about the same age. They might have been in the same class. Certainly they knew each other. Milo's firm audits the books for most of this county's governmental units."

I perked up. "That's interesting."

"It is," Adele agreed, "but it's more a connection to Charlie than between the victims."

"In an area like this, those famous six degrees of separation are probably more like only two or three," I mused.

"Certainly," Adele continued. She took another cookie and sipped some tea. She grimaced. "Cold. Oh well, it's not worth the time to make more. Let's see. Isabel occasionally brought Ham to town for Mass, and I think I recall that he sometimes gathered vines for her basket making. Milo and Colin were both Lutherans. Charlie and Faye come to our church."

She was referring to Crossroads Fellowship. I'd renewed my

faith since my divorce, and I enjoyed participating in the relaxed worship style and practical service projects of the Fellowship. But since I didn't know Faye, and didn't recall seeing Charlie at services either, I wondered how active they were.

"Maybe Milo did some tax preparation work on the side," I said. "Someone whose job involved tracking money seems much more likely to be the common thread than an artist or a person who did odd jobs. What did Colin do?"

"He'd been retired for many years. Before that he sold cars. 'A cherry of a deal in Cherry Hill.' That was the slogan he used. He probably sold cars to all the people involved, or at least their relatives. The dealership was on the west side of town, just a couple of blocks past the drugstore. Now it's been turned into a mini-mall. Well, that's another connection. There's the Curly-Q beauty salon, an insurance office, and some other small shops. One of them sold Isabel's crafts—her hand-dyed yarns, baskets, and other things."

"Just her items?"

"Oh, no. That would hardly generate enough business in this area. Mostly they have rather commonplace craft items on consignment, and used clothing. I think Isabel made most of her sales in larger cities, but she kept some things here to encourage local people to consider beautiful handicrafts."

"Where did Ham live?" I asked.

Adele angled her head to the side. "Isn't that odd?" she asked in return. "I don't know. He was a rather secretive man."

I picked up another cookie and stood up, stretching my back. "Maybe there are too many connections."

Adele countered, "Maybe that's what a killer is counting on."

4

Aside from the gray stone courthouse that had been featured on the news, the next most imposing building in Cherry Hill was the old red brick school. It had been revitalized as the Forest County Museum and temporary home of Fanning Fitness. The museum stood alone, on the north side of town, backed up to the Petite Sauble River. With a vacant lot across Liberty Street, anyone who drove north on Peach had a full frontal view of the magnificent two-story building with a pair of diamond-paned dormer windows projecting from the front roof. Ten wide concrete steps, flanked with brick railings, led to the door. Vertical banners hung on each side of the door, bearing the names of the two occupying entities.

The terms of Mavis Fanning's lease were ending in a couple of months. At that time, my friend Cora would gain complete control of the facility. Ten months earlier, she had remarried Jerry Caulfield after he presented her with the building as a gift, and Mavis had been granted use of the gymnasium and office space in return for a confession of minor wrongdoing.

It was Friday, and I wanted to pick Cora's brain about the situation involving Charlie. Adele's forte was gossip, but Cora usually had historical documentation to back up assertions she made. If there were meaningful connections between any of the dead people, she could dig them up. Since the opening of the museum, Cora had been trying to keep somewhat regular hours. She was almost always there, meeting with the public from Wednesday through Saturday. On Tuesdays, I helped her with the immense database project she had undertaken. She'd begun working toward that goal back when the extensive collection of local artifacts was housed in her private pole barn on Brown Trout Lane.

I climbed the steps and entered the foyer, which had a mosaic tile cherry bomb set into the floor. "The Cherry Hill Bombers" had been the school nickname. The former school office was directly to my right, and this was now the museum's primary interface with the public, where tickets were sold through a sliding glass window. Cora was not in that room but a high school student was. Forest County Central had organized a work-study program for juniors and seniors to help at the museum for a few hours every week almost as soon as the building opened to the public. The kids loved being released from school, and Cora got much-needed help, excellent for the most part. This freed up her time to work on the exhibits and organization.

"Can I help you?" the teen girl asked. I didn't know her; I'd rarely been in the museum on a Friday.

"Is Cora here? I'm her friend and data entry person, Ana Raven," I answered in what I hoped was a breezy but authoritative tone. I didn't want to be forestalled by some schoolgirl who thought she was in charge.

The teen matched my tone and fired back with assurance, "Sure. She's in the records office. I guess you know where that is."

"I do," I said with a smile, and took a right turn, and then another into the first room beyond the office. The former classroom had been adapted to its new purpose. Shelves lined the walls and the central area contained two rows of white tables where acquisitions could be spread out and studied. The remaining space was filled with Cora's computer and peripherals, which had also been brought in from the Brown Trout Lane location.

"Oh, hello, Ana," Cora said, looking up from a pile of short fat twigs with tags tied to them. I wondered what kind of special meaning those could possibly have.

"Hello, yourself," I answered. "Why are you sorting baby logs?"

"These were brought in by Milo Sendak's son, Roy. It was a Scout project of his dad's from long ago, and he found it in the garage while they were sorting things after the funeral."

"OK," I said, drawing the sound out. "But why is the museum interested?"

"It's quite wonderful! These sections of wood just need remounting on a display board. They're still all labeled, so it will be easy. I might have a state forester check them, but it's a good addition to our Natural History section."

"I still don't understand what it is." I was feeling stupid.

"These are samples of the native trees of the county from about forty-five years ago."

"Won't they be the same trees that are here now?" I asked.

"Probably, but it's beautifully done. You can look at the grain patterns and the bark. Somehow the squirrels and other vermin didn't get into this and ruin it. There's even a typed page of information about where each sample was collected." Cora was in her usual exuberant condition when she had a new find in hand.

I didn't understand why this was exciting. "Why does it matter?"

"I'm sure the forester will be delighted to explore the locations to see if those tree species still grow there. And look! Here's an attached list of the largest trees in the county. I know he'll be interested in that. There are societies that track big trees," Cora said.

I shook my head. This is why Cora is the county historian, and I'm not. Although twenty years my senior and very slight of build, Cora is a bundle of energy attached to a very sharp mind.

"This is Friday, not Tuesday," Cora pointed out.

"I know. I have questions."

"Let me guess. You want to know more about Charlie Dixon." Cora looked up at me sideways, and a grin spread across her face.

"You figured out I'd come by, didn't you?" I accused, but with a light laugh.

"It wasn't difficult," she retorted.

I felt a need to justify my plan. "The last time we had a mystery I tried very hard to stay out of things except to poke around a little to satisfy my own curiosity, but everyone thought

I was involved in the whole process of catching the killer. This time, I might as well admit I want to find out as much as I can."

"You're going to try to figure out if those four deaths are suspicious? The police don't even know that yet."

"That's exactly why I think I can make a difference," I said. "Until those bodies are exhumed and autopsied, nobody official can do anything. But I can start finding out about connections between any of the four victims."

Cora shrugged. "This is a small town. There are lots of connections."

"Yes, I've already heard quite a few from Adele."

"I'll bet I know some she doesn't," the small woman boasted with a sly look, rising to the challenge.

I grinned back at her. "I bet you do, too. Can we talk about it?"

Cora laid the diminutive logs aside and headed for a hot water pot she kept on a small table near her desk. "Let's have tea."

If there's one thing I've learned since moving to Cherry Hill, it's that information in small towns always comes with cups of warm beverages and a secretive tête-à-tête.

"There's one fact I'm pretty sure Adele doesn't know, just because she doesn't have access to as many old documents as I do," Cora began, dipping a bag of raspberry tea in her cup of hot water. "You want plain tea, right?"

"Please. I don't like those herbal things much," I said. I took the cup she handed me and sat in the extra office chair.

"I'm not sure what Adele told you already, but the closest connections are probably with Isabel Adams and Milo's family."

"Adele said Milo's daughter was about the same age as Isabel."

"Yes, they were in the same class. The Sendak girl's name is Wanda, but Isabel was sweet on Roy for a long time."

"Roy? The man who brought you the wood collection?" I asked.

"The very same. Roy's just a year older, and the three kids were real pals through junior high and a bit later. I pulled out a Thorpe yearbook because I was curious, myself."

"But I thought the consolidated school was built in 1972. That would be way before these kids were in high school. Isabel was, what, thirty-two? That means she graduated only about fifteen, maybe fourteen years ago."

Cora smiled her historian's smile, signaling she was ready to bring me up to date on more local facts. "You've figured that out very well, but Thorpe was always a very tight community. They held out with their own school system until the bills just couldn't be paid any longer. Their final two years they even held community yard sales to keep the building open."

"Towns can do that?" I asked.

"Sure. But the number of students simply was too low to bring in enough money from the state. Thorpe gave up and started bussing seventh grade on up to the consolidated school in 2002. They still have their elementary."

"I think I knew that. Anyway. So, you have pictures of Isabel, Roy, and Wanda in one book?"

"Right here," Cora said, thrusting a padded tan volume into my hands. Scraps of paper stuck out from the top edge. "You look at those bookmarked pages while I get something else."

She jumped up and scurried to the far wall to pull another yearbook from a shelf stacked with books. "Cora, you've been expecting me. You had this information all ready to share."

"That's true enough. I was curious, too." She handed me another Thorpe yearbook, this one from 1975. "Look at the senior pictures."

"Wait. I already know that Charlie Dixon's wife was from Thorpe. Is she in here?"

"She is. The seniors," Cora said, stabbing her index finger at the book.

I spread the covers and began turning pages, slightly wrinkled with age. The distinctive odor of yearbook paper and ink permeated the air around me. There were twenty-three seniors, arranged alphabetically, with Faye Anderson on the first row. "Charlie's future wife," I said.

"Right. Keep going."

I scanned the pictures of fresh young faces, not sure exactly what I was looking for. I turned the page and found Milo Sendak, dark, handsome, and looking very Slavic. "Well?"

"You missed it. Try again." Cora looked smug.

I went back to the beginning. There, directly below Faye Anderson, was Charles Dixon, with the slim face of youth and a full head of wavy hair. "All in the same class. All from one very small town."

Cora summed it up. "It's certainly an interesting connection, don't you think?"

5

"Well, yes it is. But so what?" I protested. "Lots of people marry locally. We knew Faye was from Thorpe, so it's not a big surprise that Charlie is."

"Maybe the relationship that's important isn't Isabel and Roy or Isabel and Wanda, but Milo and Faye instead," Cora mused. "Faye was from the family in their town with money. Milo went into a profession that deals with tracking money. Maybe he wanted her, but Charlie got her."

"Cora, this is ridiculous. Even if it were true, what would be the motive for Charlie to kill Milo almost forty years later?" I picked up my cup and sipped the cooling tea.

Cora wiggled her eyebrows and looked coy.

I smacked the cup back down on the table. "Are you telling me Faye and Milo were having an affair?"

"Oh, no. I have no such knowledge." Cora was backpedalling hard. "But such things do happen."

"Adele said that Charlie and Faye attend Crossroads Fellowship, and Milo was Lutheran. Good church folks don't do that!" I blurted. But I immediately realized my argument was hollow. People's emotions run amok and get them into trouble all the time, no matter whether they attend church or not. Was it possible there was a hidden love triangle here? A new one, or an old one?

Cora gazed at the floor and softly said, "Well, ideally..."

"OK, I get you," I responded. "I guess I don't want to believe that sort of thing happens here. Small town life has been so good to me... mostly nice people and wholesome values."

My friend's voice hardened. "Have you forgotten the three murders you've helped solve? What about the way that horrible man Bert Fowler treated our dear little Jimmie? People are just as flawed here as they are in the big city."

She was right, but it didn't make me feel better. "One of those deaths occurred years before I moved here, and one was a man we didn't even know. Let's talk about something else. How is Jimmie? Have you seen him lately?"

Cora was always happy to talk about Jimmie Mosher. She'd unofficially adopted the boy as a grandson, mostly because she'd nearly married his grandfather, for whom the boy was named.

"He turned fourteen this summer," Cora said with pride, as if she'd been personally responsible for the change in his age. "Of course, he's tickled pink that he can qualify for a work permit now. He's determined to learn the restaurant business inside and out."

I had a brief mental picture of Jimmie turning pink and giggling uncontrollably, but Cora didn't even notice how odd the old-fashioned expression sounded.

She went on. "He's growing like a weed. The last time I saw him he had shot up so fast his pants were way too short. I think he's taller than you are."

I'm only five-foot-five, so this didn't make Jimmie huge yet, but he'd only come up to my eye level the last time I'd seen him. This did sound like quite a change.

"He's trying to get Jack Panther to hire him at the Pine Tree Diner, but I'm not sure Jack wants to train the future competition."

"Jimmie's still got his heart set on re-opening The Cherry Blossom?" I asked. The Cherry Blossom restaurant had been owned by Jimmie's father before he was killed in a car accident when Jimmie was a baby.

"That boy is single minded. He's already been poking around the property, whether he should be or not. He brought me some old papers he found under a big piece of that green corrugated roofing behind the building."

"Oh? Anything interesting?"

"Not really." Cora sighed. "I'd hoped for some juicy letters or something, but it was just a bunch of placemats and ad flyers. I kept a few that weren't too badly damaged for the files. Let's get back to Milo Sendak."

"All right. Speaking of juicy letters, I don't suppose you've got any from Milo to Faye or vice-versa."

"No, I don't. But maybe you should go talk to Wanda and Roy."

I wandered over to the hot water pot. "Do you want some more tea?"

She answered in the affirmative, and I refilled our cups and got out fresh tea bags. Cora left the room, saying she was going to look for a better box to store the wood samples. I sat at the computer and idly fingered the keyboard while my tea steeped.

At the moment I couldn't think of any questions I could ask Milo's grown children that wouldn't make me look like a worse nosy parker than Adele. My resolve to become an amateur sleuth was proving weaker than I'd thought. I had no valid reasons to be poking around in other people's business except to satisfy my own curiosity.

Maybe I should just butt out and leave the investigating to the experts. But, then again, I'd really been helpful with solving several other crimes and had discovered things no one else had thought of tracking down.

Of course, I'd done it with Cora's excellent help. She was the one with all kinds of information about people's roots. The sort of stuff residents of small towns never forget. The sorts of things that lead to decades-long resentment and desires for revenge.

She would always help me find things behind the scenes, but I knew she probably wouldn't go for any active snooping. She didn't like spending much time with anything or anyone outside of her museum.

I sipped my tea and pondered what I really wanted to do about this set of questionable deaths. Should I forget them or figure out some way to get involved?

Cora returned, carrying a solid carton with flaps that weren't broken and floppy. She placed it on the work table and reached for her cup, dipped the tea bag a few times, then pulled it out and squeezed it against a spoon.

"What have you decided, Ana?" she asked.

"About what?"

"Whatever you're contemplating so deeply."

"I don't know," I admitted. "I don't know."

6

I stopped for a quick lunch—my favorite tuna melt—at the remodeled Pine Tree Diner. Jack Panther, the owner, had fixed up the formerly fly-specked and greasy diner and re-opened almost a year ago. He still served the same good, home-style food, but the cleaner atmosphere attracted more local patrons. Although he'd always had a regular breakfast crowd and some mid-day stragglers, many people who worked in town now stopped there for lunch.

The empty building connected to the diner had gone up for sale, and Jack had purchased it, opening a second seating area which had tables instead of booths. There still wasn't anything you'd actually call decor, but the small restaurant was much more inviting than previously.

I arrived back at my own home, on East South River Road, in the early afternoon. Renovations to the old farmhouse had been required, and I had worked hard at the project ever since moving to the area a year and a half ago. The house was a basic Midwest farmstead style with one wing at right angles to another. The biggest change I'd made was to add a second floor to the wing that faced the road, making the whole house two stories, and I also added a screen porch above the concrete terrace in front. I had frequented that space this summer, enjoying the breeze and looking out over Dead Mule Swamp, the wooded floodplain of the Petite Sauble River.

Probably should tackle the kitchen next, I thought as I pulled in past the lovely maple that shaded my mailbox. It was starting to turn gold, teasing hints of a beautiful autumn just beginning in the north country.

I parked my Jeep Cherokee in the wide space beside the house that served as driveway although it wasn't graveled. Several cars could park there comfortably. Of course, I had to admit the only times that had happened were when the local and county police had searched my property and the neighboring Thousand Lakes State Forest. Maybe I should throw a party.

My thoughts drifted off along those lines as I entered the house by the kitchen door. The kitchen was, indeed, now out of context with the rest of the interior. In fact, it was downright shabby. The wallpaper was at least fifty years old, with twining ivy crawling over a yellowing background. The flooring was cracked and curling in spots. It probably wasn't quite old enough to be true linoleum, but it was certainly an early vinyl product. In a dark brick pattern, no less. I'd purchased secondhand appliances when I moved here. They served the purpose, but I wasn't going to win any House Beautiful awards. Maybe I'd qualify for one of those free kitchen re-dos.

Not that I needed the financial help. My ex, Roger, had bought his freedom at a great price. At age forty-five I had all the money I really needed. I simply hadn't had time to get to the kitchen yet, and I enjoyed making changes slowly since I was doing a lot of the work myself.

As I walked in the door and tossed my keys in a basket on the counter I realized that, once again, I'd come home to a nearly empty refrigerator. It wouldn't have been difficult to bring home groceries. My friend Adele is also the owner of Volger's Grocery, a thriving enterprise, just a few doors down the street from the Pine Tree Diner. But, had I thought to stop and shop? Of course not. And now I faced the prospect of a rather eclectic dinner, as was way too often the case.

I resolved to look up recipes, buy a freezer, and make giant batches of main dishes to divide up and freeze in individual portions. After all, it was fall. This was the time of year when our energies are supposed to turn to gathering and preserving food for the winter months. Then I thought about all that chopping and washing and composting and buying containers whose lids I would immediately lose, and I sighed. There was peanut butter in the cupboard, and I'd enjoyed a good lunch at the Pine Tree. Maybe I'd leave the autumnal food hoarding to the squirrels.

I ran upstairs to freshen up. My bedroom and the bath made up the second floor of the old house. The new upper story was a large open workroom where I could spread out projects, or exercise, or do nothing at all if that's what I wanted to do. I was enjoying my single life more than I ever thought I would.

Glancing out a front window, I saw a strange car in the yard. A moment later, someone knocked on the front door.

It took me a minute to get downstairs, and the person outside must have been impatient. Another knock urged me to hurry.

"Coming!" I called

When I opened the door, a tall dark man with a beetle brow and a shorter, blocky woman with too-tight clothes, perhaps on her way to becoming fat, stood there.

"May I help you?" I asked. Unknown visitors were pretty unusual at my out-of-the-way home, the last house on the unpaved road.

"I hope so," said the man. "I am Roy Sendak, and this is my sister Wanda Sendak Reese. May we come in?"

7

"Sure," I said, stepping back and motioning them toward the pale blue and gold pinstriped couch and a matching wing chair. Roy took the chair, Wanda eased her spreading bulk onto the couch, and I sat in an antique straight chair that had taken my fancy this summer at an estate sale.

"You probably are wondering why we are here," Roy began.

I nodded. That seemed like an unnecessary observation.

Roy cleared his throat. Wanda squirmed and twirled a strand of her straight brown hair, but neither one launched into any sort of explanation.

"I'm assuming this is about your father's death," I stated. Maybe that would help them get started.

"Yes. Yes it is," said Roy. He cleared his throat again, but still didn't offer anything more.

We sat there silently while the seconds passed, and I became increasingly uncomfortable.

"Pardon my manners," I exclaimed at last. "Would you like some coffee or tea? I think I might have some soda and a couple of beers, too."

"A cup of tea would be nice," Wanda said.

"Yes, I would like that very much," Roy added.

I went to the kitchen, leaving them to their silence. As soon as I began moving things around, filling the tea kettle and placing mugs and spoons on a tray, I heard the buzzing of their voices. However, I couldn't make out any words. Apparently, they had something to say but couldn't figure out how to begin. I wasn't sure how to help them any more than I already had. The murmurs from the living room continued, and when the water boiled I filled a pot, draped several teabags over the side, and snuggled it into a crocheted blue tea cozy Adele had made for me.

All in all, Roy and Wanda had been given about ten minutes to get their story straight. I hoped they'd let me in on it, since I had to assume they'd come with some sort of idea of including me.

I returned to the living room with the tray and placed it on the sturdy coffee table. Over the past year I'd gone to a number of antique shops and estate sales and now owned an eclectic assortment of furniture that pleased me. The room was no longer nearly bare, the way it had been for months.

"There's sugar in the bowl, and the packets are stevia. I only have milk, no cream, so I hope that will do. I don't have any cookies or other treats," I apologized. "The tea's steeping. You might want to give it a couple of minutes."

"This is fine," Roy said. "Very nice of you with no notice at all. The truth is, we aren't sure quite how to begin."

I tried to be encouraging. "Since you've indicated you'd like to tell me something about your father, maybe you can just fill me in on some of his personal history. I already know he graduated from Thorpe High School with Charlie and Faye Dixon. But that's about all I know."

Wanda spoke up for the first time. Her sentences came out in staccato bursts. "Dad wouldn't have killed himself. He was somewhat unhappy. Mother left. They'd been separated since June. But she was at their house that weekend because I was home. Roy isn't married. I married late. And Dad was going to meet his only grandchild. A girl. She's mine. Mother's watching her today. She's just a baby. Carolyn, not Mother." She stopped as abruptly as she'd begun and turned sad eyes toward Roy.

Roy seemed to realize the ball was in his court. Nevertheless, he took his time working his way toward any sort of comment, let alone the point. He leaned forward and poured tea for his sister and then a cup for himself. He deliberately added two spoons of sugar, then milk, and stirred it slowly. Wanda appeared to be all done talking. She pulled a wrinkled tissue from a pocket and wiped her eyes occasionally while she sipped her tea.

"My sister is right," Roy finally said. "We just don't believe our father would have taken his own life. My reasons for believing so are less emotional, but Dad was solid. He was a completely logical person...all wrapped up in accounting. That was his line of business. Did you know that?"

I nodded in the affirmative.

"It's most of the reason our mother moved out. He was so un-emotional, she just couldn't take it any longer. But he was as excited as I'd ever seen him because of Carolyn, Wanda's baby. He'd been a bit down about not having any continuing blood line, so meeting the fulfillment of his hopes was something he wouldn't have missed. On purpose."

"Could you give me some background?" I asked. "Sendak is an unusual name. I don't personally know any other Sendak families."

"It is a Polish name. Dad's grandparents sent their son, his father, to the United States as a child when World War II was raging. He grew up working hard and not giving in to any of life's difficulties. He taught Milo, our father, to do the same."

"So your father was not outwardly emotional," I echoed. "Perhaps he kept all his feelings inside, and they finally overwhelmed him."

"No, no, no." Roy said, shaking his head and placing his mug back on the tray with an unsteady hand. "I'm telling you, my father did not do this."

"Well, that could be true," I admitted. "Actually, I don't know enough about the situation to have any particular opinion. Of course the police are wondering if it's connected to those other three deaths."

"We think it must be," Wanda blurted. "Please help us find out."

Roy ducked his head and turned brick red. "Wanda, more slowly, please. You are rushing things." His speech was deliberate, as if English was his second language. I was curious about this, since he'd just explained the family had been here for three generations.

"I have to admit I was wondering why you came to see me. How do you think I can help," I prodded.

Roy apparently regained his composure. In a strong voice he

said, "We've heard that you are a very successful amateur detective. We'd like you to look into this. Try to find out who poisoned our father."

Secretly, I was thrilled to be given a reason to poke around, but there were difficulties. "I'm not a licensed detective," I protested. "I don't work for any law enforcement agency, and I have no authority to ask anyone questions or demand any kind of information. My sleuthing might irritate the police. At the very least, I'd need to turn anything I find over to them."

"That's just what we want you to do. We will pay you for your time," Roy said.

"I don't know if that's even legal," I responded.

"Please help us," Wanda whined, and she began shredding her tissue into the empty tea mug. "The police won't do anything until they've dug up all the bodies of those other people, run all kinds of tests. That's going to take weeks. By then, whoever did this could be far away."

"Or covered his tracks really well," Roy added.

"His tracks?" I asked. "Do you think a man did this? Do you have someone you suspect?"

"There is the druggist," Roy said quietly. "He had means and opportunity in all four cases."

"Yes, but where's the motive?" I questioned. "People don't kill other people just because they can."

Roy looked at me without blinking.

"Not usually," I added as an afterthought.

Wanda and Roy glanced at each other. What secret communication passed between them?

"Look," I said, "if I say yes, I'll have to ask really hard questions. Of you, even. Like... were your father and Faye Dixon having an affair? Or your mother and Charlie? That would give Charlie motive at least in the one case."

Wanda sank deeper into the couch. She looked like a deflating balloon.

"I have told you this could be a bad idea," Roy shot in her direction.

8

"I, we... don't believe our mother was involved with Mr. Dixon," Roy said. "But it's possible she may have been seeing someone."

"We don't know who," Wanda blurted.

"If anyone. Not with certainty," Roy added.

"Do you suspect someone in particular?" I asked.

Roy and Wanda shared another look, but he replied, "No, that's not what I meant. We don't know for sure that there was someone else. She was, well... gone sometimes... for longer than seemed necessary. Before she left. Actually, you need to ask Wanda about that. I've been away."

"Oh?"

"I traveled to Poland, to Gdansk specifically, during my college years. I've hardly spoken English in ten years. Discovered our family roots, became enamored of the Baltic coast, and have lived my entire adult life there. I teach the chemistry of construction materials at the University of Technology. Concrete, you know, or steel processes."

Roy was as focused on the non-emotional side of life as his father, but I only said, "That sounds very interesting."

He pushed his dark hair away from his jutting forehead. "It's quite boring really. I should come home, I suppose. But the job is good. I like the area. There is someone..."

Wanda smiled for the first time. "At long last, my brother may have found love," she said quietly.

I smiled back. "That must be wonderful."

Roy turned dark red again. "Elka is patient, but I must return to Poland soon if I am to keep her. That is why we need you to help us answer the questions about our father's death. We need this to happen quickly."

I sighed and leaned back in my chair. "Well, that's something I'll need to think about. Really, I'm pretty sure you can't pay me to snoop around unless I have some sort of license. And if you don't pay me, then I'm just that... a snoop."

"But we've heard so much about your other successes," Roy protested.

"I don't know what you've heard, but for the most part I just happened to become personally involved in some unpleasant local circumstances. I didn't go looking for trouble."

"Please, Mrs. Raven," Wanda pleaded, getting my title wrong. I let it pass.

My desire to get involved overcame my good sense. "Let me do some checking, and I'll get back to you. Give me your phone number, OK?"

I stood, and Roy and Wanda followed my lead. We exchanged contact information, and they reluctantly agreed to wait for me to call them, although they urged me to make a decision as soon as possible. I had a difficult time getting them out the door.

After the brother and sister left, I headed for the kitchen and opened the refrigerator door. A wilted clump of celery occupied the center shelf. I pulled it out and thumped it down on the counter. Brittle, yellowing leaves broke from the stalk and littered the old Formica. With perhaps more force than necessary I grabbed a knife and cutting board and began chopping away the nasty parts. Soon, a significant pile of leaf bits had fluttered away from the salvageable portions of stalk. I pushed them around aimlessly with the tip of the knife wishing they would, like the proverbial tea leaves, arrange themselves into some sort of answer to my dilemma.

Here I had the exact opportunity I'd been hoping for, and yet it looked as if it wasn't going to result in any workable scenario. At least I ended up with some edible celery from the heart of the bunch.

In back of the peanut butter jar I found a snack size box of raisins. They were pretty dry, but I studded a plate full of PB-stuffed celery with them, grabbed some crackers, and a beer from the fridge, and headed upstairs to my screen porch.

Finishing the interior had been my summer project; the room was bright and cheerful with teal walls and white wicker furniture.

Dead Mule Swamp was lovely, and the late afternoon sun cast long shadows and highlighted the trees with golden edging. A crow cawed, sounding lazy in the warm sunshine. I'd found real peace and friendships here in Forest County, so why had I been drawn into every local violent crime, past as well as present? Reluctantly, I admitted to myself that I found the various circumstances fascinating. I could walk away from this puzzle, but that might change the perception local people were forming of me. Had I gained a reputation for solving murders? Me?

Sure, I'd gotten lucky, or unlucky, when I'd found myself in the wrong place a few times. All right, maybe I had done a little investigating. But my ideas about that bloody hatchet had been wrong. I ate slowly and pondered the possibilities of looking into the death of Milo Sendak.

The celery and crackers were gone, and the sun was low enough to shine in my eyes through the western screens. I decided to talk to Tracy to see if she had any suggestions. After all, Roy and Wanda had been in agreement that I would need to work with the police, not be at odds.

Becoming a private eye probably meant I'd have to learn how to use a gun. I could do that. The problem was where would I carry it? I hated purses. Occasionally, I'd lug a tote bag if I needed more items than I could carry in a hand. My years as a college professor had resulted in shifting all my cards and papers to a small zippered planner booklet. Cash I kept in a pocket or tucked somewhere more intimate. I tried never to buy clothes without pockets. Yes, the gun would definitely be a problem.

The house phone rang, a startling jangle. I'd kept my landline, although I had purchased a cell phone at my son's insistence. I usually knew where the ringing phone was, despite the cordless handsets. There were chargers and extensions in the kitchen and my bedroom. I ran for the handset on my nightstand and on the third ring scooped it to my ear while giving the customary greeting.

It was Cora. Since she and Jerry Caulfield had become a couple once again, they'd often invited me to join them for brunch at their home on Saturdays. This was another such invitation. I'd managed to reciprocate a few times, most recently with a hot dog roast and other portable fare at the stretch of river frontage on my property. My son, Chad, now a senior at Michigan Tech, had rebuilt a small cabin in the clearing by the water over the summer months. When he'd visited me before the start of fall classes, my closest friends had joined us there for a picnic. So I had thrown one party.

I dragged my mind back to the caller and agreed to be at the Caulfields, in town, at ten in the morning.

"Can I bring anything?" I asked.

"No, of course not," Cora responded with a light laugh. She knew me well enough to realize that unless I offered something specific it meant I didn't have a thing in the refrigerator.

9

The next morning, I parked in front of the newspaper office on Mill Street. Just north, part of the empty lot that separated the Caulfield's huge Victorian home from Mill had been transformed this past summer into a small annex of the larger city park. Their house actually faced Cherry Street, but few people went to the front door. A picket fence delineated the grassy public space from Jerry's private back yard.

I swung open the white gate and entered Jerry and Cora's house by the kitchen door where I was welcome to walk in without knocking.

This was where I'd first met Jerry, over a year ago, and learned that he was a tall, handsome, and charming man. He also was the owner, publisher, and prime reporter for the local weekly paper, The Cherry Hill Herald. As a result, that made him one of the richest men in the county. The paper had begun as a daily, founded by his great-grandfather, but Jerry would probably be the last generation of Caulfields in the newspaper business. His grown children had moved far away and showed no interest in journalism, publishing, or a small town tucked into a rural wooded county.

The century-old mansion that was the Caulfield family home had continuously been renovated to include the most modern conveniences. Even though Cora once again shared the house with Jerry, the kitchen was still stark in black, chrome, and polished wood. But evidences of Cora's touch could be seen. There were cloth covers over the small appliances, the fabric a pastel floral print. Canning jars filled with homemade applesauce sat in rows on a terrycloth towel. A bright red stepstool seemed completely out of place, but I knew Cora's small stature required her to stand on something to reach the upper cupboards.

"Ana, come in, come in," Cora called cheerfully from the sink where she was rinsing the grounds basket of their fancy, programmable coffee machine. Although when I first met her, she was living simply in a house that was designed as a summer cabin, she was equally relaxed here with all the latest gadgets. Cora was comfortable with herself, and she hadn't altered her usual attire just because she now lived in a classy house with a sophisticated man. Faded denim overalls were buckled neatly over a pink plaid shirt, and her long silver hair was wound in braids around her head.

Jerry entered the kitchen from his home office, the former parlor of the house. He was dressed casually, for him, in gray flannel slacks and a pale blue shirt, open at the neck. His full head of wavy gray hair was combed back from his forehead, and the matching mustache was neatly groomed.

"Hello! We're glad you could join us again. I think we should do this every week," he said, walking toward the sink where he towered over his tiny wife. He took the basket from her and reached the central island in a single stride, where he assembled the coffee maker, poured beans into its hopper, and pushed some buttons. For the next few seconds the whirr of the grinder drowned out any possibility of conversation.

Even though our Saturday brunch dates weren't a weekly occurrence, we met often enough to establish a routine. I set places at the island counter and sliced a loaf of Cora's delicious oatmeal bread for toasting. Jerry handled the toaster oven, and Cora whisked a bowl of eggs for omelets. Chopped vegetables and ham for the filling waited in containers on the counter. Jerry pulled a bowl of Cora's applesauce from the refrigerator.

Shortly, we were sitting on the high bar stools, chatting. Naturally, I told them about my visit from Roy and Wanda.

"I told you talking with them would help," Cora said between bites of crunchy toast.

"I know you did, but it certainly went in a different direction from what I expected. I thought they'd feel hostile, or at least reluctant, toward having their lives dissected."

"People can certainly surprise you," Jerry said. "I'm always amazed at things I'm told, even when they know it will go in the paper and be known by the entire county on Wednesday."

"That's no surprise at all," Cora added. "As Adele would be sure to point out, by Wednesday it's old news. Seeing it in print just confirms what everyone has already heard."

Jerry smiled. "Oh, once in a while I get a scoop on Adele. Sometimes things happen just before press time and I can beat her at her own game." He stood to refill his coffee cup and then raised the pot high. "Anyone else?"

"Please," I said, and passed my mug his way. "You bring up an interesting point. Namely, it's nearly impossible to keep secrets here. So, how is it that someone has managed to slip an overdose of drugs into Milo's pills? And maybe those other people's, too."

"You're now assuming four murders, Ana?" Cora asked. "Not three accidents and one suicide? Or four accidents? Or, maybe Colin Mueller was in pain and decided to do himself in. That would make his the suicide. Not so unusual a desire when people get old. Isabel's and Ham's deaths seem to be clearly accidents, although I suppose Ham might have been high, causing him to drive in front of that train."

"Hmmm. Would that make it manslaughter if they could prove someone had dosed his pills?" I asked.

"Certainly it would," Jerry answered quickly.

"And all these scenarios depend, initially, upon whether they find significant drug levels in the bodies being exhumed," I added.

Cora asked, "How's that coming? Does anyone know?"

Jerry said he had checked Friday afternoon with the police, but everything was still in the paperwork stage. He assured us it could take quite a while before anyone had useful results.

"That's where you come in, Ana," Cora said.

I was confused. "Doing paperwork?"

"Of course not. Get involved with the people. Ask questions; find out whatever secrets the interested parties have managed to keep from Adele and the rest of us."

"But this brings us right back to the real problem," I protested. "I do have a streak of curiosity, but I have no desire to acquire Adele's reputation. People love her anyway because she's so generous and honest, but everyone pokes fun at her behind her back. We just did it ourselves."

Jerry had been looking thoughtful during the last exchange between Cora and me. He tapped his fork on the counter, causing us to focus on him. He looked up. "But you can write," he said.

"Sure, but I'm not interested in becoming a 'true crime' author," I told him.

"Maybe not yet. Meanwhile, would you like to be a reporter for the Cherry Hill Herald?"

I think my jaw dropped.

Cora clapped. "That's perfect. You can ask all the questions you want. Write up what you can and keep the off-the-record parts to add to your files of information. I should have thought of it."

"But that's your job," I said to Jerry.

He chuckled. "I have too darn many jobs at this paper. I'd like to spend more time with my bride."

Cora blushed. "I'm hardly a bride."

"Close enough," Jerry said, leaning over to kiss the top of Cora's head. Then he turned to me. "Seriously, Ana, the paper is doing pretty well. I could pay you for local news features. Or maybe you'd like to have the exclusive crime beat."

Cora reacted to the kiss by jumping off the stool and bustling to the sink with her hands full of dishes. "Do it," she said.

And that is how I became a journalist in Forest County.

Before I left, Jerry popped over to the newspaper office and made me a press card and a laminated name tag clipped on a lanyard. He told me I was official but also pointed out this meant he wanted eight-hundred words for a column about local crime in his email inbox before noon on Tuesday. Every Tuesday.

This brought up another problem. I still didn't have an internet connection at my house. I didn't even know if it was possible to get one, out at the end of East South River Road. The laptop computer I'd used when I was a college professor had hardly been out of its case since I'd moved here, but I could write the articles on it and deliver them on a flash drive to Jerry or Cora. Or I could type the stories at the museum and email them to Jerry from there. For now, we'd just have to deal with the inconvenience.

That afternoon, I called Lucille Mueller, widow of the first known suspected victim. There were a lot of qualifiers in that description. How far back had the records been checked for deaths following prescription refills? Was Colin Mueller really the first? Was he a victim of anything, or had he just died of old age as had been assumed? Why was he taking a pain killer? Lucille agreed to talk with me Sunday afternoon and gave me directions to her house, an old farm property southwest of Cherry Hill.

After church, I ate heartily at the refreshment table. Adele, of course, noticed I was eating more than usual and raised an eyebrow at me. However, since I drove south out of town when I left, in the direction of my house, there was nothing to heighten her suspicions that something might be out of the ordinary.

I pulled into the driveway of an extensively remodeled house, vastly different from the old farmstead I expected. There were no shabby outbuildings, just a small greenhouse and a tidy shed. Sprawling ornamental gardens were overgrown, but the hardscapes included a brick serpentine wall defining niches containing benches. Several statues dotted the grounds.

Lucille, slim and tall, but slightly stooped, greeted me at the door in a worn, but originally expensive, fleece robe and slippers. Colin had been an octogenarian, and she looked at least that old. Her gray hair was thin and long, hanging loosely over her shoulders.

"Come in," she said in a high, reedy voice. "Excuse my appearance. I just don't have enough energy to bother dressing if I'm not going out."

"Not a problem, Mrs. Mueller," I said. "Do you live here all alone?"

"I do, indeed. The ladies of the Lutheran Aid Society check on me every day and bring me meals several times a week. You may call me Lucille," she added.

We chatted a few minutes about her current circumstances, and how badly she wanted to stay in her own home. She explained that she was eighty-eight, slightly older than Colin. Their two sons lived in the Chicago area. Colin had been a successful car salesman, owning the largest dealership in the county before he sold it and retired. They had been sad when the new owner moved the business to Emily City.

This rang true with what Adele had told me, but that was no surprise. Adele rarely got things wrong.

Lucille continued her life story. They had bought and updated this country house for themselves as a retreat. They were a compatible couple and liked to garden in the summer and travel during the colder months.

I made sure she understood I was asking questions for a news article and steered the conversation in the direction of her deceased husband. "Why was Colin taking pain medication?" I asked.

"He didn't use it very often. His primary medical problem was a bad heart that was failing, and he spent most of his time in bed. However, he had also developed kidney stones, and when those would flare up, he'd take the oxy."

"And that happened the day he died?"

"No, not that I am aware of." She changed her tone and took a new direction. "This whole business with digging up his body is disgusting and unnerving. I refused to sign the document they shoved in my face, but they came back the next day with a court order and the Sheriff. Accused me of not wanting to see justice done. It frightened me."

"So you did agree to the exhumation?"

"Yes," she said. The word sounded as if it tasted bitter.

I pressed on. "But he could have taken one or more capsules? Was he in charge of his own medications?"

"We sorted his regular pills every Sunday night. Into one of those little boxes, you know. But the pain medication he could take when he needed it. It was in a bottle in the nightstand. He never abused it. But we did ask for one of those caps that's easier for seniors to open."

"And there wasn't any way someone could have tampered with the bottle, or the pills?"

"Now you sound like the police," she said. "How should I know? I wasn't in the house every minute. I had much more energy back then. I was spending a lot of time puttering around in the gardens. It had gotten to be too much for me, of course. All of it."

"You hated to give it up, I'm sure."

"That's true. I still tried to keep up one little corner where we could sit and enjoy summer evenings. I had just started clearing around the spring bulbs. The snowdrops had bloomed, and I felt so optimistic about the year." She stopped speaking and looked out the window.

"But then he died?" I asked.

"Yes. I came inside all muddy from digging and called to him. He didn't answer me. But I never heard anyone else come around, and we'd had no visitors that week. Very few of our friends are left."

She straightened her back, and I saw a spark in her eye.

"I'll tell you what I think," she said. "If there was something wrong with those pills, it happened before they ever came into this house."

"So you think it was surprising that he died so suddenly?" I asked.

She slumped forward again, the spark gone. "I have no idea. He was old and very sick. I may have been deceiving myself as to how ill Colin was. I miss him."

I didn't want feelings of sadness to overwhelm her, so I stood and examined the multitude of photographs that were crowded along the top of a polished upright piano. There were three wedding pictures. Judging from the clothing styles, I assumed two were of her parents and Colin's, and the third might have been Lucille and Colin themselves. There were shots of a young couple holding the hands of two small boys, the boys as young teens holding tennis racquets, paddling a canoe, and posing awkwardly in formal attire with smiling girls, the inevitable prom pictures.

"Are these your sons?" I asked.

"Oh, yes. Lawrence and Peter. Such fine young men. One is a dentist, and the other has succeeded as an investment broker."

"Do you see them often?"

"They have families of their own, of course. Grandchildren! I'm a great-grandmother, and soon to become a great-great, I'm told." She smiled at me.

One of the other portraits was a young man, probably high school or college age. "Why do you have a photo of Charlie Dixon with your family pictures?" The question popped out.

"Oh, you must be mistaken. Charlie, the drugstore owner?" Lucy asked.

I pointed at the picture that looked very much like Charlie's senior picture in the Thorpe yearbook.

"That's Lawrence as a young man. Perhaps the hair styles make him look like Charlie. They are of an age, after all."

But I wasn't dissuaded. "It looks a lot like Charlie. May I borrow this picture?"

"Certainly not," Lucille said. But she looked at my

point-and-shoot camera which I'd pulled from a pocket. "You may take a snapshot of the photo if you wish, though."

I did just that. I'd hoped to take a nice photo of Lucille Mueller, too, but she wasn't dressed, let alone dressed for the occasion. I thanked her for her time.

As she let me out the front door, I hoped that Lawrence or Peter would start paying a little more attention to their mother before she faded away, as Colin had.

11

Isabel Adam's sister, Julia, had agreed to meet with me at four in the afternoon at Paula's Place. She hadn't sounded thrilled when I called on Saturday and asked to talk to her, and she had suggested the restaurant rather than her home in Emily City.

I knew Paula; she and her diner had been part of the enigma of what happened to Sunny and Star Leonard's mother. But it was a popular eatery, so I wasn't expecting any special attention from the owner.

A solid, bottle-blonde woman in her forties, dressed in jeans and a purple Mickey Mouse sweatshirt, was waiting in the entrance space. I didn't know her, but she apparently knew me. She greeted me by name, and we took a booth near the back. She said she remembered me from the Harvest Ball the previous year. Despite the pleasant introductions, Julia seemed aloof and stiff.

We ordered sandwiches, chatting about the weather and traffic, until Julia initiated serious conversation.

"I'm not sure what you people hope to accomplish by dragging this up again and putting more garbage in the newspaper for the public's feeding frenzy."

I should have refreshed my memory about Isabel. She was thirty-two when she'd supposedly died of anaphylactic shock in the spring, but that's about all I could recall. I opened my mouth to defend myself, but Julia didn't let me get a word in.

"Isabel was a wonderful person. So talented. We were never close, but I spent my teen years raising her after our mother took off, watching out for her and making sure she had her epi pen at all times after the allergy was discovered. I can't imagine why she left it in the house that day. It's just a shame. And now people are saying she died from drugs? I don't believe it."

"People will say all kinds of things," I began, "but no one really knows, yet, if she took any oxycodone the day she died. But she did refill her prescription shortly before her death."

"So what? Lots of people take medication."

"Yes, but that's what ties Isabel to Colin Mueller, Ham Nelson, and Milo Sendak. They all got new bottles of the pain killer within a day or two of dying."

"Phooey, that doesn't mean anything."

"Maybe not, but the official investigators want to be sure. Can you tell me why Isabel was taking oxycodone?"

Julia squirmed and her eyes shifted to the waitress who arrived with our sandwiches. She didn't continue speaking until we were alone again.

"She broke her ankle skiing last winter. Isabel— she never had a nickname— loved winter sports because the bees and wasps weren't a problem. She could spend hours on the slopes or cruising through the woods without any worries. The exercise kept her slim. Not like me." She patted a padded hip. "But they put two pins in her ankle after she fell, and it was hurting her a lot. Getting up and down clearing the garden beds, you know. Gardening was her warm weather delight. For her, that was the high-risk sport. Ironic isn't it?"

Julia grimaced, stopped for breath, and swallowed some coffee. She hadn't touched her sandwich, but I'd been packing mine away. The after-church snacks had worn off. I watched as she seemed to disappear inside her head, and a shiny droplet emerged at the corner of her left eye. She ignored it.

"Look," she continued, "I don't want to be rude, but this is all very painful. Our family wasn't the greatest, and now I'm the only one left. Isabel and I managed to make something of ourselves, no thanks to the drunk who begat us. I wouldn't use the word 'fathered.' Don't you dare print that."

I thought I'd steer the conversation in a more pleasant direction. "I understand Isabel was a great handcrafter. I've seen some of her baskets. Tell me what else she made."

"She was artsy from the minute she was old enough to choose

her own toys. Always painting or weaving or making something beautiful with flowers and a bunch of weeds. She made little blank journals with homemade covers, herb sachets, placemats, anything with natural materials."

"And she managed to turn that into a livelihood?"

"One of the few people I've ever known who could make that happen," Julia said. "I had to get a real job."

"What do you do?"

"I'm just a secretary. I never even had a chance to try college. As soon as I finished high school I needed an income to support Isabel and myself. Been there ever since."

"Where?" I asked.

"It's strange, you know. I work for the same accounting firm that Mr. Sendak did."

Here was a connection neither Cora nor Adele had apparently known about. "Did you know him personally?"

"Just to nod to in the hallway. I'm on the income tax side of the building. Mr. Sendak did audits."

"Did you ever talk to Isabel about Mr. Sendak?"

This "case" was turning into a huge hairball of connections.

"Not that I remember. He was just a guy at work."

That seemed to be a dead end.

"You mentioned that no one else is left. Isabel has no other family?"

"She never married, not even a long-term relationship, never had kids. I've got a permanent boyfriend, but we don't have children either. Couldn't afford to find out why, and doctors don't like couples who aren't hitched. Just as well we don't pass on the loser genes we came with." Her mouth twisted in a wry semblance of a smile again, and then she nibbled at her club sandwich, but switched to eating the French fries.

My Reuben was already gone. While she ate, I thought.

Finally, I asked, "Did you or Isabel know any of the other people whose deaths might be connected?"

She pondered this question for a minute. "I'd met that handicapped guy, Ham, but I'd hardly say I knew him. He would bring in grapevines and wood for Isabel. She paid him for the materials."

"And Isabel sometimes drove him to church?"

"Not that I know of, but I haven't darkened the doors for years."

"Any of the others?"

"I don't think I'd ever met the old man. What was his name again?"

"Colin Mueller. He owned a car dealership."

"Nope. Doesn't ring any bells, except what I've seen on the news. That M. Jack Smith on Channel Seven is pretty cute. I like to watch his reports." She smirked. "Michelangelo. That's what the 'M' stands for. Michelangelo John Smith. Guess who his brothers are?"

I shook my head.

"Doctor Don, here in Emily City, he's Donatello Mark."

I was afraid to think where this was going.

"Leonardo Luke goes by Lee. He flies charter planes in Wyoming somewhere, and Raphael Matthew's the baby. He was always called Cubby." Julia snorted. "Good thing the Smiths had four boys. But I guess Raphaela would have worked, although it would have been tough to get that fourth gospel in. Raphaela's actually kind of pretty-sounding."

It seemed I had heard one of the three names before, in addition to the newsman, but I couldn't pull it out of the mire in my brain.

"What does Cubby do?" I asked.

"No idea. He took off for parts unknown a few years after he finished school. I guess he's been back a few times, but mostly not. Couldn't stand the jokes. Can't say's I blame him."

The waitress had begun wiping down tables, filling ketchup bottles, and generally cleaning up in preparation for closing, although it was just barely past five. Paula's Place stayed open till six on Sundays.

One thing I was learning anew was that people handled loss in different ways. Julia tried to appear hard-nosed, although she clearly missed her younger sister. But I had to be tough.

"I apologize for asking, but is there anything you can think of that would have led Isabel to take too many pain pills?"

"Nothing. She wasn't that kind of person." Julia pushed away her unfinished sandwich, stared me briefly in the eyes then stood and walked to the cash register without waiting for the check.

12

It was about five-thirty, with a couple hours of light left. I hadn't gotten much help from Colin's widow or Isabel's sister. The prospects for information about Ham Nelson were even lower. No one knew of any living relatives, nearby or far away. The man had apparently been alone in the world.

I drove back to Cherry Hill and carefully entered the cemetery through the narrow wooden lych gate. I didn't know where Ham was buried, or if he was even in this cemetery, although I didn't think Cherry Hill had more than one. The newer section seemed to be toward the rear, so I headed there and parked beside an open area, free of trees, with almost no ornate monuments typical of the front section.

The evening was cool with a light breeze, and I found a Michigan Tech sweatshirt in the backseat, a gift from Chad. I pulled it over my head, then strolled among the headstones, reading the names out loud. "Tangen, Hobbs, Wolcheski, Ericson, Falconer, Brown, Heikkinen..." Our little village seemed to be a genuine Midwestern melting pot of ethnicity. I suspected I'd find a larger number of Finnish family names in the older section, but I was looking for one name in particular, and it should be back here with the new graves.

Wandering aimlessly quickly became boring. The modern headstones didn't have much in the way of decoration to hold my interest, although one large slab of granite had been laser cut with the images of an eighteen-wheeler and a beer can. It was easy enough to tell what kind of person Louis Rathborne had been. He had died the year before I moved to Forest County. His wife's name, Karen, was engraved beside his, but the dates were not filled in. She, at least, was still alive. I looked around. Lots of dead people here. Were the four deaths I was interested in actually connected?

With more purpose, I strode to the far corner of the new section and walked between the rows, first back to front, then to the back, and forward again, scanning the family name on each grave marker.

It was getting dusky and the sky fading to a bruised purple when I came to an unadorned marker with the name Nelson on it. However, it bore two unfamiliar names: Theodore and Yolanda. Theodore had died in 1992, and Yolanda in 1999. Beneath the names in script was the sentiment: love never dies.

"Huh," I said, and took another step forward to the next plot in the row. There it was, stuck in the ground on a wire stake. A gaudy but faded bouquet of fake flowers in a narrow plastic urn, with a medallion attached. "Hamilton James, their son, 1957-2013." No permanent gravestone, no comment on his life or what had been important to him. It eloquently confirmed there had been no one left in the family to spend money on his burial. His mother had probably bought a plot large enough for the three of them when Ted, or Theo, died, but maybe there hadn't been enough money for Ham's marker. Maybe his mother was superstitious, not wanting to buy one when he was alive.

And then she died; it was too late. Someone had spent a few dollars to place this temporary marker. Maybe the cemetery did that as a courtesy.

Had Ham ever come here to look at his parents' grave? Had he thought about such things as a stone for his own plot? Surely he never expected to die suddenly in a terrible wreck.

I shivered. It was such a cliché but a natural reaction to the setting and the thoughts filling my mind.

If this scene had been in a book it would be the time for some shadowy figure to emerge from the trees surrounding the older section, to approach me with a ghostly and cryptic message pertaining to the Nelsons, or perhaps a riddle related to the whole puzzle of the deaths connected to oxycodone and Charlie Dixon, the druggist.

But no one appeared. The evening grew darker and colder. I snapped a picture, went back to my car, and drove home.

13

"Ana. I made a horrible mistake! You have to come in to the store so I can make it up to you and straighten things out." Adele's voice pounded through the phone just after eight o'clock, Monday morning.

I was on my second cup of coffee, but I needed three. I'd trained my friends not to call early, but to Adele's way of thinking she'd already sat on her news, whatever it was, for a couple of hours and this was late enough.

I cringed at the thought of going out just yet, but had to admit that a trip to the store was a good idea. I agreed to come to town as soon as I dressed. However, time for that third cup of coffee was necessary before facing Adele's enthusiasm. I dawdled another half hour or more.

When I finally stepped outside, the air was crisp, and patches of frost skulked in the shadows, reminding me that colder weather was coming soon. The windshield was clear, but I felt under the seat to be sure my scraper was still there. I did find it, along with a bunch of other junk that needed to be thrown out.

The sidewalk in front of Volger's grocery was turning gold with leaves from the large maple that shaded the front door. Although the side door that opened onto the parking lot was wide plate glass and handicap accessible, the front probably looked the same as it had in 1900, except the tree would have been a sapling then. Two stone steps led up to a wooden screen door that squealed on its hinges when opened, and a bell inside tinkled. The plank floor creaked, and a century of pleasant grocery smells absorbed by the wood filled the air. I preferred to use this door.

My serene feelings of nostalgia for a Cherry Hill of the past were shattered by Adele's shriek when she caught sight of me.

"There you are. Finally. Where have you been?" she

demanded. "I called you an hour ago."

I looked around the store, hoping no one was listening to her tirade. I didn't see any shoppers. No surprise. It was early morning, post Labor Day. "What's so important that it couldn't wait a few minutes? I had to finish my breakfast and get dressed. I made a shopping list, too." I pulled a torn, used envelope from the pocket of my jeans and waved it, as proof.

"Let me see that," Adele said, grabbing the scrap of paper and studying it. "Humph. All right. I guess you did make a list."

She didn't need to know the list was a month old. I'd happened to discover it in the car when I'd been hunting for the scraper.

Adele grabbed my arm and steered me into the small office. Its large interior window allowed her to keep an eye on the business while doing daily paperwork. After we were inside, she turned toward the store and craned her neck in one direction and then the other, studying the aisles. Apparently, she didn't see anyone either.

"I do know where Ham Nelson lived," she whispered, even though we'd verified no one else was in the building.

"Why is that such a secret you couldn't tell me on the phone?" I asked, perturbed.

"He always tried to keep people from knowing. He did such a good job, I forgot I'd found out."

I laughed out loud.

She looked hurt, probably embarrassed that she'd forgotten something so delicious.

"Adele, stop whispering. The man is dead. He doesn't live there any more, wherever it was. And there's no one here but us. So, where is it?"

"What?"

"Ham's house. What did you think I meant?"

"That's just it." She continued to whisper. "I don't know exactly. But I sort of know. It's been described to me. I'd have to go with you, and together we might be able to find it."

"Why do we need to find it?"

"He lived alone. Maybe no one has cleared it out since he died.

We might find something interesting. A clue of some kind."

I couldn't imagine what clue might relate to his death in a car crash, but perhaps there were papers that could lead to a long-lost relative. Maybe the man had siblings who never showed up after his death because they didn't care for him. It was worth looking.

"Great," I said with guarded optimism. "When can we go?"

Adele's eyes dropped to study the floor. "That's the problem. Now that all the college kids are back in school, I've pretty much lost my employees. I'm here alone. I can't leave until after I close at six."

"And you opened at eight? Adele, those are terrible hours to keep. There must be someone in the county who wants a part-time job."

"Maybe. Let me know if you hear of anyone. They have to be trustworthy. And over seventeen," she added. "Jimmie has been bugging me to learn how to do ordering."

I rolled my eyes with understanding sympathy at Jimmie's ability to be persistent. Jimmie Mosher was nowhere near seventeen, but he was determined to re-open the Cherry Blossom Restaurant as soon as he was old enough. He was single minded. We both loved him dearly, despite the pestering.

Adele and I agreed I'd pick her up at her home at six-thirty, which would give her time to change clothes. She lived only a few blocks from the store.

Before leaving, I filled a grocery cart with pantry items, meat and produce. Adele deposited a deli carton of potato salad in my bags and a half gallon of ice cream.

"I'm so annoyed I didn't remember this last week," she fumed. "It might have saved us precious time. This is my penance."

I smiled and thanked her. She'd never understand that I would have appreciated an apology for shattering my morning routine more than for forgetting Ham's address.

After putting the food away, the rest of my day was spent working on the article for the Cherry Hill Herald that had to be turned in Tuesday. I was disappointed with my efforts. I certainly hadn't learned much, but I was able to say that every one of the victims' relatives could not believe their loved one would have committed suicide. That hardly seemed like news.

Adele was waiting outside her house when I arrived that evening. We agreed my Jeep was the better vehicle to take.

"We've only got about an hour of good light," she fussed as she opened the passenger door. She swept crumbs and dirt off the front seat with her hand.

"Well, get in, and we'll make good use of it," I countered.

She pulled a sandwich from her large purse, peeled back the plastic wrap, and handed it to me. Then she opened one for herself. I thanked her and bit into the chicken salad.

We drove quickly to the west side of Forest County, which only took about fifteen minutes on the main road.

"Turn south here, on Porter," Adele commanded.

This seemed easy enough; I wondered what was going to be so difficult. I soon found out.

The highway crossed a narrow bridge over some creek I did not know. I'd never explored the back roads west of town. The surface quickly changed to gravel and soon after that to sand.

"Now, it's one of these dirt paths off of here," Adele said, squinting west as the low sun tried to penetrate the dusty car windows. Every tenth of a mile, sometimes more frequently, we passed a turnoff into some sort of drive. Some looked like roads, all bare dirt. Others looked like driveways with two ruts and a strip of grass in the middle. Some were completely overgrown with weeds, as if they hadn't been driven in years. None were marked with any sort of road sign, address number, or name. I saw "Keep Out" painted on paint can lids nailed to several trees.

"Try this one." Adele pointed down a linear opening that surely hadn't been driven this season.

It looked iffy, but my Jeep could handle it. I turned west, flipped down the sun visor and drove slowly into the woods. Deeper and deeper we penetrated. After a mile, the road ended in a clearing with a fire ring and a high crossbar nailed between two trees.

"Nope. Deer camp," Adele explained.

I drove around the clearing and headed back to the so-called main road, not a major thoroughfare, but one the county maintained. A few minutes later, Adele again pointed, "Maybe this one."

This road had clear sand tracks but tall weeds grew between them. The daylight was fading, and it was decidedly dusky in the woods. Light beams strobed across the road as tree trunks alternately hid and revealed the sun. I'm not easily spooked, but I was glad someone was with me. What if I got stuck? I wiggled my elbow against my jacket pocket to check for the presence of my cell phone. I hoped Adele wouldn't notice what I was doing. At any rate, she didn't comment on my motion.

The two-track quickly forked. Adele shook her head and shrugged. We would have to explore both paths. I tried the left one which ended abruptly at a creek, maybe the same one we'd crossed on Porter. There was no place to turn around, so I backed up slowly to return to the fork.

"I hope there aren't going to be a lot of places like that. It's getting too dark to back up easily."

We tried the other fork and ended up in another deer camp where there was plenty of turning room. A bit of light still brightened Porter Road when we emerged from the woods again.

"Just one more, please, Ana," Adele implored.

"OK," I said, but I had little interest in continuing after nightfall. If we found Ham's house, the electric would probably be off, and we wouldn't be able to see anything anyway.

Adele shook her head as we reached the next dirt turnoff. "It doesn't look right," she said.

It looked like all the others to me.

"This one! I think this is it," she pointed down a curving lane with two sandy ruts. The greenery in the middle was short.

"Someone's been using this one," I pointed out.

"I see that, but I'm pretty sure I'm on the right track."

I refrained from guffawing at her pun. She was concentrating so hard, and was so serious about her snooping, I knew she wouldn't appreciate being laughed at.

We rounded the first curve. Here in the thick woods it was now almost fully dark. The headlights picked out nothing but trees, looking grim and ghostly. It was the same after the next curve, and the next. A large leafless oak, straight ahead where the road widened, blocked forward progress. In the stark light, the dead branches reached for us with an abnormal number of gnarly fingers.

"The road turns left," Adele said in a matter-of-fact tone. She was all business.

We took the sharp corner slowly and in a few seconds pulled up short in front of a wooden gate frame strung with barbed wire. It was covered with "No Trespassing" signs but not a single reflector or other warning that the way was barred. My headlights glared through the wire, down the drive, and illuminated a dilapidated trailer with a small deck. It was surrounded by piles of old tires, broken down lawnmowers and bicycles, rusting oil drums, unidentifiable junk, and a few shabby outbuildings.

The sound of a small motor reverberated through the otherwise still forest. A generator. There were lights on inside the trailer.

A large dog leaped toward us but was brought up short by a stout chain. The bull-headed beast barked furiously, revealing long white teeth between curling lips. It must have been sleeping until our lights penetrated the yard. In less than a second, a savage chorus of barking was set off in chain reaction. The woods sounded filled with dogs of all sizes, but we couldn't locate any of them, except the one lunging against its collar. It snapped and growled but couldn't reach us.

"Kill the headlights," Adele hissed. "This is it."

I twisted the control to "OFF." We sat still letting our eyes adjust to the darkness. The door opened, and a male form appeared on the deck, the silhouette of a long gun in his hands.

I began to be sorry I'd agreed to explore any more roads in the dark.

"Oh, mercy me," Adele moaned. "Can you turn around?"

"Not until we get back to that oak tree," I said through clenched teeth.

The figure raised the gun and pointed it in our direction. He yelled, but with the car windows closed we mostly had to guess at the words. I'm willing to bet it was something like "Get off my land."

He raised the barrel a bit higher and a blast of noise exploded in the woods, echoing off the trees. Twigs and leaves spattered on the hood of the Jeep.

"Shotgun." Adele identified the sound. "He's just trying to scare us away."

"It's working," I said as I backed incautiously between the dark trees, toward the corner.

14

"You've got to bring me better copy than this," Jerry said with a shake of his head, reading over the article I brought to his house Tuesday morning. "And you need to email it to me. I'm not going to re-type it."

I was already feeling foolish about the events of the previous evening and didn't want to share with him what Adele and I had done. Jerry's critique of my bland report stung, as if I'd been given a C instead of a B by a school teacher whom I respected.

"I agree," I admitted. "But it's all I had time to find out so far. What else can I do? I can't make stuff up."

"Maybe you'd better tell me what you discovered that isn't in this article," Jerry countered.

"How do you know I left things out?" I asked, surprised.

"Oh, come on. You and Cora always discovered nitty-gritty things on all those other murders you solved."

"Jerry!" I protested. "I had no role in solving the one that was supposed to be you. Everything I looked at was wrong." I could feel my neck getting hot.

"Sure, but you put the pressure on. That forced the situation to come to a head," he said, shaking the page of text at me. "This isn't even as juicy as a junior-high school-girl's journal. I'll use it this week, but if you want to be an investigative reporter, I need the dirt."

"What if I offend your readers? All the dead people are local, with families and friends here. Well, maybe not Ham Nelson, but you'll get complaints."

"Sure. But I'll sell papers," Jerry said. "Everyone is going to speculate anyway. You can give them information to speculate with. Don't bother filling me in; I don't keep track of enough gossip to be any fun. Spend the afternoon with Cora, I want something hotter for next week."

On Tuesdays I work on Cora's Forest County historical database. While driving the few blocks to the museum, I wondered if investigative reporting was going to be a bad career move. I liked most of the people I had met here, and ruffling feathers on purpose didn't suit me. I did like figuring out these local riddles, but I couldn't have it both ways.

Cora greeted me enthusiastically and asked what I'd been up to, but before I did anything else, I plugged my flash drive into the computer and emailed my tepid article to Jerry. I printed out a copy for Cora and handed it to her.

She read through it, wrinkled her nose, and said, "Now fill me in on the serious parts."

I told her everything I could think of: Lucille Mueller's depression, the easy access to Colin's medicines, the picture that looked like Charlie, Isabel's broken ankle and Julia's bitterness. I even remembered to tell her about the Ninja Turtle Gospel brothers, although they didn't seem to have anything to do with the deaths. She laughed hard and slapped her small hands on her thighs when I related the shotgun story and backing away from Ham's trailer with Adele.

"Oh, my goodness," she said, wiping her eyes. "Adele wanted to be involved. I guess she got her wish."

"What do you think I should look at next?" I asked. "Jerry's pretty disappointed. He even told me to get your help."

Cora pulled a tissue from the pocket of her overalls and blew her nose. "I can help most with finding out who lives in Ham's trailer now, and we should definitely look at that picture. Is your snapshot good?"

"See for yourself," I said. Last night, I'd copied it from my camera card to the flash drive, and now I pulled it up on the screen.

"I'll print this out and look through some old albums. You call Tracy. She can tell you who's in that trailer."

"But," I protested, "this was way out in the country. She's village police."

"So. She'll call someone else." Cora made it sound so easy.

"There's no electric service. Probably no gas either."

"You didn't see a propane tank?"

"I was a little too busy to look that carefully," I said dryly.

Cora rummaged in a desk drawer. "Here's the county plat book. Try this first." She tossed me a slim spiral-bound book.

It wasn't hard to find Porter Road and the bridge we'd crossed. South of that, there was no way to know which thin slice of property we'd been on, but I began reading names. The big chunk which included the creek was labeled Porter. Next were Harrison, P. Timm, W. Roe, Nelson.

"Nelson," I said. "Ham owned his property."

"Good. Now you just need someone with authority to find out if the property changed hands. Call Tracy. She'll get the information."

I had to agree that Tracy Jarvi was a resourceful police chief, and so I made a call on the office phone while Cora left to retrieve research materials. Her many books and photo albums now had their own library, well on the way to being sorted and catalogued.

A few minutes after I hung up, Cora returned with a box piled high with books.

"Mostly old yearbooks," she said, depositing the collection on a work table with a grunt.

The phone rang. It must have been the private line, because Cora answered with a simple, "Hello."

She listened for a minute and then echoed, "Still in the name of Hamilton Nelson," then added, "Ask her," and handed me the phone.

Tracy wanted to know if I was sure someone was living on the property. All I could say was that Adele was positive it was where Ham had lived, and someone was certainly occupying the space. I told her about the generator and being more or less shot at. She said the county took a dim view of squatting, and she would call the sheriff's department to have them deal with it. Since everyone knew no relatives had shown up when Ham died, it was hard to imagine the trailer was being used legally.

Meanwhile, Cora was spreading old school annuals on the

tables, weighting corners with pretty rocks to hold them open.

"Here we go," she said. "Here's Lawrence his senior year. This one is Peter. I've got the rest of their high school years, too. And I brought back the one from Thorpe with Charlie in it that we looked at before."

I went over to stand beside her, and she placed the printout of my photo of a photo in the lineup.

Disappointed, I said, "It's not any of these pictures. Why did I think it looked like Charlie?"

"It does look like him," Cora agreed. "Look at the eyes and the chin line. Who did Lucille say it is?"

"Lawrence."

"Well, it also looks like him," Cora said, her eyes darting back and forth between the pictures.

We hunted through the yearbooks from other years but couldn't find this exact picture in any of them.

"Here's an album of photos from a Thorpe Days Festival. One of the last they held, but the year is about right. Let's see who attended."

We studied photos for the next half hour. Most of them were taken from a distance and were of such things as a small cluster of cheap midway rides, people lined up waiting to fill plates at a barbeque, various people throwing balls at the target for a dunk tank.

Cora squinted at the fat man sitting on the seat. He wore Hawaiian print shorts, and his hair was plastered to his head. "Looks like the mayor was getting wet that year."

We found a few closer shots of faces. Most were younger kids standing beside prize rabbits, goats and calves, or women smiling over baskets of produce and jars of home-canned food. We hunted and hunted, even scrutinized photos with a magnifying glass, and thought maybe we spotted Faye Anderson huddled with a group of girls. But we found no one we could identify as Charlie Dixon.

I straightened up, and my neck cracked. "I think I'll just go ask Charlie who it's a picture of," I announced. "That might shake things up a little."

15

Plenty of light remained when I finished at the museum, just before five that afternoon. Cora had supplied me with Charlie Dixon's home address and the information that he'd been allowed to return to work at the drugstore. After initially questioning him, a week before, the police had not found evidence strong enough to issue an arrest warrant for involvement in the oxycodone deaths, so he had continued his normal routine. The drugstore closed at five, so I hoped to catch him as he arrived home. He might be tired and a little off-balance; perhaps not sharp and on guard against an admission of some kind.

I couldn't think of any reason for Charlie's picture to be in the Mueller's photo collection. But neither was I convinced the smiling face in the black and white print was Lawrence. Cora and I had studied their annual photos from all four high school years: Charlie, Lawrence and his brother Peter. This was definitely not a photo of Peter. He was blond with a thinner face and resembled Lucille. It was true that the hair styles had a lot to do with the similarities, and the teenage Charlie looked very little like the well-padded, bald man of the present. And yet, either Lawrence and Charlie bore an uncanny resemblance to each other, or it was, indeed, Charlie. If it was Charlie, why had Lucille lied to me?

I wanted to see what Lawrence looked like now. Other pictures on Lucille Mueller's piano had only showed her sons as young men. She must keep photos of them as adults, with their families, elsewhere. Probably her bedroom.

Charlie lived in the same neighborhood as Adele, on the north side of town. These streets were quiet and respectable with houses built mostly in the early twentieth century. They didn't scream old money and founding families like those on Cherry

Street where Cora and Jerry lived, but they were kept up nicely. It looked as if owners here had steady jobs and cared about paint and gardens and neatly cut edges where the sidewalk met the lawn. The trees were primarily aging maples with a smattering of ornamental crabapple. The latter were covered with small round balls, shriveled by yesterday's frost.

I easily located 302 Wing Street, a Craftsman bungalow with a front dormer and large open porch. It was painted an unassuming gray with white trim. There was a dark blue sedan in the driveway. I parked on the street, even though there was room in the drive. I climbed the steps to the porch with the photo printout in my hand and rang the doorbell. I heard it chime, and then I saw, through the window to my right, a hand jerk the curtain sideways. After a second, the fabric dropped back into place.

The door opened and a well-proportioned woman I'd never met, wearing neat black slacks and a gold sweater, frowned at me. Otherwise, her expression was a mask. The suggestion of a mask was heightened by the fact that she wore more makeup than most women in Cherry Hill, and her glasses were tinted pale amber. I assumed this was Faye Anderson Dixon.

"I know you. What do you want?" she asked bluntly, plucking with long dark-red nails at a dangling string of black beads. Her right hand held the edge of the door, as if ready to slam it in my face.

I had wanted to be on the offense, but I was so surprised at this harsh greeting that I was taken aback. "Is Charlie here?" I asked with feigned confidence. "Charlie Dixon."

"Why do you want to know? Charlie's a good man. He hasn't done anything wrong. Are you working for the police now? Coming around asking questions."

"Mrs. Dixon? Faye? No, I don't work for the police, but I am going to be writing some articles for the newspaper. I'd just like to ask Charlie if he recognizes an old photograph." I tried to be non-threatening.

"He's not home yet," the woman stated without verifying she was Charlie's wife. I could only assume that was the case. She continued to fiddle with the beads, rolling them nervously between her fingers. Her gaze lit on the page I held, and she reached for it. "Let me see that."

Quickly, I thrust it behind me. I wasn't liking her attitude, and it made me suspicious. Maybe she recognized the photo. "I'd rather show it to Charlie. You haven't even told me if you are Faye Dixon."

"I'm Faye. Charlie's not home yet. Who's that a picture of?" she asked, craning her head to the side to see the image.

A car pulled into the driveway, and I turned and saw a near twin of the dark one already there, except this car was white. Charlie stepped onto the blacktop and looked questioningly toward us. This distraction was all the opening Faye needed. She snatched the paper from my hand and held it high in front of her face, so I wasn't able to see her initial reaction.

A second later, she snorted and pushed the paper back in my direction. "I have no idea who this is," she said. "From the clothing and hair style, I'd say it was taken about forty years ago. Surely you don't expect us to remember people we might have known as children."

While Faye was completing this performance, Charlie had reached the porch, eased past me and Faye, and positioned himself behind his wife's shoulder. He looked down at the picture, which she was still holding.

I did not miss his first reaction. He recognized the photo.

"Go on and wash up. I brought home Chinese," Faye ordered.

Charlie obediently turned away. I was going to miss my chance.

"Who is this is a picture of?" I asked, grabbing the paper from Faye with one hand and clutching at Charlie's arm with the other.

"I don't know," he replied calmly, pulling away and shaking his head. "It looked familiar at first, but no, I don't recognize this boy."

Faye backed up, pushing Charlie into the house while shutting me out. I stood there staring at the dark gray steel replacement door, wondering what conclusion I should jump to.

16

The phone again rang at eight in the morning. This was becoming an unpleasant routine.

By contrast, I was trying to develop a calm wake-up habit, without disturbances. I was sitting in my bedroom watching the early light play over Dead Mule Swamp. I'd purchased a small walnut writing desk to put by the window, and I spent time here almost every day, reading a short devotional and thinking about life and my friends. Maybe I was even learning a bit about prayer beyond "God, please bless me." Maybe.

My favorite midnight blue ceramic mug with brown and cream glaze drippings down the sides was filled with steaming coffee, my first cup of the day. Letting my brain awaken slowly was one of the best parts of not needing to hold down a regular job.

Immediately, I felt annoyance with Adele for interrupting this important part of my day twice in one week. Those feelings were certainly in conflict with the inner peace I was trying to cultivate.

But the caller was not Adele. Chief Tracy Jarvi was on the line.

"Good morning, Ana. Sorry to call you so early, but I'm wondering if you could come in to the station this morning."

This was a bit alarming. "Sure. Am I in some kind of trouble?" I asked.

"Not at all. But I have something for you," Tracy said mysteriously.

"Do I get any hints?"

She laughed. "OK. Dogs."

"Oh, that helps a lot," I threw back at her. "In about an hour?"

"Sure. I'll be here."

Pleased that I'd been given time to finish my morning rituals, yet very curious, I managed to get out of the house in forty-five minutes. About a minute before nine o'clock, I pushed open the door to the Cherry Hill police station, located in the gray stone courthouse. It was like stepping back into an old sitcom. The walls hadn't been painted in years. Wanted posters, calendars and memos were taped to every vertical surface, and old beat-up desks and file cabinets still saw heavy use. But despite appearances, I knew our three-person force was quietly efficient in the small village.

Tracy sat at her desk, looking through files. Today, her long blonde hair was pulled back in a single braid. She was a large-boned, open-faced woman who inspired trust and confidence. You felt safe around Tracy.

"What's this about dogs?" I asked. "The only dogs I've encountered recently were at Ham's place. Did you go out there?"

"Three sheriff's deputies and I did just that," Tracy said. "You may be amazed at what we found."

"So, tell me."

"The occupant was indeed a squatter. His name is Myron Lake, aka Martin Pond, aka Manny Poole."

"He must have liked watery places. Was he related to Ham Nelson?" I asked.

"Not that we know of," Tracy answered. "He's not local. There was an open warrant for his arrest from Indianapolis. Suspected of dealing heroin. Illegal firearms possession."

"You've sent him back there?"

"Soon. He's in the county jail."

"Can I go out to the trailer and look around," I asked.

"If you want to." Tracy said, waving a hand to dismiss the idea, as if it hardly mattered. "I doubt you'll find anything we didn't. It's a real mess. But Myron isn't the most interesting part."

"Right. No dogs in the story yet," I said, grinning.

Tracy matched my expression, then her face closed down in a frown. "Yes, now we get to the dogs. Did you know that snatching and selling dogs can be quite the business?"

"Selling them? To other owners?"

"Selling them to medical research labs."

I felt sick to my stomach. "You mean to be used for testing?"

"Yes, with drugs, for procedures. If they outlive their usefulness they are euthanized. When there is a rash of missing pets in an area that's usually a really bad sign," Tracy explained.

"That's been happening here?" I asked. I hadn't heard about anything like this or seen "Lost Dog" posters on utility poles.

"Not in Forest County. But west of us, in Kerr County, a lot of dogs have been reported missing."

"There must have been a dozen or more dogs out at Ham's old trailer. They were really loud."

"Nineteen," Tracy said somberly. "Eighteen in wire kennels out back and the one mixed breed on the chain. That one was trained as a guard dog. We had to shoot him. One-hundred-four pounds of tortured hatred there."

"And the others?" I asked, hoping some of them might be able to be returned to their owners. My heart constricted at the idea of shooting a dog, even a vicious one.

"Here's where we do have some good news. We called the Kerr County Animal Shelter, as well as the local one. Many of the dogs we found had been reported missing. So some families, at least, will have good news."

"Could you match all the dogs with their owners? That's a lot of dogs."

Tracy shook her head slowly. "Really a lot of dogs. There were some that had been reported missing we didn't find. We can't let ourselves think about them too much."

"What about the ones you found that aren't claimed?" I asked.

"They were found here, so right now the extras are in our county. It's a no-kill shelter, so that's a good place for them. And there's some good news for you, personally."

I couldn't imagine what. "I don't have a dog." Then I thought of Paddy, the Irish setter I'd kept for my cousin, who now lived with Sunny and Star Leonard. But wouldn't they have called me if Paddy had gone missing? I looked hard into Tracy's eyes. "Oh, no! Paddy wasn't taken, was he? And not found?"

Tracy looked alarmed. "Gosh, no, Ana. I didn't mean to scare you. I'll get to the point."

"Please do," I said, trying to ignore the adrenalin burst that had shot through me. Paddy was a wonderful dog. I had a sudden knowledge of how at least eighteen other owners felt.

"It's like this," Tracy explained. "There were a lot of reports, and even some flyers circulated, but two of the dogs had a reward offered for finding them. You and Adele will have two-hundred fifty dollars to split. In fact, I have it already. The happy owners claimed their pets and brought cash, a hundred from one and one-fifty from the other."

She thrust an envelope into my left hand, and shook my right as if posing for a big news photo. Which reminded me, now that I was a reporter, this probably was news.

"I... I'll be sure to talk to Adele right away. Maybe we can use this to help someone," I stammered.

"You'll do the right thing, I'm sure," Tracy said with a smile.

Then she relaxed and gave me a little hug. Where else but in a small town?

<h1 style="text-align:center">17</h1>

From the police station, I went directly to Volger's Grocery and shared the whole story with Adele. She was excited, to say the least, and not even annoyed that I'd gotten the news before she did. She agreed we couldn't keep the money for ourselves.

"Ana, this is great," she said. "I can buy a hundred dollars of pet food wholesale and give it to the animal shelter. That will be worth way more than half the cash. Then maybe we could put the other one-fifty into the Family Friends account. Is that all right with you?"

"I think it's perfect," I agreed, and counted out the hundred dollars which I stuffed into Adele's hand. "Put the rest in your safe until you see Geri." Geri Longcore was currently the treasurer of our church committee which helped people with all kinds of needs.

"Good idea," Adele said.

Apparently I was starting to think like a journalist, since I said, "We should probably get Tracy, you and me, Geri, and a rep from the animal shelter in one place for a photo. Jerry will want this in the paper next week."

Adele threw back her head and laughed. "Now you've got the idea, Ana. We'll make everyone in the county believe they had a hand in getting rid of a dangerous man and saving family pets. You'd better find one of the dogs that had a happy reunion, too."

I drove back to the police station, got the information from Tracy about the owners who had offered rewards, and then headed home slowly, thinking about how we could set up a photo opportunity. Maybe I'd go back out to Ham's old place and take some pictures there, showing the shabby kennels where the dogs were kept. This would also give me a chance to look around some more.

My cell phone was on the front seat, connected to the car charger, so after turning onto little-used East South River Road where I lived, I flipped open the phone and dialed one of the dog owners. A man answered, but quickly said his wife was the person I needed to speak with. He shouted, "Nancy."

Nancy was clearly an organizer. Her enthusiasm was contagious, and almost before I knew what had happened, I was committed to show up at her home on Friday morning with my camera and notebook. She promised to have a bunch of happy owners with their dogs there for a photo. They had informally joined together for support when so many dogs went missing, and she was certain they'd all want to meet me.

I wasn't convinced I was the hero she made me out to be since I'd discovered the dog-napping jerk pretty much by accident, but her appreciation felt good, anyway.

By the time this call finished, I was approaching the end of the road and my house. The final mile, on both sides of the road, was unbroken forest except for my property, the old Mosher place, where a large lawn kept the encroaching woods at bay. There were no other dwellings anywhere near me, not even any decrepit barns or sheds in clearings. The early October woods was developing color nicely with mottled reds, greens and yellows. The large maple at the end of my driveway was on its way to becoming pure gold.

I pulled across the dirt road, stopped at the mailbox and slipped the Jeep into park. It made no difference, way out here, that I blocked part of the lane. Years ago, the road had continued across Dead Mule Swamp and the Petit Sauble River, but a flood had washed out the bridge decades before. It had never been rebuilt. Past my property, there remained only an unmaintained track to the river's edge. I loved the isolation and peace of what I'd come to think of as "my piece of heaven."

The pull-down door of the mailbox screeched in protest. As I reached inside, I absently reminded myself to oil it sometime soon. I reached inside for the contents, which stuck annoyingly to the floor of the box. I had to lean out the window and use two hands to scrape the flat papers into my palm.

There was a flyer from a satellite dish sales rep and an offer for a free hearing test in Emily City. My credit card company wanted me to save money by borrowing with them. The bottom item in the stack, however, was curious—a cheap white envelope with no address or stamp, obviously hand-delivered. It was simply labeled Ana Raven, printed in both upper and lower case letters. It didn't look as if the sender was attempting to disguise the writing.

Of course, I tore the envelope open immediately.

> Ana,
>
>   Meet me at Turtle Lake Dam tonight at 6 pm in the small pavilion. Bring the photo.
>
>   Charlie Dixon

I knew it! I'd been right about Charlie recognizing that picture.

My thoughts swirled for the rest of the afternoon. I attempted to clean house and do laundry, but over and over I found myself leaning on the handle of the vacuum without moving it or staring at a half-folded garment without seeing it.

Charlie hadn't tried to hide his identity from me, but yet he'd chosen a rendezvous that would almost certainly be deserted on an October evening. Clearly, he didn't want people to see us meeting.

Turtle Lake Dam was within the state forest recreation area east of town. It was out of the way for Charlie, and a serious detour for me, by car. Even if I walked two miles upriver to the old railroad bridge and crossed on foot, I'd have another six miles to hike before reaching the dam. Too far to walk in a reasonable amount of time, and it would surely be dark when Charlie and I finished talking. He wouldn't want to give me a lift home; that was a safe conclusion. I'd need to drive.

Should I go through town on main roads and take the same route that Charlie would likely be using, or should I go south? I could cross the Thorpe, a tributary of the Petite Sauble, and then work my way east on dirt roads. This would take me down the steep and curving Mulberry Hill near where I'd been rescued by Paddy the Irish Setter, more than a year ago. Funny, how that had led to my new role as an investigative reporter, I thought. I decided I'd go that way, and went to the Jeep to make sure the county map was in the glove box.

Then I began to wonder why Charlie wasn't worried about hiding his identity from me or telling me about the picture of the young man. Maybe Faye hadn't told him I was now a reporter.

My first article was due to appear in the next day's Cherry Hill Herald. Then everyone would know. I'd have to tell him about my new role. What if he wanted his information kept off the record? Could I do that? Probably, if it would later lead me to more in-depth information. Maybe he just didn't want his wife to know.

So the afternoon passed, and at five o'clock, way too early, I pulled out of the driveway. I wore a fleece jacket and took my camera. With wispy clouds in the sky, the setting sun over Turtle Lake was bound to be enjoyable even if Charlie's information turned out to be boring. I wasn't the one worried about being seen, and skywatching was as good a reason as any to be parked at the edge of the lake.

The parking lot by the dam at Thousand Lakes State Forest was deserted. Actually, I was a bit surprised, even though it was a week day. I couldn't have been the only person in the area to think of enjoying an evening drive to catch the sunset.

I left the car far from the small pavilion and killed the extra time by walking out and back on the trail that crossed the dam itself. The pavilion was to my right, on a grassy area beside the lake. A lone kayak hugged the shore far to the east. I returned to the empty parking lot.

I made my way toward the building that was our designated meeting place. I passed a large rectangular pavilion that had one closed end with a stone fireplace and many picnic tables, but the small one, all alone at the end of the mowed area, was hexagonal, walled on three sides. It was now five minutes before six and there were still no other vehicles in the lot or on the visible portion of the road. I wondered if Charlie had been delayed closing the drugstore.

Stepping into the small stone hexagon, I was surprised at how dark and cold it was. The concrete floor chilled my feet right through my shoes, and the walls that were probably designed to block wind also eliminated the late-day light and warmth of the sun. Just for a moment, there in the shadows, I began to have the creeps. I shook off the mood and glanced back at the parking lot again. Still nothing except my blue Cherokee.

Behind me, a voice said, "Ana."

I whirled around, my heart pounding in my chest. A word I don't usually use escaped my lips. A man stood in the shadows, holding a long pole. A weapon?

I grabbed the edge of the table that occupied the center of the space. My greeting was anything but cordial. "Charlie Dixon! How did you get here? You scared me half to death."

Charlie looked crestfallen. He took a step sideways into the section of the pavilion that was still illuminated by the sun and became the unassuming rotund druggist, hair combed over his bald spot as usual. He wore a t-shirt, cargo shorts, and rubber sandals. Wet footprints showed where he had stepped onto the concrete. The pole was a kayak paddle.

"I'm so sorry," he apologized. "I told Faye I wanted to go for one more paddle this season, after work. It's an escape from my boring life."

"But where's your car?" I asked.

"I paddled from the boat launch. It's off Kirtland Road."

"Oh, right," I replied, remembering how I'd taken Star and

Sunny out in boats.

Charlie moved toward the table, placing the double-bladed paddle on the floor. "Did you bring that picture?" He swung his leg over the bench that surrounded the six-sided table.

"I did." I sat down beside him and pulled the folded printout from my pocket. I spread it out on the table, although it was too dark to see the features clearly. Charlie reached over and briefly touched the face on the paper as if it would feel three-dimensional.

"Not that I really have to see it again," he said with a heavy sigh. "It's me, you know."

18

Charlie and I sat quietly, side by side, for a long time. We found our voices simultaneously.

"Why was this picture on..." I began

"Where did you get that..." Charlie said.

We both exhaled sharply.

"You first," I offered.

"I'm just wondering where you found that picture. I thought I had the only copies that were left."

"It was on the piano at the Mueller's house. Mrs. Mueller, Lucille, insisted it was a picture of their son, Lawrence."

"Ah," Charlie said, and fell quiet again, resting his head in his hands.

I decided I would wait until he was ready to tell me more. The subject was obviously emotional. I watched the shadow of a support post reach a crack between the concrete floor sections. I shifted positions. The bench was hard and cold. Still, Charlie didn't move a muscle. The shadow swallowed the crack and continued biting into the next segment.

"Colin must have told Lucille it was a picture he had taken of Lawrence. I'm sure she never knew," he said softly.

"Never knew what?" But I suspected the answer.

I saw Charlie open his mouth to continue, but with a sense of guilt, I rushed to interrupt.

"Charlie. Wait. Don't tell me anything yet. You need to know I've begun writing for the Cherry Hill Herald, so talking to me isn't quite the same as it used to be."

Charlie sat quietly for another minute.

"But you don't have to print things I tell you. You're not compelled to do so. I don't know you really well, but as far as I can tell you aren't a person who sets out to hurt people on purpose. If something ended up in the paper it would only be because it was actually news, right? I mean, you aren't writing the gossip column, are you?"

I laughed at that. "No, not a gossip column."

"So if I explain the picture, you'll promise me it's off the record?" he asked, pleading.

"You know I can't make that kind of promise, Charlie. But I can say that unless what you tell me is pertinent to some real news item, there would be no reason to put it in the paper."

"Fair enough," he replied. "I already told you it's a picture of me. It was taken on my eighteenth birthday."

"How did Colin and Lucille get a copy?" I asked.

"My father had it taken," Charlie continued, as if he hadn't heard me. "I had just graduated from high school. I took the bus to Detroit. Can you believe there was actually Greyhound service to pretty much anywhere back then?"

"Your father was in Detroit?" I asked.

"He was there for a convention."

I shook my head to clear it. "I'm confused. Why did you need to go to Detroit to see your father?"

"Not to see Bill Dixon. Because Colin Mueller had written to me and explained that he'd be there for this dealership thing. He'd have lots of free time and no one would recognize us."

"So, Colin is your father?" I asked, recalling that Adele had told me Charlie wasn't biologically a Dixon.

"Yes. I'd been adopted by the Dixons. I always wondered who my birth parents were, even though Mom and Pop were great. They were my real parents, the ones who did all the hard work of bringing up a son. And yet, there was a piece of me that wanted to know where I came from, genetically speaking."

"I can understand that," I said.

"Even though we were raised in Thorpe, we shopped in Cherry Hill because it was bigger. Colin Mueller saw me often enough. He knew who I was; he'd arranged for the adoption privately and the records were sealed. There was a strong resemblance between Lawrence and me. Colin made sure that Lawrence always had a different haircut than I did when we were growing up. I mostly had buzz cuts. Lawrence went for the long-haired hippie look, much to his mother's chagrin."

"Until you were teenagers," I pointed out.

"Almost graduates. I think Lucille must have insisted he get it cut for his senior pictures, and as a result, there was a striking similarity in our looks that summer. However, Lawrence had gone away to college the year before, and I was just getting ready to do the same. So no one locally ever saw us together that year. And, Thorpe and Cherry Hill were almost two different worlds forty years ago."

"Lucille never knew that Colin had a third son... a son with a different mother?"

Charlie shook his head. "I'm sure she didn't. Colin asked me to keep our relationship secret. He said it would only hurt her terribly, and it was 'water over the dam.'"

"How did that make you feel?" I asked.

Charlie sighed, entwined his fingers and stretched his arms above his head. "Well, I was a kid. His kid. I wanted him to care about me. So... I was hurt, but I got over that long ago."

"Did you stay in touch?"

"No. Not at all, really. Except, of course, we both owned businesses in the same town. Thank goodness, there's enough of my mother's looks in me that I don't look just like Colin. Not that I ever found out who my birth mother is." he added.

I recalled seeing the pictures of Colin and Charlie together in the newspaper. They were similar, both slightly overweight and bald, but that could describe half the male population over fifty. Suddenly, I realized this story might be more than gossip.

"But, Charlie, this relationship could be important. It might give you a motive to want Colin Mueller dead," I said.

"Good Lord! Whatever for?" Charlie stood up and stared at me in astonishment. "Look, it's going to be dark soon, and I have to paddle back. Can we wrap this up?"

He pulled a small package from the pocket of his cargo shorts, unzipped the side and gave the whole thing a couple of shakes. A lightweight nylon jacket appeared magically in his hand. He slipped the anorak over his head.

I had a hundred more questions, or at least I thought I should have. Actually, I couldn't think of any good ones to ask at that precise moment. Why, indeed, would their relationship be a motive for murder?

"Maybe the weight of being rejected for decades finally crushed you," I suggested.

Charlie laughed. "Really, Ana. I thought you had at least a little common sense. And, if I had wanted to hide the relationship, I simply could have ignored you. You'd never have found anything out with certainty."

He took a couple of steps and picked up his paddle.

"Wait," I said. "Does Faye know?"

Charlie turned to face me again. "She does not. I'd also prefer that stayed the way it is. You can see that my chances of keeping this secret are better by telling you up front, rather than having you continue to snoop around. Why hurt Lucille and Faye for nothing?"

"How would it hurt Faye?"

"She's very sensitive to social issues. I assure you, I had no reason to harm Colin Mueller. In fact, I felt a real sense of loss when he died. There's probably no way left at all to trace my birth mother. Now, I really have to leave."

With that dismissal, he walked out of the pavilion and pushed his kayak into the dusky water.

19

Thursday was the regular meeting day of the Family Friends committee. I'd gotten involved with them even before I joined Crossroads Fellowship Church. It was a good-hearted group of people who tried their best to help those in the county who were in need of some kind of immediate aid.

Adele was chairman, but I wondered if she'd be able to attend, since she had been keeping the store open all alone lately. Even John Aho, who owned the service station and was perennially late, had already arrived.

At eleven-o-nine, just as we were about to begin without her, Adele breezed in, waving her arms and puffing. "Thank goodness. Suzi showed up," she heaved.

She was referring to Suzi Preston, who was attending Sturgeon Community College in the next county to the east. Suzi had worked in the store last year, but I hadn't seen her lately. Everyone, myself included, breathed a sigh of relief. Although Adele could be dramatic, and was certainly the town busybody, she was a great organizer, and no one else particularly wanted to lead our group.

After the routine old business was taken care of with minutes, and reports on who had received casseroles, rides to medical appointments, and such things, Adele announced "New Business," and turned to me. "Ana, tell everyone about the dog incident." At the same time, she pulled an envelope from her purse. She was smiling and definitely smug.

Adele held the envelope in her lap while I explained about the rescued pets and the reward money. Knowing that despite her other faults Adele wouldn't toot her own horn, I also told how she had leveraged the hundred dollars by donating dog food to the shelter for the wholesale price. That brought me to the remaining one-fifty, which I explained we'd decided to invest in Family Friends. At this point, Adele flourished the envelope and handed it triumphantly to Geri Longcore, our treasurer.

"The dog food is being delivered on Monday, and we can talk about what to do with this today," she announced.

"Personally, I'd like to hear a little more information about these possible oxy murders," Melanie Renton said. She had only been a member for a couple of months, and so far she hadn't done much except annoy the rest of us.

"That's not on the agenda," Adele pointed out.

"It certainly should be," Melanie pushed. "If we've got a serial killer in Cherry Hill, the Family Friends ought to be concerned with catching him."

John chuckled. "I suppose you're sure it's a man."

"A woman serial killer?" Melanie scoffed. "Ridiculous."

"What's ridiculous is wasting our time on this," Adele intervened. "John and I, at least, only have an hour. I don't know of any way the Friends can really help the police. Our mission is to aid individuals and families in need."

This sparked an idea, and I jumped into the conversation. "Maybe we could help someone related to all this, indirectly at least."

"The chair recognizes Ana," Adele said, suddenly getting formal. Probably to forestall Melanie from continuing.

"Everyone tells me that Ham Nelson was such a kind soul. I didn't know him well, but I did visit his grave and he doesn't even have a headstone. He's buried next to his parents, and there's just a plastic marker that's breaking down in the weather. Could a simple but permanent one be purchased reasonably?"

"Now that's a practical idea," Adele said. "Do I hear a motion?"

"So moved," I said.

"Second," Geri added. "I liked Ham. He was always big-hearted, even if he did smell terrible. He helped my sister-in-law move a mountain of firewood the year Lloyd died." She was referring to her deceased brother.

Adele called for further discussion, but the only comment was that we should keep the expense at a minimum, since a slab of granite didn't really help anyone alive. That came from Melanie, and I saw Adele wince in response.

I understood what she was thinking. It was hard to imagine anyone who didn't appreciate visiting a loved one who had passed away, even though we knew of no living relative of Ham. But the motion carried; even Melanie voted for it. John was assigned to research the cost, and the meeting was adjourned.

In the parking lot, Adele called my name. She and Geri approached. "Can you find out if Tracy would be available for a photo at three this afternoon? Geri wants to take lunch to Mrs. Vanhala right away. She's ninety-two you know, and then do some errands. We want to be sure our action gets in the paper as part of the dog rescue story."

"Sure," I said, glad I didn't have any particular afternoon plans that conflicted with Adele's.

"Just let me know if it will work. Geri will check in with me when she's free," Adele instructed. She was in her glory when in charge of arrangements.

So, at three o'clock, Tracy, Geri, Adele and I arranged ourselves, at Adele's bidding, in various poses against the courthouse wall, while Bob, the all-purpose police office assistant, snapped photos. He took pictures of us shaking hands, with Tracy passing an envelope to Adele or me, some with Tracy wearing her hat, some without the hat.

After a few minutes, I broke in. "That's probably plenty to choose from. Thanks so much, Bob."

He handed me the camera, and Geri bid us farewell. She headed for her car.

"Need a ride back to the store?" I asked Adele.

"Suzi's got things covered for now. We don't get any after-school rush since the consolidation. I should probably be back by five, though. A lot of folks do stop in after work."

"And, this means you have another plan?" I asked.

"Well, if you don't mind."

"You'll have to clue me in," I said. "What are you thinking of?"

"I'd like to see where Ham is buried. I guess you found the

spot, right? It's so sad. I want to know what it looks like before we buy a stone. Afterwards, it will be like all the others."

"That's what we want, right?" I questioned.

"Yes, but it would be good to have a record of how much we were able to improve things. Let's go take a picture."

We drove to the cemetery; it only took a couple of minutes. The well-traveled lanes between the grassy sections were narrow, and a parked pickup blocked the one I wanted to take. I turned at an intersection and pulled around the other way to the newest portion, which was also the farthest from the gate.

As soon as Adele opened her door, we heard a small motor and quickly realized the owner of the pickup truck was blowing leaves into a huge pile in the roadway. He wore muff-type ear protection, and obviously hadn't seen or heard us arrive.

"The Nelson plot is toward the back," I said, steering Adele in the right direction. "Maybe the fourth row in, or the fifth."

She read inscriptions on headstones as we walked, commenting on many of the names. I didn't know any of the people she chatted about.

I pointed. "Over there. That reddish one with a square top. That's it." The space looked different, but I couldn't tell how until we were almost there. Something lay on the plot, not at the base of Theodore's and Yolanda's stone, but clearly beside Ham's plastic marker.

"Someone's been here." Adele stated the obvious.

Tied with a pale blue, but new, ribbon was a small bunch of late Queen Anne's Lace and purple asters. It hadn't been obvious what it was because of wind-driven leaves mounded against the bouquet.

"Here! You!" Adele called to the man with the blower, but his back was toward us.

She strode purposefully in the man's direction, while I knelt down beside the simple offering to see if it held any clues. I snapped a photo before touching it, then brushed away the leaves. It was hardly wilted at all, and the ribbon was crisp—suggesting it hadn't been rained on. There was no note, no attached card. I couldn't see anything written on the ribbon. The sound of the leaf blower cut off abruptly.

A man's voice bellowed, "Holy hades, Adele. You scared me half to death."

I took another picture and stood up, awaiting the results of Adele's enquiries. She and the man were walking toward me.

"Ana, this is Fred Quimby. He does lawn work on contract with the village," Adele said.

"Pleased to meet you," I answered.

Fred nodded.

Adele peppered the man with questions. "Fred, were you here all day? Did you see anyone back here who could have left these flowers on Ham Nelson's grave? Did you see anyone at all?"

"Hold your horses, Adele," Fred drawled. "One gol-durned question at a time. Although they all got one and the same answer. No, no, and no."

"What do you mean?" Adele demanded.

"No, I ain't been here all day. Got here 'bout one. No, I didn't see no one back here 'cept you two ladies. And, no, I didn't see no one else a-tall. I'm mindin' my own gol-durned business, and you should, too. There, I said it."

And with that pronouncement, Fred replaced the ear protectors, pulled the starter cord on the blower, and walked away, spraying red and yellow leaves in every direction.

<h1 style="text-align:center">20</h1>

My appointment to meet the grateful dog owners was for ten in the morning. Following the directions I'd been given, I pulled in the driveway of Nancy's house, a modest ranch with an adjacent pole barn, on a paved road, surrounded by open fields.

When I opened the car door, I immediately heard excited barking from both small and large dogs, coming from behind the house. I was reminded of the barking I'd heard around Ham's trailer, but the tone here was different, not desperate. These dogs sounded happy. A slightly dumpy but neatly-dressed woman, middle-aged, appeared from around the corner of the house.

"Back here," she called, motioning for me to join her. "I'm Nancy Mankowitz. You must be Ana Raven. We've got lots of rescued dogs for you to meet."

With camera and notebook in hand, I followed her. She lifted the gate latch in a chain link fence that surrounded a large yard. There were dogs everywhere, and I managed to count six, but I might have missed some. A large black lab romped with a frisbee in its mouth, trying to keep a young man from taking it away. A long-haired dachshund was jumping at the same frisbee. A beagle diligently dug underneath a wooden sandbox. Dirt flew. As I watched, the dog withdrew his nose and sneezed.

Two golden retrievers were chasing each other around the perimeter, and a frizzy terrier-mutt stood on the picnic table surveying the riot— a monarch overseeing his kingdom. He appeared oblivious to the several people seated at the table, but barked with enthusiasm. The people didn't seem at all bothered by the sharp noise so close to their ears.

Nancy said, "Come meet Duke," and led me to the patio. I thought she was going to introduce me to her dog, but Duke turned out to be her husband, the man I'd spoken with briefly on the phone.

Another dog, a fluffy little golden thing, was cradled in his arms. "Hello," Duke said, after we were introduced. "This is Mitzi. She's a little shy when all the others are here playing. Joyeux— we call her Joy— the black lab, is our other dog. She's the one that was taken."

"But she's home safe, thanks to you." Nancy beamed at me. "Our son is so grateful. He's the boy out there with Joy. Oh, that rhymes." She giggled.

Duke seemed to feel some explanation was in order. "Justin's our youngest. He's living at home, just between jobs." He turned to his wife. "Nan, why don't you see if you can herd the troops over this way? I'm sure Ms. Raven doesn't have all day."

"Good idea," Nancy said, turning on her heel and heading for the picnic table.

In short order, people and dogs were sorted into sets. Leashes were snapped onto collars. A few of the dogs obeyed voice commands. Strangely enough, the beagle was one of the obedient ones. The people arranged themselves in a staggered row with the dogs in front of them. I snapped several pictures, and the dogs were released to continue their playing.

All the names, both human and canine, were recorded in my notebook. I listened to their stories, making careful notes. The goldens' story was particularly heart-wrenching. The dogs were sisters, but only one of them had been stolen. The remaining one, Chloe, cried and moped and wouldn't eat while Zsa Zsa was gone. Her owners thought they were going to lose both dogs, one to an unknown cause and the other from a broken heart.

I spent almost two hours in the Mankowitz' yard. They offered me coffee, which I accepted, since the air was cool, and I wasn't running around playing with a pet. Whenever the breeze picked up, the faint scent of burning leaves drifted through from somewhere in the neighborhood.

The only downside of the experience was when Nancy told me about several dogs that were not recovered. She'd invited their owners to come meet me, too, but they had all declined. "It was just too sad for them," she explained.

Around noon, I said I had enough information for a nice feature. I'd also snapped candid photos of the dogs playing. I thanked Duke and Nancy and asked if there was a place nearby to get some lunch. I wasn't planning to go straight home.

They apologetically told me there wasn't anywhere closer than the Buck Lick Bar, about five miles farther west, which didn't open until four. Nan offered to make me a sandwich. "Oh, no, I'll be fine," I lied.

I had decided to go back to Ham Nelson's trailer, which was on my way home, and poke around a little bit. The place was now empty, and Tracy had given me her blessing to look things over. Since she didn't think I'd find anything of interest, I was motivated to look hard and prove her wrong although I wouldn't rub it in. There had to be some clue that would lead me to the person who had cared enough to leave flowers on Ham's unmarked grave.

The choices for lunch were to go back to Jalmari, where there was a small pizza place, or to go hungry. With summer over, I didn't think the pizza place was open at lunchtime. I had passed a small gas station near the county line. It could hardly be called a convenience store, but they might carry a few snack items.

Soon, I was fortified with a bag of stale corn chips, a candy bar and a Coke. I vowed to eat nothing but vegetables for dinner and drove the back roads to Ham's former home, munching and slurping.

The woods, and the clearing surrounding Ham's trailer, weren't menacing at all in the daylight, just depressing. The old trailer did not sit quite level, and the factory paint job was faded and scratched. Of course, no one had cleared any of the junk from the yard. The front door wasn't latched and it repeatedly opened a few inches and then closed again, as a light wind moved through the clearing. Every time the door hit the jamb, I heard a soft thud. I was amazed someone could live in such a dump. Yet, I'd never heard that Ham was a complainer. Maybe he just liked his privacy and didn't care about other amenities. I recalled that Adele had said he tried to keep the location of the place a secret. Now, I wondered what secrets he might have had that were worth hiding. Did he have secrets so big they got him killed?

The small deck on the front was the newest thing on the property. It was solidly built of treated lumber, completely out of character with everything else. I mounted the steps and opened the door. What a stink! Mold and decay. Decaying flesh. The second shock, when I stepped from the deck to the inside, was the soft flooring. Probably water damaged, and I hoped I wouldn't break through. The floor was only about three feet above the ground, but who knew what was underneath the trailer?

With a quick look around the cramped interior, I located the origin of the foul smell. A dead raccoon was liquefying in the back bedroom. There was no apparent reason it had died there. As much as I didn't want to get anywhere near it, I was determined to search the trailer, so I returned to the yard and found a shovel with a badly weathered handle.

I held my breath as I entered the bedroom, scooped up the body and headed for the woods. Giving a ninja yell to boost my strength and buck up my courage, I flung the remains as far into the brush as I was able. "That should help," I told myself. Out loud. Then I pulled a sliver from the palm of my hand.

From the car, I collected a bandana, jersey gloves and a flashlight. I tied the bandana over my nose and mouth, bandit style. I reminded myself that Tracy had given me permission to be here. The odor inside was still strong, but tolerable.

Even though it was daytime, the interior of the trailer was dusky. Tattered curtains didn't block much light from entering, but the glass was gray with dirt. From my previous visit, I knew there wasn't electricity unless the generator was fired up, so the flashlight was helpful.

Realizing that others had searched the place when Myron Lake was arrested, I didn't spend much time checking cupboards or drawers. Anything that looked really new had probably been brought in by Lake. But, even though it seemed ages ago, Ham had only died in August. Yet, I reasoned that if he'd been hiding something it would have been a long-term project, secreted somewhere comfortable and old.

I rooted around under the bed and checked for loose pieces of paneling or removable sections of the vinyl flooring. I pried the bottom boards off the kitchen cupboards and checked the narrow spaces beneath them. Nothing.

Finally, it seemed as if there was nowhere else inside to look, and I resigned myself to crawling underneath the trailer. I found two large pieces of cardboard in the yard. They'd been rained on more than once, but were currently dry and not fragile. One section of the old skirting was loose, the obvious access point to the crawlspace.

I placed one cardboard on the ground just inside the hole and got on my hands and knees. A beam of light directed through the gloom revealed piles of sagging cartons, a stash of rusting pipe fittings, pieces of eave trough, and crumbling partial sheets of drywall. This was going to be a challenge. I thought about that soft flooring that was now over my head. Would the whole trailer crash down on me? Stacks of concrete blocks here and there seemed to serve as foundation pilings. It would be good to avoid bumping into those. Instead of covering my face, for this excursion I tied the bandana over my hair.

I pulled the second piece of cardboard in front of me, crawled on it, and by repeatedly switching cardboards worked my way to the boxes. Fortunately, they contained rotting clothes and didn't take long to look through. I'd been afraid of finding papers or books that would take hours to search. The piles of construction junk also didn't take long to examine. I found nothing of interest and saw no evidence that the dirt had been disturbed recently, assuming Ham's secret, if it existed, was something he checked on every so often. If he'd buried something years ago and left it alone, I had little hope of finding it.

When I came out from beneath the trailer, I was covered with cobwebs and dirt. The afternoon was passing, and I was frustrated and hungry. But I resolved not to give up until I'd checked everywhere.

Not wanting to enter another stuffy closed space right away,

I looked into crates and metal barrels scattered around the yard. Most of the fifty-five gallon drums were open and partially filled with stagnant water or were rusted out and collapsing. I tipped them all to check beneath. One had been used for burning rubbish and was full of wet and charred remains. I left that one alone. It didn't seem like a good hiding place.

Finally, I was ready to search the outbuildings. I counted four small sheds on the property. First, I looked through the one in the worst shape. It had only a dirt floor, and the roof was caving in. Again, I saw no evidence of recent digging. Peanut butter jars filled with rusting nails and screws, and a small bench, were the only items inside. The studs were visible with no inside walls. I couldn't see anywhere to hide anything.

Next I approached a low shed that looked more like a doghouse. Probably a well cover. One whole side was a door. When I pulled it open and aimed the light downward, a block-lined pit was revealed, about six feet deep, with a pump and tank in the bottom. A ladder was propped against the side. This space looked newer than anything else on the property, with the possible exception of the deck. I stuck the flashlight in my pocket, folded my body through the small opening and climbed down.

Once at the bottom, I played the light over the machinery. It seemed strange that a house with only intermittent electricity would have an electric water pump. However, when I thought about it, my own well system hadn't suffered during electrical outages. It just hadn't worked until the power came back on. Maybe Ham had filled jugs of water in the trailer when the generator was running. I shook my head in wonder as I contemplated the difficulties of his chosen lifestyle.

The walls were ordinary concrete block. Heavy foam insulation lined the roof and the above-ground portions of the walls. Nothing seemed unusual except its good condition. Could something be hidden between the foam and the upper walls? Pulling all that apart didn't appeal to me.

My enthusiasm was waning. Around the top edge of the blocks, a sill of planks had been laid to support the wooden structure. Idly, I shone the light around the juncture. One of the blocks in the next row down was cracked. I held the light steady and studied it. The crack extended to the mortar, and in fact, followed the edge of the seam. A tiny chunk of concrete was missing.

I picked up a screwdriver that was resting on an extra block beside the water tank, forced it into the gap, and applied leverage. The wall section moved easily and nearly fell on my foot. I moved just in time. Then I realized it wasn't a whole block at all but just the face of one. I pulled out the rest of the thin piece of concrete, revealing a space lined with metal. An ancient rectangular gas can had been fitted below ground, on its side, to keep dirt from falling into the hole. Inside that space was another metal box; the words "Premium Saltine Crackers" flaked from the side I could see. But there was no rust.

Carefully, I removed the box from its space and pried off the lid. A smile cracked the dirt which had stiffened my face. "Found your secret, Ham," I said.

21

I felt so self-satisfied with my find I went straight to Volger's Grocery, but not to tell Adele anything. Not yet.

A pint of kale salad from the deli balanced in my lap, I spooned it into my mouth while I drove home. There were two bags of healthy groceries in the back seat. I arrived, put the food away, and called Cora. "I'm bringing egg and spinach casserole and a tin cracker can to breakfast tomorrow, sans crackers."

"Oh, my! That should be quite interesting," Cora teased.

I attempted to put a mysterious tone in my voice. "All will be revealed as the clock strikes nine." Immediately, I hung up.

My evening was spent sorting through the contents of the can, organizing the items.

Actually finding something as an investigative reporter was energizing, and I had no trouble getting up the next morning in plenty of time to chop the spinach and green onions, assemble the ingredients and get the casserole in the oven at eight. It's not that I can't cook; I just don't like to.

Cora opened her kitchen door wide as I approached with the towel-wrapped hot dish in one hand and the saltine tin tucked under the other arm.

"Come in here," she urged, taking the casserole. "You look like the proverbial cat that swallowed the canary."

"It's almost that good," I said.

Jerry was waiting just inside the door, and he playfully grabbed at the box.

"Not so fast, buster," I said. "Just because you're sort of my boss doesn't mean you can steal my thunder. Or my cracker can."

"OK, OK," he agreed, grinning. "But don't keep us in suspense too much longer. I think it's nine-o-two. You're late."

The center island was already set with three place servings. Fragrances of cinnamon and sugar wafted from the rolls arranged on a plate. Cora began cutting and serving the egg dish, and Jerry grabbed the coffee pot.

Despite all the anticipation, we ate first, cleared the counter, and then washed our hands because they were so sticky. The cinnamon rolls were delicious.

With elaborate ceremony, I removed the lid of the saltine tin, tipped it sideways, and fanned out the contents on the smooth black granite. An assortment of greeting cards and folded papers was revealed.

"Wait!" Cora demanded. "Gloves. I keep some here."

Chagrined, I knew she was right, but I'd already sorted through everything, several times. Nevertheless, I waited until she'd brought three pairs: small for herself, large and medium for Jerry and me. We put them on, but there was no more waiting after that.

Cora reached for the top item, a Christmas card picturing a sleigh with sparkling snow, but Jerry reached out a hand and covered her small one. "Let Ana tell us the story first."

And so I did just that, bringing them up to date about the flowers found on Ham's grave, my visit to his trailer and how I'd found the stash.

"These are all from someone named Ellie," I explained. "Only a few are dated, and the envelopes are gone, but I've ordered them as best I could based on the handwriting and the few notes of personal information. Let's start at the bottom. You read this one."

I pulled out a piece of tan wide-lined school tablet paper and handed it to Cora. She carefully unfolded it and read, "'Dear Mr. Nelson, My mama and daddy tell me you are my real daddy. I have nev'r,' she left out an e," Cora explained, "'met you. I am seven and my name is Ellie. How are you? I hope you are good. Love XXXOOO.'"

Jerry said, "May I?"

I nodded, and he took the next one, a Christmas card with Santa on the front. "'Dear Pop, It was nice to meet you. I know

Christmas is over, but mama said it's OK to send you a card anyway. Thank you for the doll. Love, Ellie XXXOOO. P.S. I like you. Calling you pop makes me laugh. But mama says you are our big secret.'"

For the next hour, we worked our way through the stack of letters, maturing in their style, always thanking "Pop" for some gift, mentioning meetings but never telling where they took place. The child became a woman, with a baby of her own. Finally, there were only three unread letters.

"If there's anything that has significance to his death, it has to be in these," Jerry remarked. "So far, Ellie and Ham have been congenial, even if not particularly close."

I nodded. It was my turn to read. The letter was dated August of the previous year. '"Dear Pop, You hinted that you might have some money someday to help me out with Rob. If you are going to give me something when you die, this would really be a better time to do it. I'm trying to make ends meet, but you know how hard it is for me. I think J, the Jerk with a capital J, is seeing someone else and he'll probably leave soon. Good riddance. I don't know what I ever saw in him. I hope your leg isn't hurting you as much now as it was. Love, Ellie.'"

"Maybe that sore leg was the reason Ham was taking oxy," Cora said as she took the next-to-last item, a birthday card.

"At least she seems to have thought of someone besides herself," Jerry remarked, pointing to the "Happy Birthday" message.

Cora opened the card—a typical masculine design with a fishing creel and pole. She read, '"Hope your birthday is nice for you. Sure wish you did email. It would be easier. J is gone and Rob is a handful now, getting into everything. Can we get together? Call me. Ellie.'"

"Humph," Cora said. "Real mail is always nicer, but young people are so impatient."

"Yes, I don't think using the computer would have been easier for Ham," Jerry said. "For one thing, he didn't own one, and for another, I'm not sure he could have mastered the skills. And to even call her he had to use someone else's phone." It was his turn to read the last card, the Christmas card with glittering snow.

"'I wish you would have brought me some of that money, but it was nice to see you. Rob might not even go to college, you know. Love, Ellie.'" He placed the card back on the table, removed his reading glasses and rubbed his eyes.

"So." Jerry made that one word an entire sentence. "We have several surprising new pieces of information."

"Ham had a daughter," Cora said.

"Who was possibly adopted or in foster care, and she now has a son herself," I added.

"Most interesting, I think," said Jerry, "is that Ham saved money, and that he could think far enough ahead to want it to be used for that child's schooling."

"I wonder why he didn't pay for an education for Ellie," Cora mused.

"Maybe that's one reason she's so hot to get the money now," I said. "A little jealous?"

Cora cocked her head and squinted. "I don't know anyone named Ellie with a baby who lives in the county."

"And that's saying something," Jerry noted.

"Maybe she's in Emily City, or who knows..." I said. "But it doesn't seem like she's really far away. They got together nearly every year."

"Right. And I don't recall that Ham was known for disappearing for long stretches of time," Jerry added.

"Do you see this money as a motive for murder?" Cora asked. "It couldn't have been a huge amount."

"We don't know that," Jerry said. "How many times have you read about people living in dumps who died with thousands of dollars hidden in the walls?"

"If he didn't have it really well hidden, it's gone now... into the hands of the dognapper Manny or Myron or whatever his name is. And I searched pretty much everywhere except a couple of outbuildings," I pointed out. "Of course, I didn't take the walls apart."

"The real question is," Cora said, sitting straighter, "who and where is Ellie? She can answer some questions."

"She's almost certainly the person who left the flowers on Ham's grave," I said.

"It doesn't seem like she'd risk being seen if she'd murdered him," Jerry pointed out.

"True enough," Cora said, and I nodded in agreement. "But we still need to find her."

"Can I put all this in an article for the paper?" I asked. "I could include a couple of the nicer notes, ones that will appeal to people. We can ask Ellie to come forward. Or would that be violating her privacy somehow?"

Jerry closed his eyes in thought. "She put flowers in a very public place. That's certainly open for publication. Anyone could have found those, or seen her, for that matter. The letters are a different story."

"But Ham is deceased," Cora said. "Doesn't that change things? They often publish letters posthumously."

"Ham didn't write these. They were written to him. It's not quite the same." He turned to me. "Ana, why don't you plan to include only one of the earliest ones? Letters from small children are rather generic. I'll check with my lawyer about the others. Let's try to get Ellie to come forward and contact us."

"It seems to me like we're finding more mysteries, rather than solving anything," Cora declared with finality. She stood up and began loading the dishwasher.

22

That afternoon, I sat at the desk in my bedroom and tried to write my column for the Cherry Hill Herald, but the theme just didn't come to me. "A young child longs for her father, but where is he?" I wrote. No. "Challenged Handyman Leaves Missing Fortune to Unknown Grandchild." Maybe. "Does baby Rob know a fortune awaits him?" Nope.

I pushed the laptop computer away and tried to assess where this case stood. We still had four people who might or might not have died from an overdose of oxycodone. Well, Milo definitely had; Colin, Isabel and Ham were unknowns. No one seemed to have a motive to kill Isabel. Ham had money a secret daughter had wanted badly. Colin fathered Charlie the druggist and kept that hidden, but would Charlie really have murdered him because of that, decades later? It was curious that two of the four cases involved children conceived outside of wedlock. And hadn't Roy and Wanda been coy on the subject of their parents' extramarital activities? Was there another unknown child in the wings? Isabel's sister had been quite adamant that she, at least, had no offspring. I sighed. It was altogether too easy for men to become secret fathers, but women became mothers in full view of everyone.

It had been a week since I'd heard anything from the Sendak siblings, or was I supposed to have called them? There had to be more information they could give me. I rummaged in my desk drawer and pulled out the folded slip of paper on which they'd written a couple of phone numbers and other means of contact.

A few minutes later, I had directions and was on my way to Emily City, with an invitation to meet their mother, Milo's widow, Valerie. Now that Milo was dead, she had moved back in and taken over the house. That was an interesting development, too.

The address was easy to find, located on a wide residential street at the south end of town, a well-cared-for tri-level. The landscaping looked professionally installed with burning bush and Japanese maples flaming against white siding. Curving layered rows of stonework, bordered with masses of hosta turned autumn gold lined the driveway that led to a two-car garage on the lowest level.

A stone stairway curled languorously between shrubs and dwarf trees to reach the wide front door. Milo's money might not have been old or as extensive as the Caulfields, but he had clearly been well off. If we were looking at money motives, should I consider someone in his family as the murder suspect?

Wanda met me at the door with a baby in her arms. She seemed more confident than she had at my house. "Ana, we're so glad you called. I'll only be here a few more days, and Roy already reserved his flight to return to Gdansk. Come in. We should talk."

She didn't offer to take my jacket but led me to a well-lit living room, warm with buttery walls and honey-colored hardwood floors. Two sets of French doors faced the back yard and provided a stunning view of a large flower garden, with some plants already neatly trimmed back for winter. An oriental rug of modern design—midnight blue with a large creamy vine twining across it—defined the seating portion of the room in front of a gas fireplace. Wanda indicated I should sit on the gold silk-upholstered Louis XIV couch.

Roy and another man sat on the dainty matching loveseat and chair and were deep in conversation. They seemed unaware of our presence.

"Roy, Martin, leave off your solving of the world's problems. Ana's here," Wanda rebuked them. She turned to me. "You know Roy, of course, but Martin is my husband. He came down for the weekend."

Martin looked up and nodded in my direction.

A woman very similar to Wanda in her generous proportions, but older, appeared from a hallway. Although stout, she wasn't sloppy. She was well-dressed, considering it was Saturday, in an aqua pant suit. Her nails were a deep orangey-red and she wore matching lipstick. The only indication she was relaxing at home was the fuzzy slippers on her feet. "I'm Valerie Sendak," she said, reaching to shake my hand, which rattled the several coral bracelets on her wrist. "Thank you for coming over to see us. The children had been wondering if you would call."

I assumed she was referring to Wanda and Roy. Wanda fitted herself beside the dark and angular Martin on the loveseat, while Valerie and I took opposite ends of the couch. Talking in a group promised to be awkward and unproductive, but I figured it was up to me to begin.

"Thanks for your patience," I said. "I've had a chance to talk to several people recently about this oxycodone business, but I won't be able to work for you."

Wanda took on that helpless, crestfallen look she'd had when I first met her. Roy leaned forward, gripped the polished Louis XIV wooden arms and gathered his legs under the chair as if preparing to launch himself at me.

I lifted a hand. "Please. That doesn't mean I'm not following up on your questions. It's just that I have a somewhat official way to do that now, and I need to tell you about it."

Roy eased back.

"The Cherry Hill Herald has hired me to do some part-time investigative reporting."

Baby Carolyn shrieked suddenly, and my eardrums vibrated. I didn't miss that part of motherhood.

Roy spoke while Wanda comforted Carolyn and popped a pacifier back in her rosebud mouth. "So this means anything you learn will become public knowledge, correct? I'm not sure I like this very much."

"Not necessarily," I answered. "I'll need to use a lot of discretion. Jerry Caulfield is still editor, and the police will be notified of anything that seems important. They'll also have some level of control over what is released. But you won't have to pay me anything." The house and furnishings suggested that the monetary consideration wasn't going to matter much, but I presented it as a positive.

"We'd truly appreciate any extra help you can provide," Valerie said. "Nothing at all has been determined by the police. I don't think they've even begun any of the other autopsies. No one's uncovered any motive at all to..." She paused and her lower jaw worked back and forth. She sat up straighter and twisted her wedding band and a moderately large diamond around her ring finger several times. "...to kill Milo."

I remembered the siblings' suspicions, but couldn't ask about lovers in front of everyone. And if Valerie was faking grief, she was a skillful actress.

"Excuse me," Valerie said abruptly. "I'll go get some refreshments." She rose and headed through a connected dining area to what I supposed was the kitchen.

"This is a very nice house," I remarked.

"Our father was an excellent accountant. He was a partner in the firm and made many good investments," Roy offered.

Martin spoke for the first time, but kept his voice low, presumably so his mother-in-law wouldn't hear. "The man made a bundle. I think Valerie did it for the money."

Wanda gave Martin a black look, but didn't respond verbally. Instead, she said to Roy, "Take Ana out to see the garden, will you? I'll help mother in the kitchen." She handed Carolyn to the girl's father and stalked away.

Roy rose and extended his arm toward the French doors. "Shall we?" he asked. "It's Mother's full-time hobby, but things got a bit out of control this summer when she was, um, elsewhere."

Even a beautiful garden has little to see when already bedded for winter, but this was my opportunity to talk to Roy alone. I wondered if he and his sister had planned this: Wanda forcing me to keep my coat, occupying Valerie in the kitchen, thrusting the baby into Martin's care.

Roy pulled the door closed behind us. "Be careful of your gestures and reactions to what I have to tell you," he said as we descended broad steps toward the lawn. "Mother can see us out the kitchen window."

23

Roy began a general explanation of the semi-formal garden—how the lawn had been bare and plain with a few scraggly shrubs. His mother had drawn out a plan and spent the better part of ten years creating the borders and beds, stone-edged pools, a knot herb garden, and walkways. The design was easily seen with all the herbaceous plants cut low for winter. A few taller shrubs and tan clumps of ornamental grass delineated the far edges. Roy pointed toward these, down a central walkway.

We reached the grasses, which were taller than either of us, and Roy indicated I should turn left onto a stone pathway that meandered among the stems. It looked like the entrance to a maze, but it was impossible for the area to be large enough for one to become disoriented.

"I don't want to stay back here very long or Mother will become suspicious, so I'll get to the point," Roy said.

"All right; what's up?" I asked, turning to face him.

"Wanda has managed to search the house pretty thoroughly while she's been here."

I was surprised. "Didn't the police do that?"

"Not really, I guess. At first, no one realized Dad had died of an overdose, and now Sturgeon County has ruled it a suicide."

"They'll change that for sure if any of those other people had too much oxy in their systems."

"I hope so," Roy said. "Will the Forest County law enforcement work with Sturgeon County? With Emily City? I suppose the State Police will get involved."

"That will probably speed things up," I told him, but I wondered if it would only create more red tape that might result in my having more time to investigate.

"Anyway... what Wanda found. There are letters, quite a few of them, from someone to Mother. They appear to be from, well... from some other man." Roy paused and looked back along the pathway in the direction we had come.

"Who?" I prodded.

"That's just it, we still don't know. The envelopes are gone, and the letters are all signed 'C.' No other name."

I couldn't help myself. "C as in Charlie?"

"We have no idea," Roy snapped. "We're doing as much as we can. Let's get going."

He pointed down the pathway. We emerged along the back fence, heading in the opposite direction, toward the right side of the gardens. Despite his warning me against actions that might rouse suspicion, he glanced up at the kitchen window. Realizing his mistake, he waved as if he'd been hoping to spot someone.

Roy gestured at various features on this side of the garden, imitating a tour guide. Poorly.

"Some of the sentences in the letters are... embarrassing," he said, extending his hand toward a trellis covered in orange and red bittersweet.

I waited to hear more.

"He was trying to convince her to travel with him to Florida." Roy pointed in another direction toward one of the small pools.

"Did it sound as if they'd been together, had a sexual relationship?" I pushed for answers. We probably couldn't continue this charade much longer.

Roy swept his arm toward the house, and as he did so, one of the French doors opened and Valerie burst from the house. Her fuzzy slippers had been replaced by yellow and green polka-dotted mud boots. The effect, with the aqua pant suit and painted nails was odd, to say the least.

She forged down the steps toward us, with Wanda right behind grabbing at her left arm. Valerie turned slightly and slapped at her daughter's hand.

Roy took advantage of the moment to hiss, "I'll have Wanda call you with more information when she can."

By that time, the two women had reached our position.

"Mother, don't" Wanda pleaded, her tone anxious and whiney.

Valerie paid no attention. "I want to know what you two are discussing out here." With her brows lowered and her jaw pushed pugnaciously forward, the woman was decidedly unattractive.

"I'm telling her what a wonderful gardener you are," Roy said.

"Bulltinkle," Valerie spat. "You don't care one iota about my gardening and know nothing about all these things you're pointing at so wildly. You're up to something, Roy Aurek Sendak, and I don't doubt for a minute that Wanda and that puerile freeloader husband of hers are involved with you."

"Mother," Wanda implored again.

Valerie turned on her, extending a finger with its gaudy nail. "Get back in the house where your sniveling isn't so apparent to the neighbors. And you," she whirled back toward me, "get off my property. I wouldn't put it past you to be trying to concoct evidence that I killed Milo."

"That's ridiculous," Roy put in, stepping toward Valerie. "You're upset, Mother. Let's go inside."

"You've got that part right, my dear son, I am upset. I'm upset at the way you've been pussy-footing around, trying to find some way to make your father's death be something other than the tragic accident it is."

This exchange was most entertaining, and possibly revealing. Did Valerie really think Milo's pills had somehow gotten mixed up, or was she protesting too much to cover guilty knowledge? I was completely unprepared for the animosity she displayed toward her children which didn't dovetail with anything I'd heard about the family.

"I'm sorry we've distressed you," I said. "I assure you that Roy and Wanda have never suggested to me that you killed your husband." I didn't mention Martin's suggestion, and he may only have been joking. But I wasn't sure.

"What you tell me means nothing." Valerie continued to rant. "Get out. You've got no business snooping in my affairs. Go home where you belong before I call the police."

Since I already had my coat on and had left nothing inside the house, I wanted to simply follow the lawn around to my car, but the low decorative fence prohibited me from doing so. Wanda provided my escape route.

She walked toward a rear door. "Come through the garage. I'll show you to your car."

"And try to give her some final secret message?" Valerie demanded. "Not on your life. I'll see her out the way she came in."

And so we all climbed the stone steps and re-entered through the French doors. Martin stood at the edge of the blue rug, watching with an enigmatic grin on his face. He said nothing, but nodded as I passed. I did not acknowledge the gesture.

Without any further suggestion of refreshments or additional conversation, Valerie hustled me through to the front entrance.

After I backed out of the driveway on to the street, I glanced at the house. The widow was standing in the doorway, watching me with narrowed eyes.

24

After that encounter, I needed a break and made Sunday a true day of rest. I attended church, as had become my custom, at Crossroads Fellowship. The music was great, and brought me peace. Having friends who offered hugs without question, and who didn't yell, as Valerie had, was worth a lot to me. The snacks afterward were a nice perk, too. Small town life agreed with me, and I realized how fortunate I was to have found a home here.

I spent the afternoon doing mundane tasks and putting off the inevitable writing of the article for The Cherry Hill Herald. This was only my second week, and already I dreaded putting enough words on paper to satisfy Jerry. It was amazing how many drawers I could straighten in order to avoid sitting at the computer. I even daydreamed a bit about upgrading the kitchen. Perhaps that would be my next renovation project.

Monday, I watched morning break over Dead Mule Swamp. With the sun swinging farther and farther south each day, between the autumn and spring equinoxes, the colors of dawn were visible through the trees from my south-east facing upstairs screen porch. Soon, I'd need to shutter this porch against the winter wind and snow, but today I sat there in a wicker chair, wrapped in a fleece blanket, cradling my favorite blue and brown glazed mug in my hands. Inhaling the aroma of the fresh coffee was as important a part of my morning ritual as the sipping.

The birds had been leaving for the season, but blue jays still called raucously. A gray and white junco landed on the window sill— the first one I'd seen this fall. I resolved to get a bird feeder set up and wondered idly why I hadn't done so last year.

I sat there a long time, until the sun was high and no orange or gold remained in the sky. The last inch of coffee had cooled, and I needed to stretch my legs.

While I was descending the stairs to refill my mug, the phone rang. It was Tracy, calling from the police station. "We have some news I can pass along to you."

"Great! More about the dogs, or is that pretty much settled?" I asked.

"That's all over and done with as far as we know. It was just a sideline for Myron. He's got more serious charges to worry about in Indiana, and I'm glad enough to have him gone."

We both laughed.

"What I wanted to tell you is that although we aren't much closer to having autopsies done on Ham Nelson and Colin Mueller, we do have some information about Isabel Adams," Tracy said.

"How come it takes so long for the autopsies?"

"Paperwork. Priorities." I heard Tracy sigh. "We don't even have the bodies exhumed yet. We can't find anyone to grant permission in Ham's case, and although Lucille Mueller signed an authorization, the county hasn't signed off on the money to pay for it yet. A backhoe operator, transportation, the doctor... all that."

"But Isabel's is done? You've learned something?"

Tracy replied, "That's where we got a little bit of good luck. We actually don't have to exhume her body."

"Why's that?" I was perplexed.

"When she was transported to the hospital in anaphylactic shock, they drew blood and did a number of other tests at the time. Even though there was no hint of foul play, for some reason the lab still had her samples in storage."

It was easy to see where Tracy was going with this.

"And they could still test that blood?"

"Yes, with some qualifications. There was no oxycodone in detectable levels in Isabel's blood. It does degrade over time... they say as much as seventy percent loss in the eleven months. But if there had been enough to kill her, some would still have been found by the lab."

"So," I said, "we can cross Isabel off the list of potential victims."

"Absolutely. I'd email you a copy of the lab results, if you had email," Tracy said pointedly. "I'm glad to see someone writing about this case, but you really need to join the twenty-first century."

I grudgingly promised her I'd set up a free account next time I was at the museum, and she rang off.

I focused on the new information I'd been given, refilled the coffee mug, grabbed a muffin, and powered up my laptop computer.

Three hours and several phone calls later, I was ready to deliver the following to Jerry.

And Then, Were There Three?

Cherry Hill Police Chief Tracy Jarvi confirmed this week that Isabel Adams has been removed from the list of potential victims of oxycodone poisoning. Blood retained by the hospital laboratory since her death in April of this year has been recently tested for the drug. A spokesperson for the hospital who wished to remain anonymous stated, "Oxycodone depresses the central nervous system until, piece by piece, the body shuts down after large enough quantities of the drug are ingested. It is impossible to say exactly how much would constitute a lethal dose for a specific person. For someone who had never used the drug, a much lower concentration could have devastating effects. How high of a cliff does one need to fall from to result in a fatality?

In addition to that variation, the drug degrades over time in stored blood. However, given that the death of Miss Adams occurred just six months in the past, and there were no opiates [oxycodone is an opiate] present at detectable levels, it is conclusive that she could not have ingested enough of the drug to have caused her untimely death."

That leaves just three potential victims. Ham Nelson

and Colin Mueller's bodies still have not been removed from the ground to be autopsied. This common scientific procedure could eliminate them from the list of possible victims, but red tape has stalled the process.

Of course, Milo Sendak of Emily City did die from an overdose of the potent painkiller, but was it suicide, murder, or a tragic mistake? Officially, the Sturgeon County Medical Examiner has signed off on the death as a suicide.

Milo's widow, Valerie Sendak, firmly espouses the mistake theory, but his children, Wanda Sendak Reese and Roy Sendak are less sure. "We do not believe our father would have killed himself." Roy stated, unequivocally. "And it's difficult to understand how he could have accidentally taken an overdose. He was familiar with the drug, and was very careful to avoid becoming addicted."

The common thread is the Cherry Hill Pharmacy, where all the prescriptions were filled. But could Charlie Dixon be a murderer? Why would he risk losing his business by doctoring pills? It's also a mystery what an elderly car salesman, an accountant, and a disabled handyman would have had in common to provoke Charlie, or a different killer, to action. Is there more to these people's lives than meets the eye?

Lucille Mueller, Colin's bereaved widow was an avid gardener in her younger days, as is Valerie Sendak. Has being wed to a gardener become a dangerous condition? Of course, Isabel also loved her flowers, the indirect cause of her death by lethal injection of bee venom.

The one true mystery concerns the fourth possible victim, Hamilton Nelson. Ham died so bereft of resources that he was buried quietly in his parents' cemetery plot. His gravestone is being purchased by the Crossroads Family Friends because there is no one alive to remember him. And yet... what has been found this week on his unmarked grave but a spray of wildflowers tied with ribbon! Yes, someone misses Ham. Is it someone he befriended in life or a missing relative?

This reporter has discovered that the quiet man may have had a daughter. At least it is certain that he received a letter some years ago, which reads, "Dear Mr. Nelson, My mama and daddy tell me you are my real daddy. I have nevr [sic] met you. I am seven and my name is Ellie. How are you? I hope you are good. Love XXXOOO."

Although the letter is not dated, based upon the aging of the paper, it is probably safe to assume that little Ellie is now an adult.
Ellie, if you are reading this, it is time for you to come forward and prove your relationship to Hamilton Nelson. You can then authorize his exhumation, and he can either be removed from the victim list or conclusively placed there. Will you do it?

Relieved, I closed my laptop and pushed it away.

25

As usual for a Tuesday, I planned to spend most of the day with Cora at the museum. It was now early October, and over two weeks had passed since Milo's death. The only significant fact that seemed directly related to the oxycodone deaths was that Isabel did not die from taking the drug.

Before I could get to my normal routine of helping with cataloguing acquisitions, I had to create an email account. Of course, I had email in my previous life with Roger, but the account on the server I used at that time was gone and I had never established another. I was being dragged into embracing technology, despite my choice of a low-tech lifestyle, by the most unlikely people. Cora was twenty years my senior, and Jerry was older than that. But they both used state-of-the-art computers.

I sighed, sat back, and let Cora create an address for me on gmail. She stood before the computer, so diminutive she only needed to bend slightly to see the screen. She added Jerry's email and her own to the contacts list then backed away and motioned for me to roll the chair to the screen. I walked it in to the desk without rising.

I'm not really computer illiterate. It's mostly that there's no easy internet access from my house in the woods, and I haven't bothered to find out how to make that happen. I'd rather spend my money on other things that don't bring intrusions into my quiet world. The only person beyond the limits of Forest County whom I really communicate with is my son, Chad, and he likes to talk on the phone instead of typing.

Resigned, I decided I could ignore most of the messages I was sure to receive, but now I'd have to check my email at least every Tuesday. What a bother.

I minimized the browser window and opened the file

containing my column, which I had previously saved to a flash drive. While I was trying to decide whether to attach the file or cut and paste the text into a new message pane, Cora was apparently reading over my shoulder.

"Oh, dear," she commented, sounding slightly shocked and worried.

"What?" I demanded, exasperated. My patience was thin, and it was only nine-ish in the morning.

"I don't think Jerry's going to be able to use some of this. Possible law suits, you know. Have you been reading Dominick Dunne?"

Dunne had been the writer of a gossipy true-crime column for Vanity Fair, and in fact, I had read some of his work recently. It was flattering to have my writing compared with his.

Laughing, I said, "Well, Jerry wanted me to shake things up a bit to see what might happen. This should do it."

"Send it along. He's a good editor. But you should probably brace yourself for a mild reprimand."

That would be a novelty. I'd never heard Jerry seriously criticize anyone, but at least I'd get some pointers as to the direction he wanted me to take. I wrote a brief introduction, inviting him to slash and delete to his heart's content. Then I hit send and swiveled around to face Cora.

"This case is so frustrating. We keep discovering things, but they don't seem to be connected to the things we need to know to uncover a murderer."

"If there is a murder," Cora replied.

"Well, there is that."

I filled Cora in on the details of the past week. It was surprisingly painful to keep the secret of Charlie's biological lineage from her, but I had promised to do so. I focused on my time at the Sendak house. She laughed at Roy's poor attempts to disguise his motives and was particularly interested in the mysterious letters to Valerie from C.

"Did you see these love letters?" she asked.

"No. You don't think Roy and Wanda are lying, do you?"

"Hardly. But if you'd been able to look at the writing, maybe take a picture of one or two of the pages, we could compare it with samples of Charlie's penmanship."

"You know what his writing is like?" Cora seemed able to produce any artifact on demand. I didn't want to admit I'd seen his printing, but that could be quite different from his longhand.

"I'll bet I can find some exemplars. He was the church clerk for a number of years, back in the eighties. Can you think of some way to see those letters again?"

"Hmmm. I think Wanda gave me her email after their first visit, but it's home on the same piece of paper as her phone number. Maybe she can take some pictures and send them to us," I suggested.

"Now you're using your head. Run right home and get it."

"But, Cora," I protested, "we aren't getting anything done on your database."

"Fiddlesticks! This is much better. We're making history one stitch at a time. Just like knitting. Go on, get out of here. I'll run over to the church and hunt up some old log books. Knit one, purl two."

An hour later I was back in the museum research room and office with Wanda's address and Charlie's printed note, just in case the love letters weren't in cursive. I couldn't show the message Charlie had left me to Cora yet, but if it was a match to the love letters, my promise to keep Charlie's secret would become null and void.

I returned before Cora and emailed Wanda, but I had no way to know how often she checked her computer for messages. I was surprised when my inbox sounded a "ding" only minutes later. Since only Jerry, Cora and now Wanda even knew I had email, it had to be either a request for editing or something pertaining to the current quest. It was from Wanda.

"You caught me at a good time. Mom is out shopping. I get email on my phone, so you don't have to worry about privacy. I'll delete the message anyway. Here are pictures of three letters. Wanda."

I was opening the attached files when Cora reappeared carrying a large and old cloth-bound book.

"Found one," she said succinctly. "I probably have no authority to borrow it, but we'll copy a few pages, and I'll take it back later today. No one will be the wiser."

"Great. I've got three letters to look at. I'll print them out."

"If the writing is really similar, we'll probably have to get hold of the real thing and call an expert," she said.

"If it's not similar, will that tell us anything? Maybe someone who writes love letters would disguise his writing."

"Maybe, but you said there were a lot of letters. That would be a big job, to remember to change styles every time you wrote to someone you cared for."

"True enough," I agreed. "But it's probably not impossible to rule out."

The printer spit out seven sheets of paper, and I carried them to the table where Cora had opened the book of church business meeting minutes. Charlie's known writing was a masculine scrawl. It was legible, but had little character. He'd clearly signed the bottom of the page: "submitted by Charles Dixon, Clerk,"

I laid the printouts displaying a cramped and precise cursive beside the words on the lined page. The writing was not even a close match.

26

"Now where do we go?" I asked, disappointed. "It looks like Valerie had something going on, but probably not with Charlie. Even so, was she serious enough that she'd want to kill Milo? It's not like divorce is difficult these days. Look at me." I raised a shoulder and pulled my mouth sideways.

"And me," Cora said. "Jerry's my second and third husband. Although John died; that wasn't a divorce. Well, we've got three purloined letters, in hand, without taking any more chances of being found out. Did you read them?"

"Ha! I haven't had time yet."

Cora took several of the printed copies, and handed me the rest. The only sound for the next few minutes was the shuffling of paper. The writing was small and tight, so there were a lot of words on each page.

Cora clucked her tongue. The room was so quiet the sharp sound was explosive. "Listen to this," she read. "'Why not come to Florida to be with me, darling? You know there's nothing but ridicule for me in Forest County, and people there would take offense at our age difference. My brothers wouldn't understand. I can't believe we'd never met until the Flower Show. Besides, we can't be together anywhere near Milo.' Blah, blah, I love you and all that. People in lust are so foolish."

"Wow. So we know C is in Florida, and he's either considerably older or younger than Valerie. She's what, fifty?"

"Yes, that's about right," Cora said. "Milo was fifty-five. I think she was a few years younger. The age factor rules out Charlie, definitively. Maybe Valerie likes older men."

"Maybe she's a cougar. That would bother people more."

"What's that?" Cora asked.

"You know, a mature woman who takes up with a younger

man," I explained.

"Oh. Well. When did we start calling them that?"

"I don't know. There was a TV show, 'The Cougar Club.' Maybe ten years ago."

Cora shook her head. "Humans," she said. "They do keep on making history for me to collect."

Her gaze returned to the paper in her hand, and she shook her head again.

"Maybe he used to live here. Why does he think he'd be ridiculed?"

"Maybe he has some disability that he thinks people would make fun of."

"Perhaps," Cora tentatively agreed.

"Although I don't see Valerie settling for anything short of perfection," I said. "Milo was good-looking, well-to-do, athletic. He had a lot of appealing qualities. And rich."

"That sort of points to C being younger. Why would she trade Milo in on an older model? I guess a desire to switch could give her a motive to get rid of Milo."

"Whoa," I exclaimed, handing her the page I'd been reading. "I'm thinking younger. This passage is pretty hot."

"Men never really get over that," Cora said with a smile, her eyes scanning the page. "But I see your point."

We finished reading the letters we had copies of but didn't find any further information that looked useful. I stared at Cora, and she returned my gaze.

"We need help," she finally said.

I was amazed to hear this from Cora.

"What kind of help?" I asked.

"Adele's kind of help. She stays on the front lines of events before they become history and pass into my domain. I hate to admit it, but we are similar except in our time period of interest."

This admission led us to share a hearty laugh.

"But she can't keep a secret. Do we want everyone to know what we've found out?" I asked.

"Roy and Wanda opened this can of worms. They'll have to accept the castings."

It was my turn to be ignorant. "Castings?"

Cora grinned impishly. "Worm excrement."

"Adele probably can't leave the store right now. It's almost lunch time, and the deli can get pretty busy."

"Let's go to her," Cora suggested. "We can stop by the Pine Tree and pick up sandwiches. Something a little different from eating her own food."

We collated the copies of the letters. Cora folded them and placed them in her purse where I knew she carried a notebook in which she could enter any important information we might learn. Cora doesn't drive, so we climbed into my Jeep and traveled the few blocks to Volger's Grocery. We easily found a parking place on Main Street almost exactly midway between the store and the diner.

The diner's owner, also our friend, Jack Panther, greeted us cordially when we entered, and before long we were headed toward Adele's store carrying paper sacks of hot sandwiches and French fries.

Reaching the grocery, we stepped into the shade of the large maple tree, which had survived its sidewalk environment for more than a century. The autumn leaves had fallen to transform the concrete to a wavy golden sea which no one felt the need to remove. At this front entrance, I could imagine it was still 1900. The bell tinkled as we entered.

Inside, the twenty-first century was alive and well. Clad in modern synthetic jackets, a number of customers stood clustered to our left by the deli case, which was being attended by Suzi Preston. Adele was in her office, at our right. Her computer glowed through the large window.

Alerted to someone's presence by the bell, she waved and bustled out to greet us. We held out the bags as an offering. Adele recognized their origin immediately, possibly by the delicious odors of hot cheese, tuna fish and potatoes that permeated the air in their vicinity. The tuna melt was one of Jack's best sandwiches. She grabbed my arm and hustled us into the office.

There were only two chairs, so she and Cora sat, while I

leaned against the wall. Adele cleared the counter that served as a desk and spread out the contents of the bags. She looked pleased and was practically bristling with expectation.

"Drinks," she said, "the drinks are on me. What do you want?"

"Ice tea with lemon," Cora said.

"Me too, but plain," I added.

"Is bottled all right?"

We both nodded, and Adele hurried off. Cora glanced at her retreating frame, leaned toward me and whispered, "She's so excited she can hardly stand it, and she doesn't even know what we want yet. I'd laugh at her if we didn't need her expertise in human affairs."

I also leaned in close. "She likes to be included, and I haven't given her much information since our trip to locate Ham's trailer. You can't blame her if she's felt left out. Shh. Here she comes."

Adele reappeared with three cold beverages. "Just let me check out these few people. You go ahead. I'll be right there." She headed for the cash register.

The smells were too enticing to be polite and wait, so we followed her advice and began eating. In a few minutes she returned and pulled the office door shut. The large window made it possible for her to keep an eye on the store.

"No one can hear us, at least," she said. "Now, I'll eat, and you talk to me. I know you've got something interesting on your minds."

Taking turns, the two of us brought Adele up to speed. There were a few breaks when she left to work the register. We concentrated on the visit to Valerie and the letters we had in hand. I told her there were more, lots more, but this was all we had copies of at the moment.

"Let me see," Adele said, her eyes sparkling. She grabbed an alcohol wipe for her greasy fingers and then passed the container to Cora. The older woman methodically pulled out a wipe and cleaned her hands before opening her purse and producing the computer printouts.

Although we'd told her our conclusions, Adele wanted to read the letters herself. We certainly couldn't fault her for that.

"Oh, my," she said, as her eyes darted across the pages. "Yes, I see what you mean... brothers... ridicule."

"We think he might have grown up here, but we're only guessing as to whether he's younger or older than Valerie," Cora prompted.

"Brothers," Adele said again, which didn't seem responsive to Cora's remark. "Brothers. This is making me wonder." She looked up, and her eyes flashed between Cora and me. "I think I'm familiar with this handwriting."

I was astonished. "No way. That would be too easy."

Adele put a hand on each side of her head and rocked back and forth. "I'll have to hunt around in the attic. Can you let me take one of these pages? It doesn't matter which one. It might take a while."

Cora glanced at me and shivered. Her eyes danced, but her mouth was drawn into a tight smile. Maybe she didn't dare trust herself to open it for fear of saying something that would jar Adele's mental workings.

"Can't you give us a hint," I asked.

"No, no," Adele said. "What if I'm wrong? I don't want to lead you down some foolish bunny trail. I may like to know what's going on in Cherry Hill, but I don't want to accuse someone of breaking up a marriage if it's not true."

"Fair enough," Cora said.

"I'll give you an assignment, though. That's almost a hint. It will be easy enough for you to do, Cora."

"All right, I'd like that."

"Go back to your museum and hunt up a yearbook with Valerie Sendak in high school. I don't know her maiden name, do you?"

We both shook our heads in the negative.

"Then, if the school she attended wasn't K through twelve, get some elementary records from the same district. That should keep you busy for a while. I'll call you when I find what I'm looking for."

27

Cora and I returned to her office at the museum, feeling both excited and deflated. Cora said she couldn't get over how Adele lit up when she saw the tight cursive penmanship on the letters. She was sure we'd know who C was before long.

I, on the other hand, was surprised to find myself slightly jealous that the primary thread of investigation was no longer under my control. I slumped into the chair at the computer desk and was silently scolding myself for being so childish when Cora placed a hand on my shoulder.

"Why do you look so sad, Ana?" she asked. "Adele's memory is terrific, but even if she can't identify the writer, we won't be any worse off."

I straightened up. "You're right. And we have work to do."

A quick call to Wanda yielded the information that her mother's maiden name was Valerie Goulet and that she graduated from Emily City High School in 1979. Emily City is large enough to have more than one elementary school, and Wanda couldn't remember the name of the one her mother had attended but thought it was on the south side of town.

I had put the call on speaker, and Cora nodded when this piece of information was given.

"I don't know Sturgeon County as well as this one, but I think that would have been Placer Elementary," Cora contributed.

"That sounds right," Wanda said, "although I couldn't have come up with the name by myself. Why do you want to know about my mother as a child?"

"We're just following a lead," I answered vaguely.

"Has she kept yearbooks or any school newspapers?" Cora asked.

Wanda didn't know of any, but she promised to look around

when she could do so without arousing suspicion.

After the call ended, Cora insisted it was silly to wait for Wanda to go hunting through a house she didn't live in any more. We could drive right over to the Emily City Library and find what we wanted.

Thus, we spent the rest of the afternoon poring over yet more old school photos. Everyone looked dorky. The late seventies must have been an anomaly. I tried to remember what my senior classmates looked like. I could recall friends' faces, but they just registered in my memory as normal. Some day I'd track down my old annuals to see if they were worthy of a laugh or ten.

Although Cora recognized a few people who were about the same age as Valerie, none of them seemed to have any connection to the people we'd been following.

Valerie's pictures showed a slimmer version of the woman I had met. Apparently, she liked makeup and dressing up even as a teen. Most of the girls had short to shoulder-length hair and wore sweaters or plain tops with long-pointed collars, but Valerie's hair was curled in a breezy Farrah Fawcett style, and she wore a blouse with layers of ruffles cascading over her large breasts. The long open front placket was tied loosely and suggestively at her throat with a ribbon. She was a girl with lots of flounce. Maybe more than was prudent.

"You should see my senior picture," Cora said with a snort. "All the girls were expected to look just alike and oh so proper. Ridiculous."

As far as finding anything of interest in the elementary photos, there was simply too much information. Boys whose names began with C were plentiful. There was a Charles and a Chris in nearly every class, with others named Cory, Cameron, Chase, Carl, Craig, Chad, Caleb, Casey and even a Cyril. To find our C by this means seemed hopeless. And we didn't even know for sure if he had attended school in Emily City.

"Remind me why we are looking at little boys' pictures from a school Valerie wasn't even attending." I said, after jotting down "Corey Roosevelt, 3rd grade 1978" on a pad of paper. It was hard to care.

Cora shrugged. "Adele asked us to. I don't mind. Old school photos fascinate me. Although I have to admit I don't know nearly so many people from these Emily City books as I would if this were a Forest County school."

Finally, Cora paid to copy the pages from Valerie's senior year since those had the largest photos, and we left the library just as they were closing. The tan concrete building was nondescript in the flat light of dusk, a fitting place to have found nothing of interest.

"Come eat with me," Cora suggested. "Jerry's always so busy with the paper on Tuesday evenings, I rarely see him. He'll just run through the kitchen for a sandwich."

"Are you sure it's okay? I already get breakfast at your house nearly every Saturday."

"Posh. Of course it's all right. Do you play any card games? Although I should warn you I'm a whiz at canasta. We'd need Jerry for bridge, even with a dummy hand."

I laughed at this novel idea. Although Cora and I had been friends almost the whole time I'd lived in Cherry Hill, we'd never done anything so frivolous. "You'll have to remind me of the rules for canasta. I do Scrabble. Or cribbage," I added as an afterthought.

When we entered Cora's kitchen, Jerry was hunkered down at the center island with a cold roast beef sandwich in one hand and his tablet computer under the other. The odor of horseradish was so strong it made my eyes water. He was furiously punching and swiping at the small screen.

"Oh, Jerry," Cora shrilled. "Take that horrid sandwich and go to your office."

The startled publisher raised his eyebrows and arose from the stool, licking his fingers. "Your wish is my command, madam." He spoke my name and nodded to me, picked up his plate and tablet, and headed for the front of the house. At the last minute, he turned and winked.

"I'll make apple crisp," Cora offered as an apparent apology for being harsh. "Ana and I are going to play some games in here anyway."

"Sounds great," Jerry said. "Have fun."

Cora opened a window and made motions as if she were shooing the strong odor out of the house. "That's one condiment I could live without, but it's his favorite."

My nose was starting to burn. "It is pretty strong," I agreed.

"You call Adele and tell her we're both here," Cora ordered. "I'll find the Scrabble board, if that's all right with you." She breezed out of the kitchen.

"Sure. You'll probably beat me, but that's OK," I called after her.

I didn't have my cell phone with me, so I dialed Adele's number from Cora's house phone. It rang and rang, and voice mail kicked in. I recorded what we'd found and that we were both at Cora's for the evening.

"No answer," I said, when Cora reappeared carrying a worn maroon box. "I left a message."

"I wonder where she is. She didn't say anything about any meetings. Maybe she had to go out somewhere to find C. More and more mysterious."

"Yeah, and maybe she's not looking for C at all. Let's play some games and forget about Adele," I said.

Cora laughed, "Oh, she's working on C, all right. You can count on that. There's no way she would perk up like she did this afternoon and then drop that ball. If she had another commitment, she probably skipped it to work on our puzzle."

Cora and I put together sandwiches without the horseradish and made fresh decaf coffee. Then we battled over words with complete concentration. I was surprised that we were quite evenly matched, and the time flew as we competed for superiority. As of quarter to nine, I had won two games and Cora had won one. But I had a Q and a J, with one vowel, an unhelpful I, and she was beating the socks off me when there was an insistent knock on the kitchen door.

28

The knocking brought Jerry in from his office. He looked around expectantly as Cora opened the outside door to admit Adele, who carried a small cardboard carton.

"I found them," Adele announced.

Simultaneously, Jerry said, "Where's the dessert?"

"Oh my goodness, I forgot all about it, but it won't take long," Cora said. She bustled to the refrigerator and brought out a bag of apples.

Adele placed her box on the kitchen island.

"We're done, right? I'll concede this game," I said to Cora.

She agreed, smiling at my concession, and I swept the letter tiles back into their container, making room for whatever Adele had to show us.

Of course, Adele couldn't reveal her secret without a decent build-up to give her credibility points with whoever was counting. She certainly was.

"I've been in the attic for hours," she began. "That's why I didn't hear the phone ring. But I got the message off the machine when I came downstairs."

By the time Adele was done taking us on a verbal tour of her third floor, without really telling us anything, Cora had the apples peeled and all the ingredients layered in a glass pan. She slipped the dish into the oven.

"Thirty minutes," Cora said, setting the timer and seating herself alongside Jerry at the island.

I was surprised that Jerry remained in the kitchen to listen to Adele. He wasn't up to speed on our mystery person, but he was willing to help things along to reach some pertinent information.

"So, Adele," he began, "you've uncovered something that's important in our mysterious deaths? I'm ready for the big revelation."

His commanding voice did the trick.

"Absolutely," Adele responded to his prompting.

Jerry reached for the box she'd brought, but Adele quickly drew it to her bosom.

"Here's what I found." But she made no move to release the carton.

"We love what you've done," Cora wooed. "It's greatly appreciated. Won't you share it with us now?"

"I knew I recognized that writing the minute you showed it to me," Adele said. "And I knew it had something to do with church."

Cora nodded in encouragement.

"Church from a long time ago," Adele added. "I started back in the far corner, but those boxes were too old."

"You explained that already," Jerry pointed out.

"Well," Adele huffed. Then she calmed down. "You're right. After all, the boxes were labeled with the year. So I knew I needed something from the 1980s. I save these things because you never know what might be important. And I was right! Where are the rest of your letters?"

I ran to my car and returned with the file of printouts we had made. When I returned, everyone was rigidly seated exactly as when I'd left.

Adele reluctantly released her death grip on the box and flipped open one of the flaps. She reached in and withdrew a sheaf of lined and punched notebook paper, stapled together in the upper left corner. She placed it on the countertop but kept her left hand spread over the writing. "Put your letters there," she said, nodding to the spot beside the papers.

As soon as I did we could tell, since she couldn't cover all the words, that the writing was very similar.

The timer on the oven produced a brutal buzz, and we all jumped. Adele knocked the cardboard box onto the floor with her right elbow.

Cora hustled to turn off the buzzer, Adele leaned over to retrieve the box thereby uncovering the papers, and as she did,

I slid the lined sheets closer to me.

Cora peeked in the oven. "Two more minutes," she announced. Then she hurried to look over my shoulder.

"They match," I said.

"I agree," Cora said. "But clearly, the writer is more mature in the letters we have. That makes sense."

Adele had recovered the box and was upright again. "Oh, let me show you, please," she implored. She sounded like a child whose surprise had been spoiled.

"You're right," I conceded. "We're stealing your show. But don't keep us in suspense any longer. We need answers."

She paused again.

"Seriously, Adele. Enough is enough," I said.

At last, Adele settled down to business. "For several years, the district ran a contest for juniors and seniors in high school. They were to enter a thousand-word essay explaining the basis for their faith. I was the local judge. That meant, in addition to choosing the top three to be sent on to district competition, I had to type those essays in a specific format. The originals were kept by the church, and when a lot of old records were dumped, I took them home rather than have them be discarded."

"Whose entry is this?" Jerry urged.

"See for yourself. It's on the last page." Apparently, at last satisfied with her success, Adele handed the papers to Jerry.

He turned the pile over and read, "R. Matthew Smith."

"What?" Cora exclaimed, reaching for the stack. "That doesn't start with C. Let me see those."

I'm sure a slow smile spread across my face as I recalled my conversation with Isabel Adams' sister, Julia. "Cubby," I said. "It's the youngest turtle, Raphael Matthew 'Cubby' Smith."

"The crisp!" Cora shouted, tossing the papers on the counter and jogging to the oven.

Despite Cora's concern, the cinnamon-rich dessert was perfect, and we topped off our steaming bowls with vanilla ice cream.

We decided it was too late, almost ten o'clock, to contact either of the two Smith brothers whose whereabouts we knew. Michelangelo John, M. Jack, was the familiar news reporter.

Although we didn't know his work hours, we could certainly contact him tomorrow through the television station. Don, who had easily taken his nickname from Donatello, was Adele's grandson's allergy doctor. His office was in Emily City. One of these men would know how to find Cubby.

"It fits, don't you see," Cora said, wiping the corner of her mouth with a paper napkin. "Those silly names. Why do parents do that? Cubby must have always felt ridiculed and couldn't bear to be called Rafe or even Matt."

"If my recollections are accurate, he even hated the color green," Adele added.

Jerry rose from his stool and placed his dishes in the sink. "Well, ladies, I have to be up very early to make sure the presses are rolling for this week's Herald. The papers need to hit the street by ten as you well know. I bid you good night."

With a sly smile, he gave Cora a peck on the cheek. Then he turned to me.

"Ana, I did some editing on that article you sent me, but I have high hopes that we'll soon have a response and can identity Ham's relatives."

"Oh?" Adele perked up. "What's this?"

Jerry left the room. Since the secret existence of Ellie, Ham's daughter, would be revealed the next day in the weekly paper, Cora and I brought Adele up to date over final cups of decaf. Giving her a head start on what was sure to be tomorrow's big news was a good payoff for what she had brought us.

It was after eleven when I finally pulled Cora's kitchen door shut behind me. The window went dark, and as I pulled away from the beautiful Victorian home an upstairs light flicked on.

29

Wednesday morning, my phone again rang at eight o'clock. Why, oh why, were my friends all morning people? I was already up, but my coffee hadn't cleared the morning fog, so I did more listening than talking. First Cora called to clarify that she would contact the TV station to speak to M. Jack Smith. She had decided she would request that they produce a short news special about her developing museum in the old school building.

"What we're doing is extremely newsworthy, and nobody's yet given it the time of day," she said curtly.

I agreed with her and knew she'd track down Cubby's whereabouts in the interest of preserving local history. Her talent for collecting minutiae while making people feel valued was amazing.

At eight-forty, Adele called. She'd already tried to reach Doctor Don but hadn't gotten past the receptionist. She did manage to extract a promise to have the doctor call her when he was free. I explained that Cora was getting a lead from M. Jack.

Both of my friends said they'd call me as soon as they learned anything. I wanted to get outside and suggested they use my cell phone to reach me. It was a good thing I'd remembered to charge it.

The sky seemed to promise another beautiful October day, providing a clear blue backdrop to the red and yellow maples and gold willows in Dead Mule Swamp. I ate a muffin and finished my third cup of coffee. Then I headed out for a walk down the pathway that wound through the wetland and came out on the seasonal extension of East South River Road. The sun was warm, but a hint of autumn chill could be felt in the breeze. Walking this two-mile loop was one of my pleasures. I tried to do it every day.

I hoped Cubby would be willing to give us some information. It seemed more likely he would react badly to having his affair with Valerie discovered, and he might clam up. And what did we hope to learn from him, anyway? Making a list of questions to ask would probably be wise.

Cherry Hill, Dead Mule Swamp, and Forest County still held the same appeal for me as I had felt when I chose to move here, but discovering so many cross-family connections and sordid activities had disabused me of believing that people here were somehow superior to those in the suburbs. Maybe small towns hid things better. Maybe the residents learned to live with it better because everyone knew, or was related to, three or four generations of their neighbors. You had to get along... probably no one was going to move away just because something embarrassing had happened.

I pulled my thoughts back to the problem at hand. Questions for Cubby. How long had he and Valerie been seeing each other? Did Milo know? Were they seriously considering marriage or living together? If so, and Milo wouldn't let Valerie go or grant her a divorce, that would definitely give her a motive to try to get rid of him some alternate way. Did Cubby have any possible connections with Colin Mueller or Ham Nelson? That seemed like a stretch, but the only death we had definitely ruled out as a murder was Isabel's. If we were indeed dealing with multiple killings, the reason had to reach beyond one person's relationship with one of the deceased. There was so much we didn't know.

For the rest of the morning I worked outside. First I raked leaves onto a tarp and dragged it back into the woods to dump, hopefully downwind so they wouldn't return to the yard. Then I hauled stones from the old barn foundation to pile around the base of the mailbox post. The box was beginning to list to the east and this solution should help it through the winter. I'd learned the hard way that the snowplow often hit mailboxes, so I certainly didn't want to do a major repair before the snow season. Soon, I'd need to cover my upstairs screen porch with the shutters my son and I had made last year, but I hoped for a few more Indian summer days before cold weather set in, and rain and snow blew across my landscape.

Just when my stomach growled, a buzzing from my pocket alerted me to another phone call. It was Adele.

"Ana, I've got an email for Cubby," she said. But she sounded disappointed. "Doctor Don wouldn't give me a phone number. Said he didn't want to invade his brother's privacy that much." Her voice took on a huffy tone. "He wouldn't even tell me where the boy lives."

"No problem," I responded. "Maybe Cora will get more out of M. Jack. In any case, you've come up with contact info, which is great. I'll let you know when I hear more."

I put away the tools and headed into the kitchen, tossing my work gloves on the table and chuckling at Adele's use of the word "boy." Cubby had to be nearly forty. I wondered if he was tall, short, cute, bald, skinny, fat, or nondescript. Then I remembered who it was that thought she was in love with him—Valerie. That probably meant he was good looking. His oldest brother, M. Jack the TV newsman, was really handsome. Maybe Cubby looked like him.

Despite the small effort I made to be patient, after eating a sandwich I drove to the museum in Cherry Hill to find out if Cora had been able to get any better information than Adele.

Cora was writing at her desk and looked up as I entered her office. She was beaming.

"Your timing is impeccable," she said. "I just finished chatting with M. Jack Smith."

I smiled in return and pulled up a chair.

Cora continued. "First of all, M. Jack told me that Cubby moved to Florida last year."

"That fits with what we know of the mysterious C. He has to be the right person."

Cora nodded. "Yes, I agree."

"Did he tell you how we can get in touch with Cubby? Adele got an email address from Don, but a phone conversation would be better. We could hear his tones as well as the actual answers to questions."

Cora backed up to relate her dialogue with M. Jack.

"Michelangelo John is the oldest of the boys, as you know. He looks much younger on the television than he really is. He credits it to good makeup and regular workouts. I convinced him that our museum is providing a service to the entire region, particularly since we employ students for on-the-job training."

"So you gave him a great local feature story," I said. "What did he give you in return?"

"We need to pick Adele up after the store closes and go to my house," she answered cryptically.

"And?"

"M. Jack said he'd convince Cubby to call my house at seven tonight, our time. We can put the call on speaker and all talk with him."

I leaned back. "But what if Cubby doesn't agree?"

"M. Jack thinks the authorities are stonewalling on connecting the oxy dots, and he wants to break the news story open. He's going to push his brother. After all, now that Milo's dead, unless Cubby was part of a murder plot there's only an affair to discuss. No one's even shocked by those any more."

I drove to Volger's grocery and picked up a copy of the Cherry Hill Herald. A copy would be in my mailbox tomorrow, but I didn't want to wait that long to see the article about Ham's daughter and the plea for her to identify herself.

Adele was busy at the checkout with the late lunch crowd, and I sat in her office reading the paper until she was finished.

My concerns that she might be jealous at the good response Cora received from M. Jack were unfounded. She was delighted to be included in the plan to talk with Cubby.

Consequently, at five minutes to seven that evening, Cora, Adele, and I were once again seated around the center island in the Caulfield kitchen. But when the phone rang and Cora picked up, we were disappointed to hear the familiar television voice say, "Mrs. Caulfield? Hello, this is M. Jack Smith."

30

However, our disappointment was overcome when he continued with, "I've dialed this in as a three-way call from my smart phone. Raphael— Cubby— is also on the line, but I told him I'd participate in the call to support and advise him. M. Jack is my formal TV name. Please call me M.J."

"Hello?" A tentative voice spoke the greeting in a higher tone than M.J.'s. It made Cubby sound smaller than his oldest brother, the only one of the four turtle-boys that I had a mental image of, to reference. Somehow he also sounded rounder than the fit and angular M.J. I shook my head. How could that be determined with nothing but a voice on a tinny speaker?

I decided I should take the lead. "Hello, Cubby, this is Anastasia Raven. Thank you so much for agreeing to talk with us. Cora Caulfield and Adele Volger, your former Sunday School teacher, are here, too."

"Mrs. Volger, how are you?" Cubby squeaked.

"I'm doing well, thank you," Adele answered.

"And I'm Cora, the local historian," Cora added.

I continued. "We don't want to embarrass you unnecessarily, but there are going to be some sensitive topics in this discussion."

"We understand that," M.J. cut in. His voice was the deeper of the two, and familiar to all of us from his news reports. He was also clearly the one in charge. "Actually we have prepared for this, in anticipation of some of your questions. And we'd like to eliminate the small talk and get right down to business. Raphael will freely admit to an affair with Valerie Sendak."

"All right," Cora said, "but then why have you moved to Florida and carried on what appears to be a secret correspondence?"

Adele added, "We certainly had to use our heads to discover

that you are the mysterious C in Valerie's letters. Only a few weeks ago you didn't seem to want anyone to learn about the two of you." She paused. "But I figured it out, you know."

"Cubby, would you respond to that, please," I asked.

We heard the higher-pitched male voice say, "Well, when Milo was alive, we, um... didn't want to make things hard for Valerie."

"But now he's not alive," Adele said bluntly.

"Right," Cubby said. "And I definitely didn't have anything to do with that. Believe me. I've been in Florida for several years."

"Let's say we do believe you," Cora posed. "But Milo is still dead, and we also have two other possibly related deaths. I assume M.J. has explained this to you. As difficult as it might be for you to consider, perhaps Valerie was involved, even if you aren't. We need to determine if you know of any connections between Milo, Charlie Dixon, and Colin Mueller."

I added, "You may feel uncomfortable, thinking we are trying to involve Valerie, but we need to get to the bottom of this."

M.J. entered the conversation again. "I'm going to stop us right here for just a minute. Do you have a way to receive a photo electronically, immediately?"

Adele and I looked at each other blankly, but Cora spoke up. "Yes, I believe so. I'll go get Jerry's tablet. You can email the file to his account or mine."

Cora gave M.J. an address, and she bustled out of the room. The silence as we waited became strained, or perhaps that was just my perception.

Before Cora returned, Cubby said, "We are sending a picture of me, taken very recently. It may help you understand some things." His voice definitely sounded tense.

In a couple more seconds, Cora was back and poking at the black glass of the tablet. I heard her sharp intake of breath, and then I looked at her directly. Her eyes were wide. She swiped the surface, spreading her thumb and forefinger to enlarge the image, and turned the thin device toward us.

The face of the man filling the screen was round. His head was nearly bald, and the features were all too familiar. Cubby was another Xerox copy of Colin Mueller, Lawrence Mueller and

Charlie Dixon. But I couldn't say anything. Even though I suspected Cora might have figured it out, I had promised Charlie I wouldn't reveal his parentage. Adele knew even less than we did; she hadn't been told anything about the similarities in photos Cora and I had found. This made it natural for her to be the first to react.

"You look just like Charlie Dixon," Adele exclaimed.

"I know," Cubby said quietly. "When I began to lose my hair I realized I had to leave the area for good."

"But what does it mean?" Adele asked of no one in particular. She blinked and rubbed her fingertips against her temples through her permed curls.

Personally, I was stuck on the fact that Cubby was not handsome or confident-sounding. He didn't seem to have any of the traits I would have expected Valerie to insist upon in a lover. My mind drifted, thinking along those lines when M.J.'s commanding voice brought me back to the conversation.

"...a good chance Mr. Dixon and Cubby are half brothers. This has caused a serious rift in our own family relations, as you might imagine. We have come to the conclusion, in light of the questionable deaths the authorities are investigating, that it will be impossible to prevent the public from learning at least some of these unpleasant facts."

"But are you certain you are dealing in facts?" Cora interposed. "Perhaps Charlie and Raphael only look alike. There are many balding men over forty who've put on a few extra pounds."

M.J.'s answer convinced us he knew what he was talking about. "We've decided that all further inquiries should be handled through Raphael's lawyer. He'll decide which parts are pertinent to a criminal investigation."

Cora took over the conversation and verified that she had received complete contact information for M.J., Cubby, and the lawyer as quickly as M.J. emailed it to her. Adele was apparently too stunned to speak, and I was lost in thought. Cubby might have left the conversation minutes ago. He did not even say goodbye.

Adele propped her elbows on the counter and held her head in her hands as if it hurt. Cora and I stared at each other across the black granite island.

31

"Cherry Hill is turning out to be a tiny Peyton Place," I finally said.

My disillusionment must have been revealed in my voice because Adele reached over and patted my arm. She said soothingly, "Every town is, Ana. It's just harder to bear when we know all the people. The soap operas make it look so sophisticated. But it's not that way at all. It just hurts everyone."

Our little group broke up quietly. We agreed that Cora and I would meet at her office in the morning to phone Cubby's lawyer, George G. Hartwick. Adele hated to miss the call, but she was expecting deliveries at the store and had to be there.

As it turned out, I wasn't able to be with Cora, either.

I was puttering around in the kitchen and finishing my third cup of coffee. A glance outside revealed light frost covering the windshield of my Jeep. I ran upstairs to grab warm gloves from the bedroom closet, the first morning this fall I'd wanted them. Coming back down the stairs I was startled to hear a knock on the kitchen door. There hadn't been any other car but mine in the driveway a moment ago.

The top half of the kitchen door had a large window, and from across the room I saw a young woman standing on the small concrete stoop. She wore maroon scrubs and a gray hooded sweatshirt that was unzipped. Her dark hair was very short, almost a brush cut. While I watched, she flipped up the hood, pulled the sweatshirt tightly around her thin frame and shivered. I had no idea who she was.

Since I live at the end of the road, people don't just happen to pass by or have car trouble before nine in the morning, or at any time of day. She must have come here for a reason. Her demeanor was anything but threatening, so I opened the door without hesitation.

"May I help you?" I asked.

"Are you Ana Raven? My name is Helen Bracket. Can I come in?"

I gestured for her to enter. "Sure. Let's sit here in the kitchen. Would you like some coffee?" I offered. The strong odor of stale cigarette smoke emanated from her clothing.

The painfully thin woman— she was quite young, I saw her as a girl— slipped into a chair angled at the table. She didn't attempt to move it out any farther. She zipped her hoodie and pulled the sleeves down over her hands. This seemed odd now that she was inside instead of standing in the cold, but as she continued to fiddle with the cuffs, pushing her thumbs through holes in the seams— which extended the sleeves into half gloves and tightened the fabric across her bony shoulders— I realized she was incredibly nervous. She also looked tired.

"I... I don't drink coffee," she said. "Some tea would be nice. I mean, if it's not too much trouble."

"Not at all. I'll just put some water on to boil."

"Thank you," she said quietly.

"You look very tired," I said.

"Sorry, I work nights. I haven't been home yet."

I wanted to be encouraging, to find out why she was here. I wondered if she'd suddenly lost her nerve after deciding to come. "That's nothing to be sorry about. I admire anyone who can operate at all on third shift. How about some toast to go with the tea?"

At this, Helen gave me a shy smile and said, "You'd do that for me? You don't even know why I'm here."

"A piece of toast is nothing," I assured her. "You know what? I haven't had breakfast either. How about if I fix us both some eggs?" I didn't mention that I rarely ate breakfast, but this seemed like a good day to make an exception.

Helen nodded her approval.

While I started another pot of coffee, got out tea bags, set the table, made toast and mixed up eggs to scramble, Helen told me a little bit about herself.

She explained that she was several years out of high school but hadn't been an exceptional student. She admitted she'd quit during her junior year. She had an apartment, half a house actually, in Proctor, a village in Sturgeon County. For income she did housekeeping at the Emily City hospital. She'd started by cleaning patient rooms, but had done such a good job they gave her special training to clean the ER examination areas and the operating rooms. She boasted of several compliments she had received from her managers.

"That sounds like a very responsible position," I agreed. "But do you like working nights?"

"I do," she answered. "I have a baby that sleeps at my mother's on the nights I work. She takes the baby— well a toddler now— to daycare in the mornings. I get some sleep and then we have all afternoon together. It works for us."

She cleaned her plate like a starved sailor. By the time we finished eating, my curiosity was beyond the breaking point.

"Helen," I said, "there must be some reason you've appeared on my doorstep today. My house isn't remotely on the way from Emily City to Proctor. You had to drive miles out of your way to get here, and this is your normal sleep time. What did you want to talk to me about?"

She smiled. It was the kind of smile that showed resignation and relief all together. The kind of smile that precedes the revelation of a secret. But at the same time there was a hint of something dark in her features. Was it greed?

"My childhood nickname was Ellie," she said, ducking her head and once again poking her thumbs in and out of the cuffs of her sweatshirt.

I'd been standing near the sink, wiping the counter and stacking dishes. Her revelation sent me straight to the chair across from her, and I sat. I couldn't believe I hadn't even thought of this possibility. My mind had been occupied with Cubby and his lawyer.

Then I thought again and wondered if the article in the paper might attract impostors as well as the real Ellie.

"What is your little boy's name?" I asked.

"Little boy? What are you talking about? My baby is a girl."

I was wise to have had reservations. The Ellie I was interested in had a boy named Rob. I sat back in my chair and pondered how to catch the little liar.

"And who are your parents?" I continued.

Helen actually looked frightened now. She worried her cuffs and began to bite her lip. "I... I was adopted by the Brackets when I was... before I remember. They got a divorce when I was in, like, sixth grade. I don't know where Dad is now. But, um... my real dad... that's what the paper said this was about. I saw it at work last night. He was Hamilton Nelson." She lifted her head with a spark of defiance. "You look like you don't believe me."

Now I was unsure of myself. She sounded very sincere. "Helen, I'm just confused. What is your baby's name? Do you have only one child?"

"Yeah, just one. Gees, that's enough. Kids are a ton of work. I love her, but I wish I'd known more when I was, well, you know."

"What's her name?" I asked again.

"Roberta, Roberta Jean. It says Bracket on her birth certificate. Is that some kind of problem? It's my legal name, not Nelson, and her dad was just a boy who didn't care about me or her." The tone of alarm in her voice was increasing.

My relief was intense. "Rob," I said. "You call her Rob?"

"Yeah, Rob or Robbie. So what?"

I reached across the table, thinking to take Helen's hand, but pulled back. Perhaps she wouldn't like that. I smiled. "I'm so sorry I doubted you. When you wrote to Ham you referred to the baby as Rob. I assumed it was a boy."

"Oh. I guess that makes sense. Yeah, I can see that."

"Helen, Ellie, forgive me if I just ask you another question. It's very important to be certain you are the right person."

"Okay. But I've got the baby. Not with me, but you can meet her. And my mom. I mean, I don't know who my real mom is. But Lisa Bracket. She can tell you how she got me. What more would you want?"

"That's great. I'd love to meet Lisa. I'm sure she's been a real mother to you. And I'll get to know you and Robbie better. But for right now, just humor me and answer one more question, all right?"

The girl nodded.

I tried to remember exactly what pictures had been used with the newspaper article. One of them was of the bouquet of flowers left on Ham's grave. But it had been in black and white.

"Do you remember the flowers you left in the cemetery?" I asked.

"Of course. I'm not that stupid," Helen declared. "Even if I was, I saw the paper and the photo. That's how I found you."

"I didn't mean it like that. I want to ask you what color ribbon was tied around the flowers."

"Blue. It was blue, my favorite color." She answered without hesitation and glared at me again.

"Yes, it was blue," I answered in relief.

I promised to meet with her again, soon, but urged her to go home and get some sleep. I wrote down several ways to reach her.

She was practically swaying in the chair from general exhaustion and the strain of the conversation.

I did explain that we needed permission to exhume her father's body to be sure he had died as a result of the crash at the railroad crossing, and oxycodone hadn't been a factor.

Helen said she hadn't ever been asked to do something like that before, but that she'd think about it.

When I expressed concern that she might be too tired to drive home, she practically sneered at me.

"I've been taking care of myself a long time now. I don't need you to worry about me."

I wanted to give her a hug and fifty dollars, but I let her go without either. What I needed for myself was another cup of coffee.

As I was pouring it, the phone rang.

It was Cora, telling me that George G. Hartwick, Cubby's lawyer, was on an eco-tour in South America and couldn't be reached for two more weeks.

<h1 style="text-align:center">32</h1>

This was devastating news to my hopes of solving the case. In two weeks the police would have lab results from Colin Mueller's exhumation and tests. Helen would probably agree to let Ham's body be tested, too. The results would lead to... to what? That was a good question. The coffee forgotten, I decided to take my daily walk and puzzle it out.

Still my favorite path, the old lane through the trees that ran parallel to the extension of my road was paved with red and gold. The entrance beckoned me as I gazed across the east lawn.

I changed my shoes, grabbed a jacket and the gloves I'd rummaged for earlier and headed out the door. It was nippy, but the crisp October air was invigorating. My pace quickened when I entered the woods, and I kicked at the crunching leaves with the abandon of a child. The leaves' edges were rimed with frost, and I was glad I'd put on boots to keep my feet dry. For a few moments all thoughts of oxycodone and complicated relationships vanished from my mind. As soon as my house was out of sight, I paused and stood quietly. The icy frost crystals had loosened the leaves, and I could actually hear the twigs releasing each leaf with a light pop as the sun melted the frost that had expanded the joints.

No breeze directed their falling, and each golden coin floated in a zippery zigzag until it reached the ground. As I watched, a sudden spear of sunlight caused them to glitter like new deposits to Fort Knox. Fall was a wonderful gift of the forested Northwoods, and I was learning to love it more each year. It smelled different from spring and summer. In Chicago all the seasons were tainted with the odor of exhaust fumes, even in the suburbs. I thought perhaps I could tell certain trees from their scent. Maybe that was just wishful thinking. I'd check with Cora;

she could ask her county forester friend if that was real.

Scuffling noises to my left, toward the river, made me turn my head. A doe with a large but still-spotted late fawn raised her head to stare at me with dark liquid eyes. The deer were only a few feet away and didn't run away in panic. I continued to stand quietly. We regarded each other, two mothers from different worlds— she couldn't know I also had a nearly-grown child. Suddenly she whirled and bounded into the swamp. The fawn hesitated and gave me one last look— the statement of a teenager claiming the right to make independent decisions—and then followed the doe.

The spell was broken. I laughed at the fawn, smiled with thoughts of my own son, and then my mind turned to Colin and his philandering ways. Apparently Lucille had no clue that her husband had fathered two boys in addition to their own two. Were there others? This whole complication made my head and my heart hurt. It was odd that all their names began with C. No, that couldn't mean anything. Cubby was a nickname and there was no suggestion that Colin had participated in naming Charles Dixon or Raphael Matthew "Cubby" Smith.

What about their mothers? Each of these women probably had strong feelings about keeping her son's lineage a secret. I didn't even know if they were still alive. That was something else to ask Cora or Adele.

Did Charlie know that Cubby was his half-brother? Cubby had made it pretty clear in the phone conversation that he knew about Charlie. Could there be a way this knowledge would have precipitated the murder of someone else? If anything made sense, it was more likely one of them would kill the other. Siblings were always murdering each other in books— usually over an inheritance. Did Colin leave anything to the two illegitimate sons? How would he dare? His secret would then be out, and Lucille would learn of his indiscretions. That scenario wasn't working, but it was another thread to follow. What was in Colin's will?

This whole line of thought was crazy, and actually off the topic. As far as we knew, Milo Sendak was the only person who had died of an overdose of oxycodone. The Colin/Charlie/Cubby mess was entirely beside the point except that Charlie, as druggist, was a suspect. And that didn't make sense. So far, at least, we'd not found a single motive for Charlie to want Milo dead.

However, Valerie certainly wanted Milo out of the way so she could run off with Cubby. Maybe she had hopes of not getting caught and ending up with lots of money to take with her. Was it just a coincidence that Cubby and Charlie turned out to be half-brothers? Might Valerie have somehow blackmailed Charlie into helping her overdose Milo? That was a thought. Maybe Cubby had told Valerie about Colin being his father. If Valerie had learned from another source that Colin was also Charlie's father, was there some additional secret she might have used to force Charlie to give her extra oxycodone?

That was silly, too. I'd seen the pills the police had taken out of the drugstore that first day. They were capsules. Valerie could have doctored them without any help at all. She only had to empty the medicine from a few into one pill casing and destroy the empty capsules. For that matter, anyone could easily have done this.

By the time I finished walking the loop and returned to my house, I was pretty much settled in my mind that almost anyone had means, but Valerie was the only person with motive and opportunity.

I rounded the last bend in the road and shook my head slowly at the sight. Helen's beat-up Honda was back in my driveway. Was that girl trying to commit suicide by driving around all day with no sleep?

33

The driver's door opened and Helen stepped out, but she didn't move away from the car. I continued up the driveway toward the house. When I was within a few feet of her, with no preliminaries, Helen blurted, "I've decided I can trust you. I've got something to show you."

She wore the same work clothes and gray sweatshirt. Her hands were concealed in the pockets of the hoodie. My walk had taken less than an hour. I wondered if she'd had time to go all the way home and return. Just barely, but if she'd been home why hadn't she changed? I glanced toward the interior of her vehicle but didn't see a child in the car seat, so Roberta wasn't what she had brought for show and tell.

"All right," I answered, "come back inside with me."

She followed without comment, trailing along like a puppy. She collected nothing from her car. Seated at the kitchen table again she raised her eyes to look at me. They were becoming dark-rimmed and droopy from lack of sleep.

"I've been driving around thinking..." Slowly, almost robotically, she pulled her right hand from the pocket of the sweatshirt, placed it on the table and pushed a ring of keys toward me.

"What is this? Your car keys?" I asked.

"Sure, but look at the little one. My bio dad sent it to me, but I don't know what it's for. Maybe you can help."

I fanned the collection of keys by pushing at them with my index finger. In addition to normal car and house keys, there was a thin flat key with no identifying marks.

"This one?" I asked, putting my finger on it deliberately.

"Yeah."

"It looks like a safe deposit box key, but..."

"What's a safe deposit box?" Helen interrupted.

I'm continually amazed at the pieces of information young people seem to be missing. This girl could probably program a smart phone to do any number of things without reading any directions, but she had never heard of this basic service provided by banks.

In the silence of my pause, Helen continued. "Is it a box like a safe, but it has a key instead of a combination? I've seen them for sale at Wal-Mart. That doesn't seem very safe. Anyone could carry it away and smash it. That man who lived in my dad's trailer probably already took it." She looked crestfallen.

"No, it's much more secure than a portable lock box," I said. "This kind of box is in the vault at a bank. Fastened into a wall. The bank has one key and the owner of the box has the other. Both keys have to be used to open the box."

"But I don't own anything like that," Helen protested. "If Pop had a box, why did he send me the key?"

"My best guess is that he left instructions with the bank that he or an heir could open the box. At any rate, you could prove you were his only heir and that would give you the right to open it. A bigger problem might be that we don't know what bank or what box number this goes to. Was there anything that came with the key?"

"Um... I think so. It had a little tag with some number on it, but I threw it away."

I tried not to roll my eyes. The girl hadn't known it was important to keep that.

"Well, perhaps the bank can deal with that if we produce papers to prove who you are. But first we have to figure out what bank this key came from. It won't work on any box at the wrong bank."

"I don't know," Helen said. "I suppose he banked here in Cherry Hill, but he could have gone anywhere. He had a truck."

My mind was racing to recall if there were any valuable papers found among Ham's personal effects. There was nothing like that in the cracker tin I'd found. Maybe Tracy Jarvi would know about papers found on him when he was killed.

"Look, Helen," I said, "would you let me take a picture of this key? Maybe I can get some help finding out what bank it came from. I won't tell anyone where I got the picture. Or let anyone have a copy."

"I guess that would be OK. I mean... like I have to trust someone, or I'll never find out what's in the box, right?"

"You could probably figure this out on your own if you took the time," I admitted.

She removed her hands from her pockets and scrunched up her short hair, then rubbed her weary eyes. "But it would be nice to have someone to help. Banks kind of scare me. I have a checking account because of my job and to pay my bills, but I don't like them."

"OK. I can understand that," I said, although I didn't, really. "One thing for sure you'll need to do. You are going to have to have papers that prove Hamilton Nelson was your biological father. Can you come up with those?"

"I'll ask my mom. I think she has all that stuff. I never needed it."

The conversation came to an awkward end.

Finally I said, "Why don't you go get some rest and call me later today after you talk to your mom. Her name is Lily?"

Helen rolled her darkened eyes. "Lisa. Lisa Bracket. She's in the Emily City phone book. And you already got my cell number."

The exhausted girl drove away after I snapped a picture of the key. I sighed and said a little prayer for her safety.

As soon as she was gone, I grabbed my own car keys and headed for Cherry Hill. Without an internet connection and no smart phone of my own, the only way to show the picture of the key to anyone was to take it to them. I was on a mission, and now I hardly noticed the beautiful fall colors flying past my windows as I drove toward the Forest County Museum.

Cora, of course, was my first choice for factual information. When I found her, I filled her in and showed her the picture of the key.

Cora shook her head. "It doesn't look like one from the bank in town. But you know we don't have our own bank any more.

The old State Bank has become a branch of Wells Fargo. Do you know when Ham rented the box?"

"Not really," I said, my eagerness dampened. "Helen said she was sent the key a couple of years ago. Right after Robbie was born. So at least that long ago."

"Now, don't get discouraged," Cora said calmly. "We'll figure it out, and quite easily, I imagine. Make a print of that picture but block out the other keys."

"How many banks are there in the area? How many of them have changed hands?" I asked, as I plugged my SD card into the computer and opened the graphics program to follow Cora's directions.

"There are a few. But they don't change the boxes and keys when management changes. Think of the headache it would be to issue new keys to everyone and be certain the right person got them."

"That makes sense. How do you know it's not the local bank?"

"Because Jerry and I both have boxes there, and this key is not at all like either one of ours."

"There's Emily City. How many banks are there?"

Cora tilted her head in thought. "Maybe four or five. And don't forget Shagway to the west. No one from here goes over that way very often, but Ham did live over in that direction. There's at least one bank there. It's the biggest community in Kerr County, after all. And he could have gone north or south. Just because the main highway runs east and west didn't limit his choices."

The printer hummed and then with a whirr, it spit out a print of the cropped picture.

"Wow. This could be harder than I thought. Will banks be willing to tell us if this is a key they issued?"

"Let's find out," Cora said, pulling her fleece jacket from the back of the chair.

34

As I drove toward Emily City, Cora checked the Yellow Pages of the phone book she'd grabbed on the way out of her office.

"There are actually only three banks, but one of them has two branches. We should be able to visit them all yet today."

"OK," I said dubiously. "Maybe we'll learn something."

Three hours later, I'd broken my promise to Helen not to tell anyone where I got the picture of the key. Asking questions without giving up any information got us nothing. What we learned was that the key was not issued from two of the banks in Emily City. At both those places, when we finally got to speak to someone with authority, an officer looked at the picture for only a moment, but both gave the same reaction. They shook their heads. Their answers were nearly identical. Each said that if the key had been theirs they could not give us that information, but since it did not look like any of their safe deposit keys they were allowed to answer in the negative.

At the third bank, the one with a branch located in Waabishki, we received more of a cold shoulder and a formal reply. The customer service person we talked with made us wait for over thirty minutes while she, apparently, went to confer with someone in a higher position. We drank slightly burned coffee from small foam cups. We nibbled at the snacks the bank had laid out to celebrate the season... cheap sandwich cookies and apples. At least the fruit was fresh and shiny—probably locally grown. I took a cookie, but Cora crunched slowly on an apple. That's why she weighs only one-hundred ten pounds, and I don't.

Cora patted her lips with a paper napkin and leaned toward me from the depths of an armchair that was way too large for her.

"I think I know how to find out what these keys look like, even if she won't tell us anything," she began.

"Shh, she's coming," I hissed.

"Thank you for waiting," the woman said, "but, unfortunately, I can not tell you very much about your key. In the first place, even though you have given me a fair amount of information about why you would like to know where this box is located, I have no way to verify that you are truly working in this young woman's interest. Helen Bracket, correct? Of course we've all read the story in the Cherry Hill Herald, but that doesn't mean much."

Cora sat up as tall as she could from the depths of the huge chair and nearly sputtered. "What? You don't think the paper publishes stories that aren't factual, do you?"

"No, of course not, but you have no legal standing in this matter. Helen would need to come here herself and have acceptable paperwork in hand to prove she was the rightful heir to any property of Hamilton Nelson. At this point, I don't even know that this key was issued to him."

"What kind of paperwork?" I asked.

"If there was a will, we'd need that. In lieu of a will, Helen would need proof that he died intestate, and that she was the biological offspring of Mr. Nelson and came by this key in a legitimate manner."

"All that, just to learn if the key even came from your bank?" Cora protested.

"I'm sorry," the woman said. "And now, you'll need to excuse me. I see someone else is waiting."

We were clearly dismissed. Cora was still fuming, but as soon as we got in the car her face took on a determined look.

"Let's go to Paula's Place," she said.

"Now? We just had a snack. Well, I guess we didn't really have any lunch," I amended. My big breakfast with Helen was wearing off, and one dry cookie hadn't taken up much space in my stomach.

"Not for food. Paula's sure to have a safe deposit box, and I'm betting she uses the branch that's near her restaurant."

"Great idea," I said, turning the wheel and stepping on the gas as we pulled out of the parking lot.

Paula was happy to see us and immediately liked the idea of possibly helping another person come into some kind of fortune or reward. She spoke warmly of Sunny and Star Leonard as she recalled the small role she had played in finding out what had happened to their mother the year before. I was spreading Helen's story around two counties, after promising not to do so. I hoped she wouldn't be too angry.

Paula did, indeed, bank at the Waabishki branch. And she did have a safe deposit box. She wasn't so keen, however, on showing her key to us because the box number was stamped into the metal.

"That's not a problem. If you could just look at the picture and tell us if the key is the same basic shape it will be enough. If the blanks could have been the same, we'll try to get the paperwork Helen needs and take her to the bank. If they aren't the same, well..." Cora's voice trailed off.

"All right," Paula agreed, squinting at the picture. "Let me take this in the back. It's hard to be sure without looking at the key."

"Absolutely," Cora said.

"Sure," I chimed in at the same time.

After Paula left the dining room I looked at my watch. It was past two. "I've changed my mind. Let's get some food," I said.

"All right," Cora agreed without sounding interested. She seemed so focused on our mission that food was only an annoyance. "Just order me a salad."

I picked up a menu and was looking over the sandwiches when Paula returned. She placed the computer printout in front of Cora and shook her head. "Not a match," she said. "Mine is longer and thinner. The head is similar, but after that they aren't alike at all."

At this news, Cora actually perked up. "Well, then, now we've got some information. And I think I know just what to do next. Thank you so much, Paula." She turned toward me and winked. "Get that food to go, Ana," she commanded.

Inspired by Cora's self-discipline, or perhaps from guilt, I ordered two large salads and coffees. Paula's coffee was excellent. "Extra dressing for the Cobb," I said quietly, hoping Cora couldn't hear me.

"What are you so happy about," I asked as we climbed into the Jeep once again. I didn't waste any time prying off the plastic lid and slathering my salad with both packets of blue cheese dressing.

"Don't you see?" Cora said, grinning from ear to ear. "The box isn't from any bank in Cherry Hill, Emily City or Waabishki. That almost guarantees it's from Shagway, and there's only one bank there." She waved the phone book at me.

My mouth was full of lettuce and hard-boiled egg, but I swallowed quickly. "So? What if they won't tell us anything? Do you know someone who has a safe deposit box there, too?"

Cora's face lit up like a little girl opening a bag of candy instead of the salad she was fussing at to pop the stubborn lid. "I do. Me."

"What? You didn't tell me that," I almost shouted.

"Don't get so excited. I'm about to go open one. I'm pretty sure a small box will cost around fifty dollars for a year, maybe even less. Well worth the expense if we get a definitive answer."

I wasn't going to argue with her. She certainly had the means, now that she was again married to Jerry Caulfield, and it would give us a clear answer one way or the other about the key.

Cora ate her salad delicately as we drove west. It was over thirty miles to return across Forest County, and then over part of the next to reach the Kerr County seat of Shagway. I'd actually never been there.

The town appeared dingy and depressed. The courthouse, a large but rather plain building, was located on the south side of a central boulevard. Next door to that, the post office was of a similar construction. Small mismatched buildings on either side were alternately boarded up or displayed aging signs advertising their purposes. "Cut and Curl, The Villa—Italian Dining, Ajax Pawn Shop," I read aloud.

The center mall of the boulevard was filled with yellowing

grass and sketchy flower beds gone to seed. There were a few benches placed haphazardly and an obelisk monument. The lettering of the inscription was too small to read without walking up to it.

"There's the bank, down past that horrid cheap dollar store. See the sign?" Cora pointed to the north side of the street at the far end of town.

"Right," I responded and drove to the end of the mall where I easily found a parking space.

"You stay here, please, so I look like some old single lady coming in to rent a box," Cora said.

"You're spoiling my fun," I joked. But I was happy enough to finish eating my salad. The bites I'd managed before I started driving had simply made my stomach growl for more.

Twenty minutes later, Cora returned. A wide grin split her face, as if she'd heard the best joke of the year. Opening the car door, she said, "They knew who I was, but it didn't matter. I had money and wanted a box. Look!" She waved a small key.

35

The drive back to Sturgeon County seemed to take forever. It was past mid-afternoon, and we agreed that Helen was probably awake. She might be at her mother's picking up Robbie, but since her phone was mobile it didn't matter where she was. Cora called the number I'd been given, and after a considerable wait she said, "Hello, Helen? This is Cora Caulfield, and I'm driving toward Proctor with Ana Raven. We've found some information that will help you determine what your father might have left for you."

They talked at length, and Cora put the phone on speaker. It couldn't overcome all the car noise, but I heard most of the conversation. Cora spent quite a bit of emotional energy calming the girl, assuring her that we were only trying to help her. Helen was upset because I'd involved another person, but Cora explained that sometimes it took an extra brain to solve difficult puzzles.

I chimed in so Helen knew I was right there although she said she couldn't hear me very well.

Cora threw in a few well-placed anecdotes about what a helpful and gentle person Ham Nelson had been. These stories must have been reassuring because Helen's tone became less sharp and she eventually sounded almost glad that we might be able to solve the mystery of the key.

She wanted to meet at her mother's house and promised us Lisa was home and would be prepared for us to arrive in about twenty minutes.

Emily City was a little closer to us than Proctor, so it only took fifteen more minutes, and we drove around a few blocks to kill time and get a feel for the neighborhood. The streets were narrow and lined with similar one-and-a-half story houses built in the 1930s and 40s. Many had porches across the gable end that faced the street. Some were in need of extensive repair, but for the most part they were neat and modest. We found Lisa Bracket's house, which was white with brown trim, nicely kept. Miniature scarecrows on sticks kept sentinel on each side of the steps that were closed off at the top with a scissor gate. Bright plastic toddler toys were visible through the white mesh of the barrier. As we pulled to the curb a small blonde head popped into sight above the gate, and a chubby hand waved to us making the single pony tail at the top of her head bounce.

The door opened, and Helen emerged, followed by a slender brunette woman wearing blue jeans and a pink sweatshirt.

Helen hesitated a few seconds, glanced at the other woman, and then called, "Let me get the gate. Come in. My mom says she thinks I can trust you."

We climbed the steps and introduced ourselves to Lisa. She invited us inside, and we were soon comfortable in the living room. The furniture was inexpensive, but the house was clean and inviting. Pumpkin spice fragrance filled the air, originating from a scented candle.

A hand-crocheted afghan covered the back of the couch. Cora commented on it, and the two women began chatting about yarn crafts. Helen bounced Robbie on her knee, and soon the child wanted to get down. She waddled directly to me and demanded, "Up."

The ice was broken.

"Well, now to the point," Cora said, taking charge. "We are quite sure we've learned in which bank Hamilton kept a safe deposit box. In this state, boxes are not sealed at death, but since you didn't know anything about this, Helen, you must not have signed any paperwork as a co-lessee of the box."

Helen shook her head slowly. "I don't know what you mean by co... col... but I didn't ever sign any papers with my real, er, birth dad."

"Co-lessee. It just means someone who leases a box with someone else, and they both have access."

Lisa spoke up. "I have all the paperwork to prove that

Hamilton Nelson was Helen's biological father."

"Good," Cora continued with authority. "The bank may accept that and allow the box to be opened. I think you can only take out things like a will until the court says so, but you can at least find out what's there."

"Court!" Helen exclaimed. "We haven't done anything wrong, have we?"

"Not at all, baby," her mother said. "It's just that when there are big changes in people's lives like deaths or divorce," she grimaced, "the law tries to make sure that no one steals things."

"Oh," Helen said flatly, "like how James didn't steal your furniture?"

Lisa shifted uncomfortably and looked around the room. "You know we agreed on that. I kept the house but he took the furniture and the car. That's a long time past, baby. Let it go. I preferred having a place to live since you stayed with me."

Helen rolled her eyes.

"But, yes, the court was involved in making sure that was all done legally," Lisa added.

My mind wandered to my own acrimonious divorce. It felt so long ago now; my new life in Cherry Hill fulfilled me in ways I hadn't realized I needed.

Robbie stuck her thumb in her mouth and cuddled against me. Helen turned her head toward us and smiled. She had smiled so little since I'd met her that the gesture was unexpected, and it warmed me from head to toe.

"It's too late today to get back to the bank," Cora said, "but perhaps we could all go there tomorrow? Actually, we don't need to be with you at all. Just be sure you have the correct paperwork."

"I want you there," announced Helen. "All of you. That is, if you don't mind." She lowered her head; once more shy and insecure.

"We'd be honored to participate," I said.

36

We all met at the bank in Shagway the next morning at eleven o'clock.

Lisa apparently considered the occasion important as she was wearing tailored gray slacks with a silky blouse and wool cape. She stood straight and clutched her purse tightly.

Helen characteristically slouched and rubbed her eyes, looking as if she had just gotten out of bed, which was almost certainly true. She wore jeans and the same hoodie as on the previous day. Robbie was not with them.

"We left her with the neighbor," Lisa explained. "I thought it would be less stressful without the distraction."

"Good thinking," Cora replied, patting Lisa on the arm.

I opened the bank door and gestured for the others to enter. We made our way to the open door of a customer service office, and a slim young man in a blue suit, who looked too young for the job, smiled and waved us inside.

After brief introductions, where we learned his name was Tim Statler, he asked, "How can I help you?"

Cora took the lead. "This young lady," she nodded at Helen, "would like to examine the contents of a safe deposit box."

Tim turned to his computer and punched some keys. He studied the screen. "You said your name is Bracket? We have no boxes rented by anyone with that name."

Helen looked frightened and turned to her mother. I was surprised but somewhat grateful that Cora didn't leap in to supply answers.

Lisa took a deep breath and let it out slowly. "Let me explain. Helen is my adopted daughter, but her biological father was Hamilton Nelson. You may be aware of the fact that he died a few months ago. There was a bad accident with a train; it was in the papers." She paused as if expecting a reply.

Tim returned her gaze without indicating whether or not he was aware of this fact.

"We understand, that is... we believe that if we can show Helen is his heir then she can open Mr. Nelson's box."

More typing. The young man's eyes shifted from one area to another of the monitor display. "That may be true. There is such a box and the payment is current." Tim drew the words out as if unsure. "What sort of documentation do you have?"

Lisa opened her purse, and Cora placed her hand on a file folder she held in her lap. Cora and I had swung by the Cherry Hill police station before our trip to Shagway and obtained a copy of Ham's death certificate from their records.

"Proof of Helen's birth and adoption," Lisa said, drawing out a brown envelope and handing it to Tim.

"Hamilton Nelson's death certificate," Cora added as she passed over the file folder.

For a few minutes, while Tim studied the documents, the room was silent except for occasional footsteps and voices from the lobby. "Do you have a photo ID?" the young man asked Helen.

She pulled a wallet from the small bag she carried and extracted a driver's license which she handed to Tim. Digging further, Helen found her clip-on hospital badge and presented it also. Finally, she placed her key ring on the desk.

Tim leaned forward and jiggled the keys, separating the safe deposit box key from the others. He looked directly at Helen, then stood.

"Give me a minute. Wait here," he ordered, adding, "Please."

He scooped up the papers with Helen's identification and left the office.

I turned in my chair and saw him knock on a closed door across the main room. It opened and he entered, shutting the door behind him.

"Is this good or bad?" Helen whispered.

"I'm not sure," Cora said. "He should have had the authority to let you open the box. But he's very young. Maybe he's not actually a bank officer."

Helen shook a cigarette out of a pack and nervously fingered it.

"You can't smoke in here," Lisa hissed in a strained voice.

"Oh. Right," Helen said, continuing to hold the pack in one hand and to roll the cigarette between the fingers of the other.

Lisa tapped a fingernail against the metal clasp on her purse. I looked at Cora and she shrugged. Minutes passed. Coffee was burning somewhere, and the automatic door to the lobby opened and closed with an annoying swish-swish-thump, followed by a cold draft of air, whenever someone entered the bank.

Finally, we heard people approaching. Tim Statler re-entered his office first, followed by an older and rounder man who looked less businesslike than Tim. His well-worn suit was rumpled and his tie crooked, but Tim introduced him as Frank Hathaway, a vice president of the bank.

Mr. Hathaway cleared his throat. His eyes darted from Lisa to Helen. He saw the cigarettes and frowned.

Helen reddened and shoved everything back in her bag.

"Well, this situation is really quite straightforward, although a little unusual," he said in a soft voice, clearing his throat again. "Mr. Nelson visited often and was well-known to us here in Shagway. We helped him as much as we could. You understand, I assume, that the man was barely competent to keep financial records. His reading skills were poor. He relied heavily on my advice. He liked to feel that he had a safe place to keep certain trinkets. He spoke of a daughter, but we thought it was just his imagination since we were unaware of your existence."

The man was beginning to sound self-important. He clasped his hands behind his back, rocked from his heels to toes, and addressed himself to Helen.

"Although we suspect there is nothing of any real value in your father's safe deposit box, and even though your documentation seems valid, since the box was not jointly rented by you and Ham, we cannot legally open it for you without a court order."

Cora sprang from her chair. As Hathaway talked, her posture

had become more and more rigid, and she had inched toward the edge of the seat. "Are you sure that's necessary, Mr. Hathaway?" she demanded.

"Oh yes, Mrs. Caulfield. State law, and all that. Mr. Statler, give the ladies a petition form." He waved a hand in Tim's direction.

Tim produced a sheet of paper and smiled at Helen as he handed it to her. "Fill this out," he directed. "You'll need a judge from this county to sign it, then bring the order back here. It shouldn't be any problem. Oh, there's a nominal filing fee, as well."

Helen handed the paper to her mother but didn't say anything. She looked numb.

Lisa stood. "We'll bring this back to you as soon as possible. Mr. Hathaway, Mr. Statler." She nodded at the men. "Come on, Helen. Now we know there is a box and what we need to do to see whatever it is that Ham Nelson valued." She touched the girl's shoulder gently.

Tim handed all the paperwork we'd given him to Cora and shook hands with each of us as we filed out.

We hadn't even reached the cars before Cora was pecking away at her cell phone. "Jerry," she demanded, "do you know a judge in Kerr County?"

37

Jerry did know a judge in Kerr County, but it was Friday afternoon, and he said he wasn't sure he could reach his friend. We knew this without being told because although we could only hear Cora's end of the conversation, she was annoyed and repeated nearly everything he said. She reluctantly agreed to wait for him to call back.

At the western outskirts of town we found the Swirly-Freez. They advertised burgers and hot dogs as well as soft ice cream. A sign with plastic snap-on letters proclaimed "CL SING NEXT WEE." The building definitely needed paint, probably more than paint. But The Villa in the center of town didn't open until four, and this seemed to be the only place to get some lunch. When we approached the window we were told it was actually their last day of the season. They had one non-dessert item left—hot dogs—but we could have them for half price. We ordered six, with fries and drinks. Three picnic tables were available for diners, and I chose the least grubby one.

None of us had much to say. Helen slid into the attached bench at the table, leaned forward and rested her head on her arms. Lisa hadn't sat down yet, and she walked to her car, returning with a blanket. She nudged Helen and motioned for her to stand up, then folded the blanket and covered the grimy seat. Helen resumed her napping position.

We could see the courthouse. It was near the middle of town, but on the opposite side of Main Street.

Cora pointed at the plain gray building. "I have half a mind to walk in there and find a judge. Surely there's one in the building, even if Jerry can't locate Winston Thorne. He's probably out playing golf."

She stood up and gazed toward the center of town, then sat

down abruptly. "I should have dressed better."

Cora was wearing her usual blue denim overalls with a pastel blouse. Today's selection was a print featuring pale orange roses on a tan background. Although she knew how to dress up, Cora certainly didn't like to.

"You're dressed nicely," she said to Lisa. "You'll have to do it. You should anyway. You and Helen."

Just then, we were summoned to the window to claim our order. Helen roused herself and grabbed the white paper bags that had been pushed through the window.

"Get napkins," Lisa called.

Cora's phone rang, and we all fell silent as she answered it. "Really?... Today?... One o'clock sharp... Jerry, you are the best of the best. I'll make you apple dumplings this weekend."

I was watching her closely and noticed that she smiled and blushed just before she hung up.

The hot dogs were nothing special, but we each had one and a half, which satisfied our hunger. We had a half hour to kill before meeting Judge Thorne, and Lisa entertained us with stories of Robbie's newest skills. While Lisa talked, Cora helped Helen fill out the form we'd gotten from Tim Statler.

Promptly at one, the judge greeted us cordially and invited us into his chambers. After the introductions were sorted out, he asked for the papers Lisa and Helen had brought, and also for Ham's death certificate.

He studied them briefly but thoroughly, raised his eyes to Helen and said, "I don't see any problems here, young lady. Let's get this petition signed, and you'll be on your way back to the bank in record time."

With exaggerated motions, Judge Thorne pulled a pen from an ornate holder on his desk and scribbled on the bottom of the form. He straightened the papers, stood and handed them to Helen, returning the smaller ID cards separately. "Let me know how it turns out," he added with a wink. "Oh, yes, I read the Cherry Hill Herald. Perhaps that father of yours was a sly one."

As we filed out, he said to Cora, "Give my regards to Jerry."

"Certainly," she replied, "and thank you so much for helping."

"My pleasure," he said and winked again.

We hurried back to the bank. Tim Statler and Frank Hathaway looked at the petition and gave their consent for the safe deposit box to be opened. Tim motioned for Helen to follow him.

"I want my mother to come, and my friends," Helen said.

"No can do," Tim replied. "Only the person named in the petition is allowed, the relative. The others can wait in our lounge area." He nodded at a grouping of plus-size chairs arranged near a bar where the overheated coffee I had smelled earlier still sat on its hotplate.

"Oh, but..."

"It will be all right, dear." Cora told Helen.

"You'll be fine," Lisa added gently. "We'll be right here waiting."

We sat and watched Helen follow Tim down a corridor; she nervously fingered her cuffs and looked back at Lisa just before turning to the right through a door.

Cora said, "Well, then," and picked up a magazine from the central coffee table.

We waited in silence, but we didn't have to wait long.

Helen emerged from the hallway, with Tim right behind her, supporting her elbow in a rather old-fashioned gesture. She looked pale and was practically shaking.

"Sit here, Helen," Tim said. "I'll get you some water."

He quickly filled a glass from a pitcher near the coffee pot, and rejoined us.

"Helen's had quite a shock," he said. "Perhaps we should go to my office."

"No, stay here. There's no one else around," Helen insisted. She gulped and took a sip of water, which brought on a fit of coughing. "You tell them," she said to Tim.

Tim squirmed a bit and adjusted his tie. "You understand that normally the bank officer would simply insert the bank key in the lock and then leave the room. However, in cases like this, after the death of the owner, a list of the contents is made for probate. So, I stayed while the box was opened. It contained two items."

Chairs like the ones provided were always too large for Cora, so she was already perched on the edge of the seat. Her eyes were bright and dark. "What were they?"

"There was a will which appears to be written by Hamilton Nelson. Handwritten. I'm having a copy made for you to take. Mr. Hathaway is comparing the signature with others we have on file."

"A holographic will," Cora declared.

"Yes. It leaves a quarter of his estate to Helen and the rest in trust for the education of her child, Roberta, and any other future children."

"What was the other thing?" Lisa questioned.

Helen lifted her head and spoke. Her voice shook and was little more than a whisper. "An envelope full of bank statements. From a big bank."

Her hands were trembling, and we realized she was unfolding a small piece of paper she had been clutching. She read, "Thirty-one thousand, four-hundred fifty-two dollars and seventeen cents."

38

The weekend passed quietly with no shocking revelations that had any bearing on the oxycodone deaths. No new information at all, shocking or boring, came to light.

Although Helen had been rocked to her core at the money her birth father had left her, those of us who are older realized it wasn't a huge sum. It certainly was a significant amount for Hamilton Nelson to have saved, since he lived in poverty and only worked at odd jobs. The bank statements showed small deposits made over time, and no withdrawals. Tim Statler and Frank Hathaway had studied the collected bank statements, and they believed tax officials would not question the sum. We were told that if the thousands of dollars had appeared in one deposit, or if there had been cash in the safe deposit box, the origins of the money could have triggered police interest.

The envelope of monthly statements also explained why Ham had visited Shagway bank so regularly. After he received each one in the mail he added it to the collection in the box. Mr. Hathaway thought someone must have helped Ham write the will, but no one knew that for certain. At any rate, it didn't look as if there was anything controversial about the bequest.

Lisa said she and Helen would see her lawyer during the coming week to determine what needed to be done next.

The pressure of writing for the newspaper every single week was already becoming a driving force in my life, even though this was only the third week I'd been the local crime reporter. After sleeping in on Saturday, I called Helen to ask if I could continue her story in my column. The girl hadn't been comfortable with the idea at first, but I told her the information was bound to get around since several people already knew. The argument that persuaded her to agree was that if the facts were made public, there would be a chance readers would understand her better. If they knew the money was mostly to go for Roberta's education, she wouldn't be hounded by scavengers who thought she was suddenly rich.

Although fewer than eight-thousand dollars were going directly to Helen, she made it clear that she felt rich, but she agreed a lot of people were always trying to get handouts.

The rest of the day was filled with laundry, cleaning and other household chores. Being an investigative reporter had not elevated me to any lofty status that exempted me from everyday tasks, and the dust bunnies multiplied without mercy.

Sunday morning, the sanctuary at Crossroads Fellowship was decorated with richly colored banners celebrating the gifts of God's harvest. I sat with Adele, which was a little unusual. She often stayed near the back door so she could leave the service early to arrange foods on the refreshment table. This day, she said Geraldine Longcore was covering the task. I learned that Adele liked the old hymns best, while I preferred the more modern praise songs. But the service included some of each, so we were both pleased.

With permission to go public from Helen, I felt no guilt about sharing the events of Friday with Adele. Since she had the day off from responsibilities after church, we grabbed a plate of snacks and cups of coffee and sat alone at the end of a long table. Despite the fact that she liked to know everyone's business, Adele's heart was pure gold. She was genuinely happy that Helen's future would be financially easier. Although she pointed out that Helen didn't exactly need Family Friends to pay for her father's grave marker any more, the only serious complaint she made was that she hadn't had a chance to meet baby Roberta yet.

Later that afternoon, I sat with my computer on my lap and began writing the column that was due on Tuesday. My first attempt had been too bland, my second too scandalous. Maybe I could find a balance with this third try.

Realizing we still didn't have permission to exhume Hamilton

Nelson's body, I called Helen yet again. After asking her some specific questions about Ham and how she felt about the money, which provided better quotes for the article than I had anticipated, I brought up the topic.

"Helen," I said, "I understand how the idea may be disturbing to you, but it would be a really good thing to find out for sure whether there was oxycodone in your father's system when he was killed. If there was no overdose, then there'd be no further police interest in trying to link his death with Milo's. Wouldn't that make you feel better?"

I thought Helen wasn't going to answer. Too late, I realized we should have had this conversation face to face so I could see her reactions. But after a few seconds, she replied, "It's all so strange. I don't feel old enough to make a decision like this."

"But you are the only one who can," I pointed out.

"Who would want to kill him? He just kept to himself when he wasn't helping people."

"That's my point, Helen. There's probably no connection at all between him and Milo Sendak or Colin Mueller, and the autopsy could establish that for sure. But it has to be done soon, while there's a chance to detect any levels of oxycodone in the body. Every week we wait the chemical fades."

"I've forgotten. Why do they think he took that drug?"

"Charlie Dixon— you remember, he owns the Cherry Hill Pharmacy— told the police that Ham was having hip pain. He filled a prescription just a few days before he died. So far, that's the only thing those deaths have in common. Isabelle Adams also got a new bottle of the pills just before her death, but tests of her blood showed she didn't have high levels of oxy in her system. That means she didn't die of an overdose. Milo did. We don't know about Colin and your father yet."

"I guess it would be good to know that. I see some awful things, working at the hospital. I don't like to think of my father like that."

"I'm sure you don't."

I waited patiently for an answer.

"OK, I'll do it."

When I reminded her she would need to make that permission official, Helen's timid side took over and she asked if I'd go with her to talk with Chief Tracy Jarvi. We agreed to meet at the police station Monday afternoon. I said I'd make an appointment and let her know the time.

After that I settled in at the computer with a box of crackers, cheese squares, tea and a serious resolve to type out a column that Jerry wouldn't have to edit so heavily.

39

Oddly enough, I didn't need to telephone the Chief. She called my cell phone just after nine o'clock Monday morning with an official statement for the newspaper. I thought that was strange, but she said Jerry had told her to give the information to me.

The results of Colin Mueller's autopsy had been received from the lab. Tests had been made on various organs and tissues with wildly varying results.

"That's perfectly normal," Tracy assured me. "What the lab techs said that was meaningful is that all the readings were an order of magnitude higher than concentrations that might be considered therapeutic."

"What on earth does that mean?" I asked.

"It means that every level of the drug was at least ten times higher than anything that would be normal in someone who took the drug for pain management. I've got results from analysis of the blood, liver, kidney tissue, urine, various muscles, lungs and vitreous humor. They really did a thorough job."

"Humor? Something was funny?"

"The eye," Tracy explained. "The fluid in the eye."

"Oh. Ick."

"Yeah, but it's pretty stable after death for a long time, so testing it gives a reliable result."

I was stunned. In my head, I'd previously filed this death as 'not suspicious' and was only waiting for confirmation. Now I was hearing the exact opposite. "Tracy, you're telling me that Colin didn't die of old age. He died of a massive drug overdose. Oxycodone."

"You've got that right. Now we just have to decide if it was self-inflicted or if we've got a murder. A cold case at this point, either way."

163

My phone made a clicking sound and Tracy's voice cut out for a second. "Hold on, I think I've got another call coming in, but I don't know how to switch without losing you," I said in frustration.

Tracy laughed. "Yeah, I can make that work on the office phone, but never on my cell. I'll let you go."

"Wait!" I exclaimed. "I'll call this person back later. Can Helen Bracket and I stop in at the station this afternoon? She's ready to give permission for Hamilton Nelson to be exhumed."

"Sure thing. I'll get Bob to type up the forms so all she has to do is sign them. Make it around one."

"Thanks, Tracy."

"Thank you. It will help a lot if we can find out for sure about his death. It's already goofy enough adding Colin to Milo. What did they have in common? Nothing I can easily see."

"Right. I don't know of anything," I said, and we ended the call.

Of course, I did know that Colin was the father of the man Milo's wife wanted to run away with. But that didn't make any motives leap to mind for doing away with the two of them.

After I hung up, I saw the symbol for a new voicemail message, and I pushed the buttons to listen. Jerry Caulfield's voice blared through the quiet house.

"Ana, Jerry here. Call me back ASAP. Tracy has new info about the deaths. We really could have two murders. Your column should be your personal take on things, but I want you to do a front page feature with Colin Mueller's autopsy results."

I poured a cup of coffee to fortify myself for the details of this new assignment and called Jerry.

What he had in mind was a half-page story with photos of Colin Mueller and Milo Sendak. I told him I'd already written my column with the focus on Helen, and he decided that was a great human interest angle, so I wouldn't have to do a re-write. The front-page newsworthy item was the two known oxy deaths. He urged me to press Tracy to speculate on what could link the two men.

I pointed out that Valerie seemed to be the only link, even

though she probably didn't know that Colin was her Cubby's biological father. Also, we didn't have permission to release that information until we heard from Cubby's lawyer. Did newspapers need to wait for permission?

Jerry grudgingly admitted that he, Cora, Adele, and I might have more information than the police at this point, and that it was probably early to release what we knew for public consumption.

His parting instructions were to collect the photos that looked so much alike of Colin Mueller and his sons: Lawrence Mueller, Charlie Dixon, and Raphael Cubby Smith, so the paper would be prepared as soon as it was free to run the story.

I also told him that before too much longer we'd have a definite answer about the presence of drugs in Ham's system when he died.

As I hung up, my mind was spinning with the realization that if Hamilton Nelson's death turned out to be an overdose, we'd be back to having no connections at all between the known people involved.

Next I called Helen. She was probably still asleep because the call went directly to voicemail, but I told her to meet me at the Cherry Hill police station at one o'clock.

After that, it was back to the computer for me. A front page news report was more serious writing than a column. More facts and less speculation. As I typed, making one false start after another, it occurred to me that being the crime reporter was going to include long sedentary stretches of writing in addition to the more interesting, but now official, assignment of running around digging up information.

Helen and I were both on time in Cherry Hill, and she signed the forms for the exhumation and autopsy. I offered to let her proofread the article I'd written about her inheritance before it was printed, but she said it would be fine, that she trusted me.

Sometimes I had a hard time understanding this girl. She alternated between being painfully shy and private, or blasé, or sometimes belligerent. Perhaps that was normal for people her age. My only real experience was with my son Chad and his friends, who were a few years younger. Even though I'd taught at a small college, that career ended three years ago. In three years the whole mentality of an age group can change. Yet, Helen was about the same age as my final class of students. No, Helen wasn't exactly the norm, but she was making her way in the world despite a lot of hard knocks. Maybe if a few more people cared about her she'd learn to be more caring in return.

After Helen left, I quizzed Tracy about additional autopsy results on Colin. She gave me a copy of the report, pointing out that since the Muellers lived out of town the sheriff's department was taking the lead. The city police would work closely with them because the pills had been purchased at the Cherry Hill drugstore. The druggist, Charlie Dixon, was still the closest thing they had to a suspect. He had no known motive— and he had told me he had more reasons to want Colin alive than dead, and no feelings at all toward Milo— but he was the person with the best opportunity and ready means to have doctored the medications.

"Detective Dennis Milford is handling the case. You remember him?" Tracy asked.

I rolled my eyes. I certainly did remember the gruff detective who'd walked all over my property and my psyche the previous year. "Great," I said. "Just great."

40

A week passed, then stretched into two. The sugar maple at the end of my driveway dropped its leaves first, creating a carpet of gold around the mailbox and spilling into the road. Since almost no one except me drives down this road, the color remained unspoiled for many days. The deciduous trees in Dead Mule Swamp were mostly red maples; they held their flaming scarlets and oranges longer, a fiery contrast with the dark green of spruce and hemlock.

Where my lawn faded into the woods, a border of purple New-England asters appeared, and I was glad I hadn't mowed the edges carefully. The acrid odor of damp and dying leaves wafted from the swamp, the smell of autumn.

Overhead, skeins of Canada geese wound themselves into balls, then unraveled in ragged hooks, heading south. Flocks of starlings blackened the lawn and rose in swarms of undulating harmony until they faded into the distance. Robins herded up as well, although in smaller numbers. I no longer heard them singing at daybreak.

I'd never seen a sandhill crane before moving here. Now I knew their raucous, rattling call and managed to catch sight of two pairs of the huge birds, their long necks extended southward.

The first week of November, a hard frost at night followed by cold rain the next day brought down almost all the leaves. Even the bright green of the wet conifers didn't succeed at making the swamp appealing. Cold, wet and dismal were the only words I could think of that morning.

We learned very little of interest during that time concerning the deaths by overdose of painkiller. Despite the permission from Helen, progress toward Ham's exhumation was stalled by the flu. A virus had laid the backhoe operator low, and the city insisted

167

their insurance wouldn't cover anyone else.

Detective Milford grudgingly acknowledged that I had some right to receive press releases from the sheriff's department, but none of high interest were issued, only notices of car/deer accidents and the standard minor crime bulletins.

The two columns I wrote during that period were beyond boring. One was a summary of ways to minimize your chances of bringing home the venison the expensive vehicular way. The other was at least slightly humorous, covering a breaking and entering at the pizza place in Jalmari. It happened that after closing up Sunday night— and they weren't open on Mondays— the owner had painted the concrete floor of the back room. The burglar both entered and left through a rear window. The police simply followed the gray footprints to a nearby house where they apprehended a teenage boy with about fifty dollars too many in his pocket.

Helen called me and asked if she could come to a Family Friends meeting to thank us for buying her father's gravestone, and I told her that would be much appreciated. She said the first Thursday in November would work best, and I alerted Adele that she'd be coming. But on the appointed day, there was no sign of Helen. Adele called the meeting to order and the minutes were read.

While I was wondering if the girl had overslept, the crash bar on the outer door banged, and a draft of cold air swirled into our meeting room. Geri was turning pages in her notebook in preparation to read the treasurer's report, so we were momentarily quiet. I heard the sounds of multiple approaching footsteps. Had Helen brought Lisa along for moral support?

No one else knew enough about Helen to be surprised, but I very nearly spilled my coffee when she entered with Tim Statler.

To get our attention, Adele rapped on the table with her pen, introduced Helen, and suggested to her that she tell us about her companion.

Helen turned to look up at Tim. He nodded, touched her back and said, "Hello, everyone. I hope I'm not intruding by coming along, but my name is Timothy Statler. I'm a junior officer at the

Shagway Bank."

Murmuring began as members of the committee turned to comment to each other.

Tim continued, "Now, folks, that doesn't mean anything. I'm really only here to lend moral support. Helen has something she'd like to say to you." He smiled his encouragement.

Helen pulled her cuffs over her hands in what seemed to be her signature gesture of nervousness. "I...I'm not very good at this." She looked at the floor, and Tim touched her again which made her straighten a bit, but even so, she kept her head bowed.

"I just want to say thank you for caring about my birth father's grave when no one else really did. I guess if you read the newspaper," Helen glanced at me with her head still lowered, "you know that Hamilton Nelson left me some money. Tim tells me it's not really all that much, but I feel like I'm rich."

There was more murmuring from committee members, which made Helen even more nervous.

She continued at double, run-on speed; perhaps she was afraid she couldn't finish her speech unless she got it all out at once. "I'm going to keep working, and Roberta will have money for college when she's old enough, and what I'm trying to say is that I want to help someone like you helped me, but I don't know who or how, so I'm going to give you some money, OK? Is, like, five-hundred dollars enough?"

We broke into spontaneous applause to encourage Helen with positive feedback, but our enthusiasm seemed to startle and frighten her.

She leaned into Tim and he put his arms around her, patting her back.

Wow, things have certainly progressed rapidly on that front, I thought.

The rest of the Family Friends meeting was business-as-usual, and Adele was thrilled to meet Helen. She cornered the young couple when we dismissed, and I slipped out the door, smiling.

After a hot, comforting lunch at the Pine Tree Diner, I headed home. My brain was racing. Helen and Tim— no one could have seen that coming. But it would certainly do the girl a great deal of good to have another stable influence in her life. Hopefully, it wouldn't turn out to be a relationship that ended badly.

We'd all pretty much stopped thinking about the "oxy case." I'd been involved in the solutions of several untimely local deaths over the past couple of years, and considering them each to be a "case" seemed logical. It also made them easier to discuss. Besides, I liked the way the word "case" sounded. Official.

However, labeling the mystery as a case did not produce further information that could link Milo and Colin. Maybe they were unconnected suicides, after all.

The mail usually arrived in the late morning, so on returning from Cherry Hill, I stopped at my mailbox to collect it. Along with the usual assortment of junk and bills was a hand-addressed blue envelope with "Francine Kelly" written in as the return. I couldn't recall meeting anyone with that name. Parking quickly, I entered the kitchen, where I hurriedly shed my jacket and threw it over the back of a chair.

Grabbing a knife, I slit the envelope and pulled out multiple sheets of blue paper covered on both sides with black handwriting.

41

Dear Ms. Raven,

You probably never heard of me. Very few people from Cherry Hill or Forest County have. Hopefully, not more than two, ha ha. I live in a Chicago suburb as you can see from my return address, and to tell you the truth, I've never been to Forest County. But my father lived there.

I've been following the news events with some interest. Yes, I subscribe to the Cherry Hill Herald. I suppose I get some sort of displaced pleasure from reading about the small town happenings that might have defined my life instead of the big city. Oh, I guess whoever does the address stickers at the paper has heard of me, but they don't know who I really am. Imagine my surprise when about a month ago, my father's name began to appear in the paper every week, even though he died last spring.

You see, my father is Colin Mueller! I've been told he was an awful playboy in his midlife crisis years. The family hustled me off to be adopted out of state very soon after I was born. I don't actually know who named me, or if Colin had any part in that. Of course, I'm married now, and Kelly is my husband's last name. But someone named me Francine Michelle. Maybe it was my adoptive family. Funny, I never even wondered about that before.

Anyway, my birth mother (I won't tell you her name because she has moved out west and likes her privacy) threatened Colin with a lawsuit unless he came up with some money to place me with a good agency for adoption. She had a family of her own and didn't want to face the embarrassment of raising me. But we still keep in touch. She never could completely let go of me, her "love child."

I also heard rumors from my mother that I was not the only "extra" child of Colin's. That's why I'm writing to you now.

Although it hasn't been reported in the paper yet about whether my father died of a drug overdose, even though he was very old, I'm sure that he did. If you are going to be a good crime reporter, you need to follow up on that idea much more seriously.

Here's why I think it must be true. Lucille knew. She knew about me, and she was mad as hell and could be mean as spit. At least that's what my real mother says. Like I said, I never knew the man in real life. Or Lucille.

It may not make much sense, but even though Colin was old, I think Lucille killed him. Maybe she just couldn't stand it any longer, or Maybe She Found Out About Another "Extra" Baby!!!!! That wouldn't surprise me a bit.

Here's another news flash. I was recently contacted by a bigshot lawyer. He said he was representing the children of Colin Mueller to make sure that justice was done. Whatever that means. I told him my husband had plenty of money and that I wasn't interested in getting involved in any lawsuit. But maybe I should've listened to what he had to say. When there's money involved, and Colin had lots, people are willing to do desperate things, right? I don't even know whose lawyer he was supposed to be. Maybe Lawrence and Peter (those are Lucille and Colin's boys, but you probably know that already) hired him to find me. Wouldn't that be something! Wait. I don't know if they knew about me.

But when people die and there are wills written

that don't say things very clearly, stuff can get very messy. I know this. My husband got tied up in a big legal battle with his siblings when their mother died a couple of years ago.

My husband doesn't know who my father is and I had sort of hoped to keep things quiet, not rock the boat after so many years, you know? But I guess if that doesn't work out I can live with it. Because if Lucille gave him extra pills everyone will hear about me. I'll be the motive! At least part of a motive, for sure. And I don't want her to get away with it.

You hunt around. I bet you can find another "love child" somewhere. Men like that just can't stop themselves.

I haven't been able to remember the name of the lawyer who called me. When he called I just didn't care. That would give you another place to look for answers. If it comes back to mind I'll send it. Maybe we could use email. Mine is frannyshelly@coldmail.com.

I've probably gone on too long, but there was never anyone to tell these things to, or even any reason to tell them. Anyway, email me if you want to. I don't care one way or another, but it does seem pretty exciting. Or maybe I should be scared. Do you think Lucille might want to get rid of me too?

Sincerely,

Francine Kelly

I read the whole thing through twice. Francine didn't know about Cubby. Did Cubby know about Francine? As far as I knew, no one except me was certain that Charlie was also one of Colin's "love children." And I wasn't supposed to share that secret, but my promise to Charlie might become impossible to keep.

Lucille Mueller as a killer? That was an image my mind could not reconcile with the tired and sad old woman I had met.

As interesting as this information was, it didn't connect anything at all to Milo Sendak.

I decided it was time to get busy writing that front page article about Colin Mueller's death from an overdose of oxycodone.

42

I began by organizing the facts: Colin Mueller had two legitimate children, Lawrence and Peter, with Lucille. In all likelihood, there were at least three other people he had fathered: Charlie Dixon, Francine Kelly, and Raphael Cubby Smith. I didn't know Francine's age for certain, but I guessed that Charlie was oldest and Cubby was youngest.

If Colin had left a will, he had probably specifically named Lawrence and Peter as his heirs, so what would be the point of any of the "love children" killing him? Only Lawrence or Peter could have wanted to hasten Colin's demise. I made a note to check on their financial status and to find out if either of them had visited their father in the month before his death.

Since we now had medical proof Colin died from an overdose of oxycodone, the only choices were an accident, suicide or murder. He'd been self-medicating for a long time, on an as-needed basis, so an accidental overdose seemed unlikely.

Had Colin committed suicide? Why would he do that? Maybe he knew that either Charlie or Cubby was about to spill the beans and expose his true character as a philanderer, and he didn't want to face the fallout. That seemed possible. If Lucille had the temper Francine claimed, Colin might not have wanted to be the target of her wrath if she learned about Charlie and Cubby. Then again, she might already know. These were certainly not topics I had discussed with her on my single visit to the widow's house.

This brought me back to Francine's theory that Lucille had killed Colin. I still couldn't visualize this. Lucille seemed truly lost without her lifelong companion. She didn't have the energy to keep up a small space in her beloved flower garden. She hadn't even been dressed when I'd visited. Nope, I just couldn't picture it.

Besides, if she had learned that her husband was the father of Charlie or Cubby and feared this information becoming public knowledge, killing Colin wouldn't have stopped the facts from getting out. Maybe she had committed some sort of mercy killing, to protect Colin from being embarrassed.

I stopped thinking and shook my head. "You are getting a little muddled, Ana," I said aloud. "That would be a really weird motive." Francine is probably at least right that Lucille was plenty angry at Colin's extra-marital activities.

Instead of writing a news article, I called Adele. I needed her ability to pry information from people.

"Adele," I said, "can you get away from the store this afternoon?"

"Right now? Well, I might. Suzi is still here. Let me ask her if she can stay."

The phone receiver clattered, followed by the slight buzzing of an open land line. This response was so Adele. She hadn't even asked what I wanted, but she didn't want to be left out of whatever it was. In a minute I heard footsteps approaching.

"Suzi is good 'til closing. What are we doing this time? Another scary back road adventure?"

"I hope not. I'd like to get some information from Lucille Mueller, and you might do a better job. You're local. I suspect she sees me as a nosy newcomer even though I do work for the paper now."

Adele laughed. "And the nosy hometown lady is better?"

"Probably."

We both laughed at that.

"I'll call Mrs. Mueller and pick you up in thirty minutes if she agrees to talk to us, OK?"

"Let me call Lucille," Adele said firmly. "Oh, and dress nicely. It makes her more comfortable. You'd better pick me up at my house so I can change. I'll leave here right now." She hung up without waiting for me to ask if I should expect a call back to let me know if Lucille had agreed to see us or to ask what "nicely" meant.

Adele had seen me that morning and knew I had on jeans and a plaid shirt. So I guessed that wasn't nice enough. I switched to a pair of olive green pants and a paisley blouse. There weren't many options for improving my hair, which I keep cut in a long-ish pageboy. But I ran a comb through it and put on a bit of lip gloss. I grabbed a fleece jacket from the closet.

As I pulled into her driveway, Adele emerged from the side door wearing one of her "church dresses," a patterned synthetic in green tones with a solid dark green jacket. She wore low heels and carried a matching purse. Apparently she was really serious about dressing nicely.

On the way to the Mueller home, I read Francine's letter to Adele. My idea was to try to find out what Colin's will had actually said—if he had left one. But if he was as rich as Francine had hinted, surely he must have. Of course, Adele knew about Cubby, but I had to bite my tongue, nearly letting it slip that Charlie Dixon was also Colin's son.

Lucille opened her front door and gave us a weak smile. "Come in. I've made some tea."

This time, she was dressed in a neat pair of gray slacks and a white blouse with a black and white cameo broach at her throat. Her hair was pulled up in a bun with no escaping hairs. She must have styled it after Adele called.

We followed her into a room off the entryway that would probably have been called a parlor in an earlier age. This was not the large room I'd seen on my first visit; this was a cozy retreat with a pink loveseat and two chairs encircling an antique coffee table. Paintings of flowers decorated the walls. On the table were a silver tea set, dainty cups and a plate of small sandwich squares the size of a quarter-slice of bread, with no crusts.

"It's so nice of you to visit me," she said to Adele. "I'm feeling quite well today and decided to show Mrs. Raven I'm not always such a bedraggled mess as I was when she called on me before." She poured a cup of tea and handed it to Adele. "Cucumber sandwich?" she added.

I hated being called "Mrs. Raven." Raven was a name I'd taken after Roger and I divorced, and I certainly was no longer a "Mrs."

I wanted to protest, but there was nothing to be gained by taking offense. Lucille was trying to be polite, so what I said was, "Please don't be formal; call me Ana. After all, you've asked me to call you Lucille."

She offered me tea and cucumbers, too. I felt as if I were in a Victorian play.

Lucille returned the tray of sandwiches to the table. She then nodded, either in agreement with me, or as some sort of signal to herself that she had decided to answer our questions, since she initiated a serious topic immediately.

"All right, then. Adele said she wanted to ask me some further questions. I can understand that. It was a horrible shock to learn that Colin had all those drugs in his body. Who would do such a thing to him?" Her words seemed addressed to us both, but she looked only at Adele.

Adele had taken two dainty bites of sandwich and a sip of tea. She placed the remaining tidbit of bread and vegetable on her saucer and patted the older woman's knee fondly. She was smiling at Lucille. "I was so sorry to receive this news. It must have been much more difficult for you. Tell me what went through your mind." This was Adele in action.

"Oh, Adele, you can't imagine," Lucille said. She produced a handkerchief from her cuff and dabbed at an eye.

"I'm sure I can't," Adele agreed, "but were you truly surprised, or hadn't you wondered about his death just a little bit?"

"I never thought... No, it seems impossible. Why would Colin kill himself?"

"Do you think that's what happened?"

"It must be true. No one would want to kill him." Lucille wiped both eyes this time. "I'm sorry," she added, at last turning to me, but then once again focusing on Adele.

"I was wondering if either of your sons visited here sometime prior to their father's death," I asked.

Lucille turned to me. "It's interesting that you would ask that. The police asked me the same question. No one could seriously believe that one of the boys would hurt their father."

"But were they here? Either one of them?" I continued.

Lucille sighed. "Yes, Lawrence was here about a month before we lost Colin." The answer was direct, but Lucille seemed to be holding her breath as if she hadn't finished the thought.

"Isn't there more to it than that?" Adele asked gently.

The widow let out her breath in a quiet whoosh, but her tone became bitter. "I suppose I may as well tell you, too. There doesn't seem to be anything I can do to stop this from becoming a family train wreck. Lawrence picked up Colin's prescription for the pain pills at the drugstore."

"The police asked you this question?" I asked.

"Yes, and a lot more," Lucille snapped. "They seem to think Lawrence could have tampered with the medicine."

I tried to soothe the older woman. "They have to cover all the possibilities, no matter how unpleasant they seem. They'll need to rule Lawrence out as a suspect, so they have to know everything he did."

"I suppose you're right, but it's no picnic having all the family business raked over the coals."

"Did Colin leave a will?" Adele probed, steering the conversation in the direction we had discussed in the car.

"That's another thing that's very odd," Lucille said slowly. "I thought he would have drawn up a will with his lawyer; he was such a detail-oriented businessman."

"And he didn't leave one?" Adele asked.

"Well, he did. But it wasn't specific at all, and he apparently didn't consult a lawyer. I found a handwritten document in his safe that said his estate was to be divided between me and his heirs. That would be Lawrence and Peter, of course."

Listening to the conversation instead of participating had one real advantage. I could concentrate on what was being said without having to formulate responses at the same time. Either Lucille had a terrible memory or she was lying. Francine had been very clear on the point that Lucille knew of her existence.

"Of course," Adele purred.

Adele had picked up on that misstep as well. "Do you think it would be possible for us to see a copy of the will? After all, it's probably been probated and is public record. It would be just so much easier if you could give it to us." Her teeth showed as she took another small bite of sandwich, a cat on the prowl cornering a mouse.

After a slight hesitation, Lucille agreed to have Colin's lawyer send us a copy. "I don't have one in the house," she protested.

We visited politely a bit longer. Lucille walked outside with us and pointed out some lovely late-blooming pink asters she'd weeded and staked.

I decided with a burp that cucumber sandwiches were not something I needed to try again. But thanks to Adele, I'd probably seen a Lucille that was closer to the norm than the Lucille I had talked to a month earlier.

Adele and I compared notes on the way home. We both agreed that Lucille did not want to acknowledge Francine, but maybe that was because she thought the secret was safe. She might only be trying to continue the charade of propriety. We drove in silence for a few minutes.

"What if Milo Sendak was another love child?" Adele blurted.

43

It was a great idea, but the more Adele and I discussed it, the less likely it seemed. Roy and Wanda, Milo's grown children, had spoken of a tight family, raised in Old World traditions. Milo certainly had looked Slavic, as did Roy. If Milo was Colin's child, the strong genes that made Charlie, Cubby, and Lawrence look so much alike hadn't kicked in. Nevertheless, I promised Adele I'd check with Wanda as to any family gossip concerning Milo's parentage.

It was late afternoon when we returned to town, and the one cucumber square I'd choked down at Lucille's hadn't filled any sort of niche in my stomach. Even though I'd been there for lunch, when Adele invited me to join her for dinner at the Pine Tree, I eagerly agreed.

Jack Panther had come into quite a bit of money as a result of establishing his Native American bloodline, which was how he had afforded the expansion of the diner. Now, everything was clean and in good repair. It stayed open all day, and you could order breakfast, lunch, or dinner. Jack still did most of the cooking himself, and it was the best place in town to eat out. OK, it was the only place in town to eat out. I smiled to myself at that thought, and wondered how many years it would be before the determined young Jimmie Mosher would re-open the Cherry Blossom. He'd give Jack a run for his money.

Jack himself greeted us as we entered, and he showed us to a booth with good lighting. There were a few other customers, but it wasn't crowded.

He brought us glasses of water, then stood up straight and pointed to several frames on the wall. "How do you like my new pictures?" he asked. "Cherry Pit Junction in its heyday. See that engine? It's a Baldwin saddle-tank switcher. Very interesting that it was used here. I think it ran short hauls between Cherry Hill and the junction."

"You sound like Cora," Adele said, placing her handbag on the seat beside her and taking a sip of water.

"I'm a railfan. If it has to do with trains and local history, check with me not Cora," Jack answered, smiling. He glanced from Adele to me and back. "You ladies are sure dressed fine. Something up?"

"We had an afternoon appointment, and the refreshments were slim," Adele said, giving out no information of value. "Let's see the menu."

"Sure thing," Jack said, pointing to the plastic jackets tucked behind the condiment rack.

Adele opened a menu, snapped it shut, twisted in her seat, and tilted her head to look directly at the owner. "Jack, how well do you remember the Mueller boys?"

"Hmmm. That was a while back, for sure. They were pretty ordinary. Couple of years ahead of me in school. Peter is older. He helped out at the dealership. I know because I liked to hang around there looking at the cars. Lawrence tried to be a 'bad boy' in high school. I remember my mother telling me to steer clear of him, but he really didn't do nothin' except drive a souped-up old rod around town and wear his hair kinda long."

"And what about Charlie Dixon? Did you know him in school?"

"Nope. Charlie grew up in Thorpe. That school was so small we didn't even play them in sports."

"But you must have known him," Adele said. "How did you know he was from Thorpe?"

"Funny you should ask that," Jack said. He lowered his chunky frame and slid into the booth beside me. "OK if I join you a minute? Don't want to talk so loud."

I slid over to make room and also so I could turn and watch Jack's face.

"Go on," urged Adele.

"The year I was a sophomore, Lawrence was a senior. Two grades was a big difference to be friends. Lawrence wouldn't give me the time of day, but I was in love with his car. It was a 1955

Chevy, red with orange flame decals. Not a cheap hand-painted job like most of us had to do. He'd fitted it with the Corvette engine his dad had pulled from the wreck that killed Billy Lincoln, and that baby could roar. You remember Billy?"

Adele nodded and looked solemn.

"Old Man Mueller wouldn't dirty his hands, but he had a shop for fixing the cars he sold, and he'd let his boys work there. They both had nice rides. Me? I had a ten-year-old Gremlin with dents and a K-Mart spray-can paint job. I used to follow that Chevy around town. It'd prob'ly be called stalking nowadays."

"So how does Charlie come in?" prodded Adele.

"I'm gettin' there. So I was hanging around Mueller's Cherry Hill Cars—that's what he called the place— and I saw Lawrence turn in off the street without his fancy car. He was riding a bicycle, of all things. He'd made some changes; his mother made him cut his long hair for senior pictures, so he looked different that year from what we were used to.

"Anyway, I yelled, 'Lawrence'— we never called him Larry; he didn't like it— 'where's your car?' And he jerked back like he'd been sucker punched and looked around to see if maybe I was talkin' to someone else. But there wasn't anybody else around."

I couldn't stop myself from saying, "And it was Charlie."

"Gees, Ana, how'd you know that? It was for a fact. Charlie Dixon was nearly a dead ringer for Lawrence Mueller. He didn't offer to introduce himself, but I pushed it, and that was the first time I met him. He said he'd ridden over from Thorpe to look at cars, but he got right back on his bike and pedaled away from there as fast as he could. It was odd enough that I've remembered it all these years."

"We discovered that the two men look quite a bit alike some time ago," Adele said with no further explanation.

I added, "Lawrence moved away, but Charlie bought the drugstore here in Cherry Hill. Have you ever talked to him about that day?"

"Never. In fact, we aren't very friendly. His wife gives me the creeps."

Adele perked up at that. "In what way?" she asked.

"Oh, for one thing Faye's an awful flirt. I'm a bachelor, you know. But she's not a bachelorette, if you get what I mean, and yet she was always touching me, or leaning over so I couldn't help but see down her front. I didn't like it, and I told her so. That's all I need, to rile up a Cherry Hill businessman by getting accused of fooling around with his wife. Anyone even caught me looking, I'd get labeled a 'dirty Indian.'"

I felt my eyebrows rising involuntarily. "After she and Charlie were married, she did this?"

"All the time. She still would if I didn't avoid her. I've always wondered if she got that position as Township Treasurer by sleeping around."

I squinted. "Isn't that an elected position?"

"It is, but there's elections, and then there's elections. Hey, I gotta get back to the kitchen." Jack pulled on the end of the table to leverage himself out of the booth, stood and stretched his back.

But then he leaned forward again to be closer to our level. "I just have one more thing to say, and then I'm done with this gossip. A person can't help figuring things out, and Faye has too darned much money for what her job pays and the measly profit Charlie makes at the drugstore. Treasurer's salary is public record, that's easy. And, unless he's lying, I know pretty close to what Charlie's making through Chamber of Commerce meetings. It doesn't add up. None of my business, but you can put that in your pipe and smoke it."

44

Tossing and turning as I tried in vain to fall asleep that night, I came to the conclusion that Charlie Dixon, the druggist, was somehow key to this whole puzzle. He just kept turning up in too many parts of the equation. Or equations, whatever the heck we had going on.

And then there was Faye Anderson Dixon. I certainly hadn't liked the woman the one time I met her. She seemed disingenuous, fake, and overly protective of Charlie. Or maybe she was trying to protect herself from something.

Before floundering into a ragged dream state some time after three a.m., I decided I had to tell the police what I knew of Charlie's family history. Keeping that secret for him was no longer possible.

I came to around ten with a headache, fuzzy mouth and bad dream memories of being chased through Valerie Sendak's flower garden by Charlie wielding a kayak paddle, Lucille Mueller jabbing a shovel, and Faye trying to snag and strangle me with a long strand of black beads. Helen was hiding in the tall grass with gauze bandages streaming from her hooded sweatshirt cuffs. When Ham's train-mangled corpse rose from the dirt, I woke up, shaking. I decided the dream was nothing more than a delayed reaction to Halloween decorations that still adorned many lawns; nevertheless, serious coffee was in order.

After two strong cups of a delicious shade-grown custom brew, which helped a little, it was time to act on my decision. I really didn't want to. I'd learned that small towns may hide secrets, but they are also close-knit communities where people care about each other. I liked Charlie, and sharing his confidence with the police might cause him unnecessary emotional harm.

Maybe I could talk to Chief Tracy Jarvi first. That would be most comfortable for me. But when I called the police station, I was told she was leading an in-service day with local teachers about safety in the schools in case of a mass shooting. That information didn't make me feel safer. And it meant I'd have to talk to the county detective, Dennis Milford. Tracy had informed me he was in charge, but Milford was not on my list of favorite people. Maybe he'd also be out of the office.

No such luck. I had another cup of coffee and a cinnamon roll to fortify my fortunes before calling, but it didn't help. Milford was in, and eager to hear from me. I was told to come right away. That gave me only twenty driving minutes to decide how I was going to explain what I'd learned. Even though the first one hadn't been lucky, I took another roll to eat on the way. Couldn't hurt.

The uniformed deputy on desk duty looked up as I entered the plain gray block building that housed the sheriff's department. I couldn't remember his name, but he knew me. "Go right on back. Detective Milford is waiting for you." He jerked his head toward the hallway.

Milford's door was open. He heaved his solid, square bulk upright behind the desk when he saw me entering. A graying crew cut accentuated his angular shape. He was wearing the same gray suit I'd come to associate with the man. Did he own three alike, or did he never change?

He pointed at the empty chair without offering to shake hands. "Sit down, Ana. They tell me you have some information that might be of interest."

The words themselves were neutral, but the tone implied I'd been concealing critical evidence. Don't be intimidated, I told myself.

"Yes, that's true," I said. "Some of this was told to me in confidence, but one person just keeps turning up whenever I learn something new."

Milford stared at me. I couldn't imagine why he had such a strange expression on his face. It was alarming.

"What's the matter?" I asked.

"You have brown stuff on your teeth."

My reaction was immediate and productive. I ran my tongue over my teeth and discovered a burst of cinnamon. Why now?

"Who?"

"Who what?"

"Who keeps turning up? You're the one who wanted to tell me something."

What I wanted was to throttle the man. "Well, it's Charlie Dixon."

"Yeah, tell me something I don't know," Milford responded as if unaware he'd thrown me off balance. Was it done purposely? "He's still our primary suspect with means and opportunity, although we've got no motive. No motive for anyone to want Sendak and Mueller dead, really. If Nelson turns out to be an overdose, too, then we'll have less than nothing."

I cleared my throat. "That's just it, I can't figure out how it fits together, but Charlie might have a motive to want Colin Mueller out of the way."

The detective put his hands behind his head and leaned back. "I'm listening."

"Colin Mueller is Charlie Dixon's biological father," I said.

"What?" Milford's chair groaned, rolled and banged the wall as his hands slapped down on the desk, and he practically lunged at me. "How long have you known this? Are you positive?"

I met his fierce gaze, but it was tough. "About a month, and yes, I'm sure. Charlie told me himself, but asked me not to let it become public."

"And you didn't think this was important enough to tell the police anyway? You amateurs. I'm tempted to charge you with... with something."

This threat was enough to give me some backbone. "What would that be? Charlie's parentage alone certainly isn't evidence of anything. I'm sure the county has plenty of illegitimate children. To be honest, I came here mostly because I've heard something about Charlie's wife, Faye. She seems like a bigger sneak than Charlie, but I suppose they could be acting together."

"All right, all right," said Milford, settling back in his chair with a sigh. "What about Faye?"

Suddenly, my big news seemed petty and nothing more than what it was: gossip. I tried not to hang my head, but may not have succeeded. "Jack Panther thinks she has more money than what he can account for with their combined income sources."

Milford perked up at this non-evidence. "Really? Money is always a good motive for murder, but how would she get money by killing Colin Mueller? Or Milo Sendak?"

I definitely felt defensive. "That's just it. Nothing makes sense yet, but I'm trying to give you the information I've got, in case you have other pieces of the puzzle. And while we're at it, Raphael Cubby Smith is Colin's child, too. Did you know that? His lawyer is supposed to be contacting everyone with authority when he gets back from some exotic vacation."

Milford nodded. "Cubby's brother—that TV guy, M. Jack—called me last week. Asked me to sit on the information as long as I could."

I tried to switch to the offense. "Have you learned more about this case than you're telling me? Things that could go in the paper without compromising your investigation? Remember, you agreed to be cooperative."

"Yeah, yeah. But, no, we don't know more than you do, I guess. This case just seems to go nowhere. We still have one death we can't even tie in or rule out as connected. What kind of mess is this?"

"A messy one," I said.

"Slippery," Milford said.

"All oozy around the edges," I said.

"Get out," Milford said. "Go find me something useful, Miss Crime Reporter of the Week."

As I was leaving I realized I hadn't told him anything at all about Francine and her suspicions. Too bad. The man really was insufferable.

45

Neither bad dreams nor the sun awakened me Saturday morning. I slept late, much later than usual. Rain fell silently through the gray skies, dripped from the eaves, and pooled in every fallen leaf I hadn't raked. Enough foliage was off the trees that I could see flat light glinting from open water in the swamp; perhaps some of those reflective spots were even the Petite Sauble River itself.

By the time I actually looked at a clock, it was after eleven, but I still felt groggy. A good day to stay home and write my news article and column.

For once, it was genuinely annoying that I had no internet connection at my house. I wanted to get more information from Francine Kelly, but she'd only given me a mailing address and email. I called Information, but they had no telephone listing for anyone named Kelly at the address I gave.

I called Cora. We hadn't arranged to share brunch that Saturday, or I would have set my alarm. But maybe she was home and I could mooch off her Wi-Fi. Jerry answered and told me Cora had gone shopping in Emily City with Jimmie Mosher and Dee, his mom. I explained my problem, and he assured me I was welcome to log in from their house in town, although he was busy in his office. "The back door's open," he said.

Within an hour I was chatting with Francine Kelly via email. She had decided she was ready to deal with whatever changes might take place in her life as a result of people learning of her biological lineage. "It really won't affect me very much, but Lucille will have a fit," her final message read.

I kept my promise to protect Charlie's secret a little longer but did tell her about Cubby. In addition, I was able to confirm her suspicions that Colin had indeed died of an overdose. Since most of the general public wouldn't know until the paper came out on Wednesday, these bits of advance information made Francine feel like an insider. She agreed to keep me informed if anyone connected with the situation contacted her. We both thought Lawrence should be looked at more closely; however, I hedged on accepting her idea that Lucille was a murderess.

Since I was comfortable at the Caulfield's kitchen desk, I stayed there and made myself type and type until I had two items I could live with— a factual article for the front page about Colin Mueller's death being an overdose and my column focusing on possible motives to kill such an old man. I was careful not to name anyone, but it was impossible to avoid bringing in questions about his will. It was hard to imagine any other reasonable motives. This all made perfect sense until one tried to connect Milo Sendak's death to Colin Mueller's.

I was doing final edits and a word count when the back door burst open and two girls entered, giggling. They were followed by Jimmie Mosher. The girls were his pre-teen half sisters, Beth and Lindsey. Dee and Cora came in last. Each of the five people carried plastic shopping bags. Jimmie had three.

The girls suddenly became shy when they saw me. It had been quite a while since I'd talked with either of them, but Jimmie's eyes brightened.

"Ana, look!" He pulled a plastic cylinder and several brightly colored objects in various shapes from his bag. "I got a thing that makes curly vegetables. You can decorate salads or turn zucchini into fake pasta. And these. Silicone everything. Ice cube trays, hot pads, a muffin tin. Well, it's not really a tin, is it?"

Before I had time to respond, the girls took their cue from Jimmie's acceptance of me.

Beth, the older girl, thrust a craft kit with beads and trinkets into my lap. "You can help me make some necklaces," she commanded.

Lindsey hung back only a moment longer. "I got a book. Would you like to see it?"

There was finally a moment for me to get a word in edgewise. "Very much."

With a sly look, she pulled the plastic bag away from her treasure like a magician performing a trick. "It's about a horse. A real horse. His name was Snowman and he liked to jump so much he was a national champion. I bought it with my own money."

Jerry appeared from the front of the house. "What's all this commotion?" he demanded, although his tone indicated he didn't mind the childish voices a bit.

"The rain finally stopped," Cora announced, as she lifted her two bags onto the granite counter. "It's actually warm out for November. Jerry, why don't you get the grill going? Jimmie's going to fix dinner for us all. Ana, there's plenty. Please stay."

"I'd love to," I agreed in a heartbeat.

While Jerry and Jimmie hurried outside to fire up the grill and make hamburger patties, and Cora bustled around pulling groceries out of several bags, Dee came over and stood beside me.

She had lost almost two-hundred pounds since I had first met her. Although she wasn't likely to ever be thin, she was normally mobile and had landed a decent job as an assistant teller at the bank. She placed a hand on my arm.

"I don't know how to thank you enough," she said with a wide smile. "The court awarded primary custody of the girls to me this fall, just before school started. I don't know where we'd all be if you hadn't... well, you know."

We shared a hug. "Anyone would have wanted you to have a better life," I said.

The girls had run for the bathroom, but returned to the kitchen. "We can help," Lindsey said.

Beth chimed in, "I know how to do the salad. C'mon, Linds, let's do that. Maybe Jimmie will let us be the first to make curly carrots." The older girl grabbed a head of lettuce from the counter.

Cora smiled and offered the sisters a large bowl. She also pushed the red stepstool toward the island for Lindsey to stand on.

Although I thought I should be helping with the meal, Dee continued to hold my arm.

"All these other purchases were sort of beside the point," she said. "I asked Cora to help me buy a new outfit for work. We don't have to be really dressy, but I want to look nice. What do you think?"

From yet another plastic shopping bag Dee extracted a dark blue suit in a soft material with satin lapels on the jacket. A baby-blue blouse with pin-tucks was nestled into the folds.

I couldn't help but smile at the idea of Cora as a fashion consultant since she rarely wore anything except blue denim bib overalls with pastel shirts. Indeed, that was what she had worn to the store where she helped select this clothing. Today's shirt was an aqua floral print.

Fortunately, Dee thought I was smiling at her purchase. "You like it, then? I'm not quite thin enough to wear anything fitted yet, but I tried this on, and at least I don't look huge. They had the same suit in mauve, but that one made me look like a giant ham." She giggled.

"Not very businesslike," I agreed. "This one is perfect."

We continued to chat. She wanted to tell me about the court proceedings that restored Beth and Lindsey to her custody from foster care.

The girls finished preparing the salad, topping it with curly carrots without Jimmie's permission.

The back door banged open. Jerry stuck his head in and called, "Burgers are ready. Bring out those buns and chips. I covered the benches and table with plastic while Jimmie was cooking. They were damp."

Cora had been loading a tray with condiments and salad dressings, and another with plates, bowls and forks. We all grabbed something and headed out to the picnic table to share a summery treat in November.

Jimmie pretended to be mad at his sisters about the carrots, but they knew he was teasing. He slipped a burger into each bun as we filed past and presented our plates. If it was related to food, Jimmie wanted to be the man.

Jerry slid in beside Cora and wrapped a long arm around her shoulders. "Pretty much like having our own grands, eh?" he whispered.

But I was standing close enough to hear him.

Cora leaned her head against Jerry and sighed—deeply contented.

These people made Cherry Hill home for me. For the rest of the evening we strung beads, read a few chapters of Snowman aloud and didn't spend even two seconds thinking about wills, pills, or murders.

<h1 style="text-align:center">46</h1>

A Missionary Conference at church kept me occupied all day Sunday, and on Monday I simply crashed. I didn't even get out of bed until the sun was high in the sky. At least I assumed the sun hid up there somewhere; everything I could see was gray. It was Veteran's Day, a good day to stay home and consider my blessings.

I was cutting up apples to make a dessert late that afternoon when the phone rang. Grabbing a towel with one hand, I picked up the handset and pushed the button with the other.

"Is this Ms. Anastasia Raven?" The voice was nasal and high-pitched, but seemed to belong to a man.

"Yes, who's calling?" The sticky apple juice distracted my attention. I tried to wash my hands with the phone crammed between my shoulder and ear. It didn't work well.

"George G. Hartwick. I was told to contact you when I returned from vacation."

Who was this person? I didn't remember meeting anyone with that name. The southern drawl really threw me. Then I remembered.

"Ah, Raphael's lawyer. You were in South America, as I recall."

"Y'all call him Raphael? Down here we call him Cubby. Seems friendlier," Mr. Hartwick twanged.

"He's pretty much Cubby here, too. Anyway. What can I do for you, Mr. Hartwick?"

"I'm not sure you can do anything for me. But Cubby seems to think you are the person to tell his story about being the love child of your local and deceased car dealer."

"He wants to go public?" I was astonished. "What purpose would that serve?"

"He's concerned that people are going to start connecting the dots, and unless he breaks the story first, he'll be accused of killing Colin Mueller for money. His financial assets are a bit strained at the moment, and that might be construed as motive."

My "something's fishy" antennae were bristling. "Really? That's an interesting idea. Why does he think he'd profit from Colin's death? Especially by killing him."

"Money is a powerful motive, Ms. Raven. Mighty powerful."

"Of course," I retorted, "but a person can't profit as a result of their own crime. Correct me if I'm wrong. You're the lawyer."

"To be sure. To be sure, that is the law. However, one tries not to become entangled by his or her own wrongdoing. Therein lies the secret to financial gain."

"Let's get back on point, Mr. Hartwick. How is Mueller's illegitimate child supposed to gain anything? He must have specifically named Peter and Lawrence, his children with Lucille, as heirs."

I heard the lawyer suck in his breath through his teeth. I imagined them yellowed and slightly pointed.

"Now there's a most interesting question. Indeed. If a legator does not specifically exclude legatees who may have a valid claim on a portion of an estate, the potential heirs may bring suit to challenge said will. If the testator does not specifically name the heirs, the testament can be adjudged to include all the biological offspring of the legator. Some rights..."

My head was spinning, and I was afraid the man would continue speaking legalese. I butted in, "Stop. Wait a minute. You're saying that the actual wording of the will is critical as to who inherits, but perhaps any biological children could, right? Have you seen the will?"

"Your first statement is a correct assessment of the situation. Very shrewd, Ms. Raven."

"Call me Ana," I said. I sat down and pushed the pan of apples away from me.

"Very well, Ana. Now, in response to your second question, no. I'm afraid I have not seen Colin Mueller's actual will, but I am fully prepared to represent Cubby's interests in this matter to the fullest extent of the law."

The man's teeth were definitely pointed and his lips thin.

"All right, so Cubby wants me to tell the world about his DNA bank. Since he already seems to know, and therefore I presume you know too, that Charlie Dixon is also Colin's child, it's not that simple. Charlie may not be ready to reveal that fact publicly."

"Be that as it may, I think the time is coming very soon when Mr. Dixon will not have the option of concealing that information."

"Are you aware of any other potential heirs," I asked, thinking of Francine, but not wanting to tip my hand.

"Not at the present time. But these situations often become quite murky. Most unfortunate for all involved."

A vision of a pendulant pointed nose was forming above the yellow teeth and thin lips.

"I'm sure it is."

"It appears that the time is ripe to begin to harvest some of the fruit of Colin Mueller's labors."

The phone made a funny noise, and I glanced at the little screen. There was another call coming in.

"Uh, Mr. Hartwick, I've got someone else trying to call me. Have Cubby contact me, and we'll discuss it." That was a good way to stall for a little time.

"Certainly, Ms. Raven, Ana. Good day."

He clicked off, and I pressed the correct button to switch calls.

"J.R. Fenton's office." It was a female voice. "Calling for Anastasia Raven."

"Yes, speaking," I said with caution. A stupid telemarketer. Well, she had saved me from more discussion with Hartwick.

The woman informed me that J.R. Fenton was Colin Mueller's lawyer. It was certainly a good day for lawyers. She told me to be at Fenton's office the next morning at ten, at which time the will would be read to those other than immediate family. The Will. Lucille was going to be present, as was Detective Milford and Chief Tracy Jarvi. That was going to be an interesting party.

47

The party turned out to be larger and even more interesting than I could possibly have imagined. Fenton's office was located in a made-over service station on the east edge of town. A lot of misguided effort had been applied to disguise the original purpose. Stone columns, brushed aluminum trim and a tiled hip roof had been added, but it still screamed "gas station." With the pumps removed and no broken vehicles filling the area, there was plenty of parking, and most of the spaces were filled.

I was shown into Fenton's office by a woman, probably the one who had phoned me the previous day. The man seated behind the desk nodded to me as I entered and announced my arrival. I looked around the room. The furniture was office basic, not ostentatious; the collection of people eclectic.

Not only was Lucille there, but a younger man stood behind her chair with a hand on her shoulder. I guessed it was her son Peter, rather than Lawrence, because he did not look at all like Charlie Dixon. He had a full head of brown hair, graying at the temples, and was more angular than round.

I was able to make a direct comparison of Peter with Charlie because the druggist was there, too. He sat with another man I did not know. That Charlie was present implied he had given up keeping his secret. So far, there were two groups with two people in each.

The next couplet was Detective Milford and Chief Jarvi. Milford looked ready to become angry at the least provocation, while Tracy was calm but alert. She was in uniform but held her cap on a knee, which released her long blonde braid.

The final person in the room was a middle-aged woman I did not recognize. She seemed to be by herself although I saw her glance at the man beside Charlie. Her expression was so hard you could have struck sparks from it.

I assumed the man behind the desk was Fenton. He straightened his tie and cleared his throat, then proceeded to complete the introductions. Apparently, I was the last person to arrive. Peter Mueller was the man behind his mother. As executor of the estate, he had traveled all the way from Marquette for this meeting, and verbalized that he wasn't happy about it.

The man with Charlie turned out to be yet another lawyer, Sanford Randolph. I wasn't quite sure where he fit in.

Imagine my surprise, however, when the woman sitting alone was introduced as Francine Kelly. Hadn't she said she wasn't interested in any of Colin Mueller's money? Hadn't she promised to tell me if anyone official contacted her?

The men completed polite handshakes, while the women confined themselves to stiff nods. J.R. Fenton stated he represented Lucille Mueller and her sons, Peter and Lawrence, and that he had urged Colin to have his will drawn up professionally, but the man repeatedly refused to do so. He further explained that the will was now being contested, and he was in no way surprised by this. He adjusted his tie again and gave the floor to Mr. Randolph, asking him to explain his interest in the matter.

Randolph was a youngish man, maybe thirty-five. His eyes, slightly enlarged behind thick designer glasses, roved from one person to another while the introductions were taking place. His clothes were expensive, and his voice crisp and commanding. He announced that at the present time he represented Charlie Dixon and was, in association with George G. Hartwick, also representing Raphael Cubby Smith. He stated that both men, as biological offspring, had valid claims on the estate of Colin Mueller. Furthermore, Francine Kelly was included in the suit as an additional rightful heir.

Lucille gasped and sagged in her chair. Peter gripped her one shoulder tightly with his right hand and patted the other one with his left. He glared fiercely at Randolph.

Francine opened her mouth as if to speak, but nothing came

out. I sensed her willing herself to stare solely at J.R. Fenton.

The host lawyer cleared his throat again and stated, "The will is straightforward in its wording although perhaps not so clear in the execution."

He rustled the papers on his desk and lifted a single sheet of what appeared to be ordinary business stationery. There was no stapled blue cover that one sees on most legal documents. He turned the page to the room so we could see a few lines of handwriting in blue ink, with three shorter lines near the bottom. I guessed these were signatures.

At last he read.

> I, Colin Edward Mueller, being of sound mind and body, do hereby bequeath to my faithful wife, Lucille Carol, the house we have occupied for all of our married life, its furniture, decorations and accoutrements, and two acres of land on which the house is located. The balance of my estate, all stocks, bonds, cash, real estate, and any investments convertible to cash, is to be divided equally to all my heirs, including Lucille.

Fenton laid the paper back on his desk and patted it, almost lovingly. His gold ring flashed. "Although Colin declined to have me draw up the will, I find this document to be legally signed, witnessed and notarized." He looked up.

Lucille found her voice. "Certainly he meant Peter and Lawrence."

"Certainly," Fenton replied. "I urged him to specifically name the heirs and he promised me he would do so."

"Then there's got to be a later will," Peter exclaimed. "What's the date on that one?"

"October 11, 2012, a few months before his death," Fenton said. "Does anyone here know of another will, post-dating this one?"

Charlie Dixon was shaking his head in the negative.

"This is preposterous," Peter insisted. "I handle Dad's assets. If they are liquidated, except for the house," he patted his mother's shoulder again, "we're talking about four million dollars. Splitting that six ways instead of three just isn't going to happen."

Now it was Francine's turn to gasp. "Four million? Even with six people to inherit, that's over six-hundred thousand each. I had no idea it would be that much." Her wide eyes darted between Charlie and the other lawyer.

"It appears," said Randolph, "that Mr. Mueller always intended for all his biological offspring to inherit but didn't want to name them for fear of starting a family row with Lucille." He crossed his legs and pinched the crease of his trousers.

"Not so fast," Fenton countered. "Colin simply thought of himself as competent to write legal documents. His expertise in making money is nearly unrivaled in the county, but that talent did not extend itself into the law. His intent is obvious. Peter, Lawrence and Lucille are the heirs he had in mind. His promise to me to name them specifically shows that intent."

Charlie started to stand, and Randolph reached over and pushed him back into the chair. "Not so obviously," Randolph said. "He had plenty of time to re-write that document, and he did not do so. That indicates that his actual intent was to provide for Charles, Francine and Raphael."

Fenton smiled, "I guess we'll see you in court, counselor."

"I'm sure he was going to change that will." Lucille's voice shook, but she managed to make herself heard.

"Unless he never had the chance," Peter said, glaring first at Charlie and then at Francine.

Detective Milford and Tracy had been whispering for a few seconds, but our attention was focused on the sparring lawyers. Suddenly, Milford stood and took two steps toward Charlie. Tracy also rose and circled behind the druggist's chair. Milford motioned for Charlie to stand.

"Charles Dixon, you are under arrest for the murder of Colin Mueller. You have the right to remain silent. Anything you say can and will be used against you in a court of law. You have the right to an attorney."

"You bet he does," Randolph snapped, jumping to his feet as Tracy clipped handcuffs on Charlie's wrists.

"Means and opportunity we had," Milford said bluntly. "Now we've got the motive."

48

Jerry was not impressed. I had been too stunned to stay on top of the crime beat. I hadn't had my camera with me to catch a picture of Charlie being handcuffed. I hadn't raced ahead of the police cars to the jail to catch a picture of Charlie being hustled into the building. Even though the meeting at Fenton's office had broken up quickly after the arrest, to be honest I never even thought of speeding to the jail.

Jerry admonished me to keep my camera on my person at all times and sat me down in his home office to write a late-breaking story about Colin Mueller's possible heirs and the druggist's arrest. He wouldn't even let me leave to get lunch, but he did make me a ham sandwich, which he placed on the desk with a polished apple and a paper napkin holding a pile of potato chips. Then he grabbed his camera and headed out the back door.

Feeling chastened, I wrote until after three p.m. about the relationships between Colin, his legal family, and Cubby, Charlie and Francine. The entire mess would be front page news the next day.

As soon as Jerry accepted my article and released me, I drove directly to Volger's Grocery. I owed Adele the courtesy of telling her ahead of time what would erupt in the county's consciousness. Also, I needed groceries again.

Much to my surprise, Faye Dixon, Charlie's wife, was at the checkout, talking with Adele. It seemed incongruous to me that Faye would be out in public so soon after Charlie was arrested, especially since everyone I knew seemed certain she was extremely sensitive to what others thought of her.

Faye was dressed very much as she had been the only other time I'd seen her. Her silvery blouse glittered as she ranted, and a long string of blue and black beads alternately caught and swung free against the metallic fabric. She punctuated her speech with slashes of bright red nails.

These details captured my attention before I registered her face. She was wide-eyed and incensed. Too-dark hair indicated a recent dye job, and the short-and-stiff pageboy made me think of a pharaoh's headdress. Her voice was loud and brassy.

I didn't want to interrupt, but I did want to hear what they were saying. Grabbing a package of donuts and a jug of cider, I headed for the cash register. More sensible foods could be added to the pile later.

"...entitled to anything we can get. That man owes the children he fathered." She emphasized the word "owes." Faye blustered on, the beads bouncing on her heaving chest. It would be more correct to say that Faye was talking at Adele— not with her— I hadn't heard my friend get in a single word.

Adele turned and acknowledged my presence with raised eyebrows, but Faye continued as if no one new had arrived.

"Of course Charlie wouldn't kill for the money. That's just crazy. He'll be out of jail tomorrow. You'll see. His lawyer is working on it right now. The insane things people in this town will believe just because some dirty old man got his medications mixed up. What about the other two? Their motives are just as good, maybe better. Cubby has no money, and who knows where that Francine person came from? I'll bet she's a gold digger who can't prove anything about Colin being her father." She tapped a hard red nail on the counter for emphasis.

"How...?" Adele began.

But Faye forged ahead. "How do I know about Francine? Charlie told me. That's how. They allowed him to call me after he was fingerprinted and stripped and thrown in a cell like a common criminal. He told me all about it. The indignity! You'd think there would be more respect shown someone who's served the community for decades. I don't think I can make myself go there to visit in person. But he'll be out in a hot minute anyway."

Faye seemed as if she would be perfectly happy to continue raging indefinitely, but her elbow brushed mine, and she jumped.

"Where'd you come from?" she demanded. "Humph. I don't

talk with people who don't know how to mind their own business." And with that pronouncement, she grabbed her shopping bag from the counter and marched out of the store, slamming the screen door behind her.

The old-fashioned front entrance was good for scenes like that. It never would have been as effective if she'd gone out the modern automatic doors on the side of the store.

Adele grinned at me and laughed. I joined in, and we nearly ended up in tears.

"She's pretty wound up," I finally said. "I guess you can't blame her."

"You don't know the half of it," Adele said, wiping her eyes with the edge of her store apron. "She'd been here maybe ten minutes before you showed up. What you heard was the adjusted Faye. She managed to get her tone and facial expressions to register shock and defensiveness for her man in that time."

"What on earth are you talking about?" I asked.

"It took her a few tries to work out the kinks in the wounded spouse act. She never should have practiced on me; she should know better. She'll have regrets later, but the damage is done."

"Stop being so mysterious, Adele."

"Fifteen minutes ago she looked like butter wouldn't melt in her mouth when she told me Charlie had been arrested."

"What does that expression mean, anyway?" I said. An unexpected giggle escaped my lips.

"You know, she was so cool about it all. Almost satisfied. Not enough warmth in that heart to melt a single pat of butter."

"Wait," I said. "Are you telling me that she's actually happy Charlie has been charged with Colin's murder?"

"That would be my first guess although I think she's got the injured innocent act down pat now."

"But, why?"

"Now that's the important question." Adele squinted. "If Charlie really is guilty, he can't inherit, so she won't be in line to get any of Colin's money."

"He wanted me to keep it secret, but Charlie told me about Colin being his father a long time ago. He said Faye didn't know."

"Hmmm. And you didn't tell me? What other secrets are you keeping from me, Ana?" A flash of annoyance passed across Adele's face. "But Faye didn't say or do anything to make me think that was a big surprise to her. I'll bet Charlie only thought she didn't know."

I had a sudden thought. "There's a lot more to Faye than meets the eye. Maybe she's the guilty one. Surely she could get in the drugstore whenever she wanted to and tamper with medications. If Charlie takes the blame, she's home free."

"Sure, but where's her motive?" Adele asked. "Unless she really hates Charlie so much she wants him out of her life and punished for something he didn't do."

"It is hard to see how she could be certain Charlie would get blamed, unless she planned to provide some kind of false evidence if things didn't go that direction. Anyway, divorce is a pretty easy option these days if she just didn't like him." Again, I thought ruefully of my own situation.

"It sure is," said Adele. "And nothing, nothing, nothing that has happened recently has anything to do with Milo Sendak's death. It's like everyone has forgotten about him."

"I know."

"So, did you really come here for donuts and cider?"

I looked down at the sugared circles in their plastic box. "No. I need real food, and I wanted to tell you about the meeting with the lawyers this morning."

Adele perked up at this statement. "Come on, I'll help you shop for something healthy. Then if you help me straighten the office a bit, we can close up, and I'll feed you a home-cooked dinner while you give me the whole story. How's that sound?"

"Perfect."

<h1 style="text-align:center">49</h1>

Not surprisingly, when the Cherry Hill Herald hit the streets on Wednesday, questions of inheritance and murder were the primary topics of conversation in the county. I made the rounds of businesses in town, doing errands, and ending with a cup of coffee at the Pine Tree Diner in order to catch snatches of what people were saying. The most creative comment came from a woman who suggested the five children should start a support group for potential offspring of a certain philandering car salesmen. It was sure to grow as rumors inflated Colin Mueller's worth.

Despite Faye's prediction, Charlie remained in jail. He was the only likely suspect, and judges are reluctant to set bail on first degree murder charges.

By Friday, everyone seemed to have accepted the gruesome likelihood that the man who had been filling their prescriptions for years had betrayed their trust and used his medical knowledge and power to kill. It was becoming unlikely the Cherry Hill Pharmacy would ever reopen. Adele shared the gloomy truth with me that the closed pharmacy was already hurting her business. If people had to drive to Emily City to get their medicines, they probably stayed to shop at bigger stores.

Also on Friday, Tracy Jarvi called me with the news that Hamilton Nelson's exhumation and autopsy had finally taken place. She was free to share the results with the public. No oxycodone in his system. So that was a dead end.

I passed the news along to Adele, Jerry and Cora. We were left with Colin Mueller and Milo Sendak, and no apparent connection between them. And no actual proof that either was murder rather than suicide.

Even though Cubby's brother M.J. was a reporter at the

closest TV station, we were so far from their base that except for the discovery nearly two months earlier that four deaths might be linked, followed by Charlie's arrest on Tuesday for one of them, there had been no other coverage. The entire run of this week's Herald sold out.

I breakfasted with Jerry and Cora on Saturday. Jerry was smiling and rubbing his hands together as I entered the kitchen with a still-warm sausage strata casserole. It was way past my turn to bring the main course, and Adele had given me the recipe and made sure I bought all the ingredients.

"Ana, your stories may win us an award for news coverage of a continuing story by a weekly paper," Jerry announced.

"How can you predict that?" I asked. "The paper just came out a couple of days ago."

"You keep up the good writing, and when this is all over I'll submit it to the Associated Press Journalism Awards competition."

Since I wasn't sure I'd even found my "voice" yet, recognition for quality work seemed unlikely to me. My columns so far had been all over the map, stylistically. But it was nice to have an enthusiastic editor.

"Have some breakfast," I said, thrusting the towel-wrapped dish into his arms.

Cora entered the room, smiling. "Jerry's got the coffee going already, and the rolls should be done by now."

Indeed, the rich smell of cinnamon filled the air.

"Sit, sit," Cora said, pulling stools out from under the island. She grabbed a pot holder and extracted a pan from the oven. Apparently she'd already mixed the icing, which she now dripped over the hot rolls.

We ate in silence for a few minutes. This was a brunch to die for, if I did say so myself. Cora licked her fingers— a childlike free spirit despite being married to the richest man in town. Even richer than Colin Mueller, I suspected, but I had never asked.

"We received the newest layout for the real estate ads this coming week. They always come in well before deadline," Jerry commented.

This seemed a complete non sequitur.

"And?" I asked.

"Interesting offering from Thousand Lakes Real Estate," he said, reaching into his shirt pocket and pulling out a folded sheet of computer paper, which he handed to me.

I opened it. There were small block pictures of houses and cabins forming streets and alleys across the page. Some of the corners featured a banner that read "Newly Listed."

"What am I looking for?"

Cora scootched her stool closer to mine and peered at the page, too.

"Right there." She pointed at one of the bannered photos. "The Mueller house. That was fast. I wonder if Lucille wants to give it up or if Peter pushed her into a quick decision."

"She seemed pretty attached to the gardens and all even if it is way too much work for her at this point," I said.

"She's certainly aged a lot since her husband died, and she probably wants to get away from all the gossip. Some of it has been rather vicious. And none of what's happened is her fault, poor woman." Cora shook her head as she stood, stacking plates and grabbing dirty silverware.

Jerry added, "I didn't know her well, but she was always much more private than Colin. Preferred the company of her flowers, I think. As I recall, she won several Garden Club awards over the years."

"Maybe Peter is taking her to Marquette with him," I said. "She'll probably be willing to tell Adele her reasons for leaving. That and the fact that Ham Nelson died only from the accident should give me plenty to write about for this week."

"Is there more coffee, Cora?" asked Jerry, holding up his mug.

50

The next few days crawled by at the speed of a wooly-bear caterpillar. I saw several of the fuzzies with a wide orange band, suggesting a mild winter. The temperature dropped anyway, and I was way behind on seasonal chores.

What I felt like doing was curling up with a warm fleece blanket like the caterpillar. Instead, I raked leaves into the edge of the woods for what I hoped was the last time, but overnight the wind blew them all around the yard again. The first snow fell. It didn't amount to much, but it provided good motivation for one last chore. I hired Jimmie Mosher to help me put up the shutters on my screen porch. The days were so short I picked him up after school and we rushed to my house to complete the task before dark. It took both of us to get the extension ladder set up. Fortunately, the sectional panels were narrow and easy to handle.

For once, I'd planned ahead, and there was beef stroganoff ready in the crockpot. All that remained was to cook the noodles. After hanging his jacket over the back of a kitchen chair, Jimmie lifted the lid of the cooker and waved the warm steam toward his face.

"Is this hard to make, Ana?" he asked. "This would be a great fall entrée at the Cherry Blossom."

I laughed. "I'll give you the recipe. Maybe you can tweak it and make it even better. I know you're still focused on reviving that restaurant."

"You bet I am! There isn't much at the high school level that helps me, but I'm cooking every chance I can get. The guidance counselor says I should take business classes in college. For now, I'm just trying to get good grades and clean up the building."

"Clean up the building? Jimmie, you aren't poking around

alone inside that old place are you? It hasn't been used for nearly fifteen years. It's dangerous."

"Aw, just a little bit. And I'm careful. My mom found out that we sort of still own it."

"Oh, Jimmie, I don't see how that can be true. Even if no one bought it after your dad died, it probably would have gone into a tax sale."

"Yeah, Mom's trying to find out more about it. She was talking about taxes and stuff. But she did pay the taxes some years. And she says she didn't get proper notices. We're going to figure it out."

"I'm afraid you're getting your hopes up for nothing, but I'm certain you're going to keep trying anyway."

"I sure am. I belong at the Cherry Blossom, but I need to grow up faster."

"Hold your horses, buster, that's happening fast enough." In fact, I had to tilt my head upward to look Jimmie in the eyes. I pulled leftover Halloween chocolates out of a drawer and tossed a handful at the slender young man whose great-grandfather had built my house.

He laughed with me as the wrapped candies rained around his shoulders.

Wednesday's paper carried my newest article about the Mueller house going on the market. I had managed to get Lucille to talk with me on the phone and give me a few sentences about her reasons for leaving. It was quite simple; she was too hurt by Colin's many affairs. She'd previously been aware of only one, which resulted in Francine's birth. The house was a painful reminder of her life with a man she suddenly didn't seem to know. She admitted it was also much too large for her. It was a sad business to go through everything, she said, sorting and boxing the years and years of mementoes, discarding many things that meant nothing to anyone other than herself. She did plan to go live near Peter. He had found a small house with garden space just outside Marquette, where she could still have her independence but be near him in case she needed help with things.

All in all, she sounded remarkably upbeat for someone facing so many difficult facts late in life. She invited me to come to her house and take pictures of the nicer items she planned to dispose of in an estate sale. I was pleased with this offer, and even though it wouldn't be part of the crime series, it would make a nice feature about county history. She had some lovely antiques, and I was confident Cora could add interesting background information.

Thursday, Charlie was released on a surety bond with the drugstore as collateral. I attended his arraignment, and although the judge bound him over for trial, she remarked that there was precious little physical evidence linking the druggist to the crime.

Of course, the District Attorney hammered on the idea that he was the only person with motive, means and opportunity, while the defense pointed out there was not even one specific fact that connected Charlie with the fatal doses of oxycodone.

Despite being free on bond, no one saw Charlie around town. Rumor had it he was lying low at home. Adele, who lived near the Dixons, said his car was always in the driveway when she passed by, but Faye seemed to be leaving and returning with her usual frequency, often with take-out food containers. I thought Adele must be driving by more often than usual to have determined that fact.

Adele also reminded me that since Charlie's wife mostly worked from home as Township Treasurer, she didn't keep regular office hours.

Thanksgiving was coming up in another week. I called my son Chad, and we agreed to meet and eat out in Mackinaw City for the holiday. It was a five-hour drive for him from Michigan Tech at Houghton, but he said he didn't mind, and it would be fun to have fudge for dessert and see the Mackinac Bridge.

Would a solution to the puzzle of Milo's and Colin's deaths be any closer in another week? It seemed unlikely.

Everything changed on Friday.

51

Adele called me early, really early. It was about six in the morning and pitch dark outside. As she told it, she'd already waited a half hour to contact me. Lucille, a morning person through and through, had called Adele, knowing she'd be up and getting ready to go to the store.

Lucille had been distraught, and wanted Adele and me to come to her home as soon as possible so she could show us something. She refused to tell Adele what it was over the phone, but she wanted our advice.

"I've asked Suzi to open the store for me, and she's glad for the extra hours. How soon can you be ready?" Adele's voice was full of anticipation.

My brain needed coffee to even think about the possibilities. Had Lucille found another will? That was about as far as I could speculate. Fortunately, my coffee maker brewed the life-giving liquid quickly, and I owned several travel mugs.

"I'll try to be at your place by six-thirty," I groaned. "Do we really have to do this now?"

"Lucille says it's urgent. You don't want her to call someone else and bypass us, do you? She wants us, Ana. Us. Besides, Suzi has a class at ten. I'll have to be back by nine-fifteen at the latest."

"Okay, okay," I said as I peeled back the warm covers and placed a tentative foot on the cold floor. "I'm up and moving."

In less than an hour, we three ladies were again seated in the Mueller parlor. This time, no tea and sandwiches were served, and no one dressed up. In fact, Lucille was wearing what could only be described as an old house dress, with a pale pink duster jacket over it. This was not the poised hostess who had welcomed us on our previous visit, but seemed more like the distressed woman I'd first met. Lucille noticed the mugs and thanked us for bringing our own beverages.

"Oh dear, oh dear. I'm so glad you've come. I just don't know what to do," the older woman said as soon as we were seated.

She wore black oxfords and I could see support hose, rolled to just above the knee.

Lucille actually wrung her hands. "This is so terrible. But we had no reason to look for anything. Now, I've been sorting everything."

Adele gently but firmly cut her off. "It's all right, Lucille. You'll be fine. Just start at the beginning and tell us what you've found."

"I was going through the boxes this morning, ones from the bedroom that were taken to the garage after Colin died. We just hauled things out there to get them out of the way. No one questioned how he had died way back in March. He was old and sick..."

"We understand," said Adele, nodding her encouragement.

"The doctor just signed the papers, and that was the end of it."

"But now you've found something unexpected?"

"Yes. Colin kept a notebook diary. It was folded in a magazine; the March issue of Time. He liked to read the news, right up until the end. I only found it because there was a big lump in the stack."

Lucille pulled a medium-sized spiral notepad from the patch pocket of her duster. The booklet was flipped open and held at that location with a blue rubber band. A pen had been forced into the metal coil. She handed it to Adele.

"It's sort of a journal. I read all the pages. They're dated. See for yourself, but mostly it's just the weather and an occasional comment about a phone call or something he saw out the window. Except the last one."

I moved to stand behind Adele so I could look over her shoulder.

Lucille pleaded, "Can you deal with whatever should be done? I just don't think I can take any more."

Adele and I had been trying to read above the distraction of the woman's shaking voice. In a scrawling hand, which looked to me very similar to what I'd seen in the will at the meeting with the lawyers, were written the words:

> The pain has become unbearable. Forgive me Lucille for so many things— I've hurt you I know, and the worst is yet to come because I won't abandon responsibilities to all my children in death. You and Fenton will figure it out. I've been saving a capsule here and there for a long time. Now I have enough. Please believe I've always loved you.
> Colin.

Lucille was truly crying now, tears running silently down her cheeks. Her shoulders shook. She lifted the edge of the duster and blotted her eyes.

Adele handed me the notebook and leaned forward to take the older woman's hands. "Everything is going to be all right, Lucille. This provides answers. There's no more guessing. Isn't that a good thing?"

"I... I suppose so."

"It is. Definitely. Shall I make you some tea? Ana can call Detective Milford. He'll have to be told right away, you know. This means Charlie didn't do anything wrong." Adele rolled her eyes toward me while she was saying this, knowing that with her head down Lucille couldn't see the gesture.

I mouthed the words, Will do.

"Come on, dear. Let's go to the kitchen and you can show me where you keep the tea bags." Lucille sniffed and nodded. Adele helped Lucille out of her chair and hustled her down a hallway toward the rear of the house.

This was my cue. I did have my mobile phone with me, and I punched in the number of the sheriff's office. I knew it by heart.

Daylight was barely brightening the eastern window.

52

Charges against Charlie Dixon were, of course, dismissed, and the community breathed a collective sigh of relief.

The man must have been crazy busy all weekend. When I arrived in town for church Sunday morning, under every windshield wiper was a neon green flyer proclaiming that the Cherry Hill Pharmacy would re-open on Monday with door prizes, candy and other treats for kids who came in after school, and bargains galore. I know this because I collected my own from the Jeep's windshield after church. The colorful papers also included several valuable coupons, so I saw people pocketing them instead of tossing them away.

Adele was extremely put out that she couldn't get anyone else to watch her store, so I agreed to be at Charlie's grand re-opening and hang around for a while to gauge the reaction of the community. I didn't expect much to happen that could be included in a crime beat story, but I dutifully took my camera and a notebook, just in case. I wasn't going to have Jerry displeased with me again for being unprepared.

There was actually a short line in front of the doors at quarter to nine. Most were women. I had expected to see the senior citizens, but there were also several young mothers with preschoolers in tow.

The drugstore was located on Main Street, two blocks west of Volger's Grocery and two-and-a-half from the Pine Tree Diner. All three buildings were part of the quintessential small town brick construction boom near the turn of the twentieth century. Cramped facades with decorative cornices and apartments on the second floor were the norm. While both Adele, and Jack Panther at the Pine Tree, had taken over adjoining buildings to expand their space, Charlie had not. As a result the store was long and narrow. And small. The line, which grew even as I approached, suggested this grand re-opening was going to be a logistical challenge.

A white van marked with the call numbers of the TV station where M. Jack Smith worked was parked at the far curb. Cherry Hill was back on their radar. A cameraman and M.J. hurriedly spilled out and began filming with the store as a backdrop, briefly covering the history of the druggist's arrest and subsequent release. M. Jack interviewed a couple of the potential customers. Judging from the meaningless responses, I deduced there would be heavy editing applied to produce a short clip for the nightly news.

At five minutes before nine, Charlie appeared. It seemed unlikely that he had just arrived; he must have had a lot of last-minute preparations to accomplish. Maybe he wanted to make an impression instead of opening the door from the inside. He wore a blue smock over a white shirt with a tie. He'd lost a little weight over the course of this ordeal, which helped his appearance. Nothing could change the genetics of his balding, rotund physique, but he did look less portly than he had in September. He wore a tweed newsboy cap. Was the hat vanity, or a foil against the chilly air?

In fact, he exhibited a bit of showmanship, perhaps for the TV camera; he'd obviously planned this in advance. The actual door was recessed between two large display windows. The stoop spanning this space was a huge slab of stone with the year 1896 carved deeply into it. More than a century of passing feet had worn down the center of this stone enough to create a slight, but visible, depression, and the date could still be easily read. The original carvers must have foreseen decades of future shoppers.

This stoop was two steps higher than ground level, and those steps thrust out into the sidewalk. The stone platform created a natural low stage, and Charlie mounted, gently but firmly encouraging people to back away from the door and step down to the sidewalk. He flourished a large golden key on a ribbon. It looked fake, and when I saw the light reflect from a small spot near the bow of the plastic key, I realized he'd simply fastened the real one on the same ribbon.

Nice flourish.

Before he put the key to the lock, Charlie turned around and raised both hands, palms outward. The eager crowd quieted, except for one crying toddler. The mother scooped her up, and I realized it was Helen Bracket with Roberta. We made eye contact, and she smiled. Her mother, Lisa, was there, too.

M. Jack Smith sidled in and held a microphone near Charlie's face. The druggist glanced sideways, looking surprised, but he took it in stride.

"Thank you all so much for coming and supporting Cherry Hill and me," Charlie began. "As you are reminded by this stone every time you enter, my building was constructed in 1896 and has been in continual operation as a pharmacy ever since. I'm beyond happy to tell you that it's my plan for that to remain true. In the middle years, there was also a soda fountain and lunch counter. Does anyone here remember that?"

"Of course," an elderly lady called out. "Ben and I used to come here after school for nickel Cherry Cokes." She made a noise that might have been a giggle and poked the man next to her, presumably Ben. He nodded and grinned, took the woman's hand and raised their arms in a victory gesture.

Charlie continued. "Of course, lunch counters went out of fashion. When the school moved out of town, it was the end of that era. But the space has been filled with sundries and toiletries more appropriate for modern times, and I surely appreciate that you approve of my selection by your hometown buying habits."

I thought he might be getting a little too caught up in his own eloquence, but he must have sensed it was a good time to quit. He announced that because of the limited space inside, ten people would be allowed in at one time, but that hot cider and donuts would be served on the sidewalk. On cue, a young man I didn't know appeared from around the corner, wheeling a cart decorated with colored leaves and cornstalks. As promised, there was a pile of donuts on a plate and a steaming pot, which turned out to be the cider perched on a propane hot plate.

Charlie pulled a handful of small items from his oversized smock pockets. These turned out to be finger puppets, which he distributed to the small children who immediately began having finger wars. Then he turned his attention to the door, applying the real key hidden behind the large gold one.

The TV crew and ten eager shoppers followed him inside pulling green coupons from their pockets.

I snapped a few pictures, but the excitement was pretty much done. I was thinking about heading over to Adele's to give her the scoop when I heard a vehicle door slam, and a man dressed in jeans and a maroon nylon jacket, who could have been Charlie's double, albeit a few years younger, came around the front of the TV station van.

"Uh, oh," I said involuntarily. "Here's Cubby."

53

I approached the man. "Hello, I'm Anastasia Raven. You must be Raphael."

"Sure, but call me Cubby. We talked on the phone, right?"

"We did. I thought you were in Florida. What brings you back home?" I wanted to add "at this particular moment."

As this was happening, out of the corner of my eye I saw a woman in the waiting line recoil. Her cider slopped onto the pavement. She immediately handed the cup to a woman beside her, pulled out a cell phone and started poking at it, but my attention was drawn back to Cubby.

"I thought it was time to reconcile myself to the reality of my relatives. Besides, Charlie's ready to accept his parentage, so there shouldn't be any unpleasant waves."

I'll bet it's the money, I thought. "You came with M.J?" I asked, which was obvious, but I couldn't think of much else to keep him talking.

Cubby must have sensed I was fishing. "He picked me up at the airport this morning. Now, if you don't mind, I'll go in and let Charles know I'm here." He wore glasses, and he tipped his head slightly to stare at me over the top of the frames.

"Uh, no, I don't mind at all," I said, stepping aside.

Adele would kill me if I missed this, so I followed Cubby inside, expecting immediate fireworks. In that respect, I was disappointed. Charlie nodded at Cubby, but he remained where he was, answering a woman's question about pain relievers.

What a let-down! I could only assume the two men had been in previous contact. Cubby's earlier comments had implied as much.

Cubby and M.J. held a whispered conference. The newsman was pointing at the door and Cubby was shaking his head. A minute later, the camera crew and M.J. left. I heard the van start and pull away.

Charlie took Cubby by the arm and led his half-brother toward a back room. I heard him say, "Not too long. Today is about customers. You couldn't have waited a day?"

Their conversation was cut off by the closing door.

I wandered around looking at displays and trying to figure out when Charlie had time to make the small store look so festive and attractive. He'd certainly succeeded at making people happy today. Shopper after shopper took multiple items to the checkout, which was operated by the young man who'd brought the refreshments. This local shopping would make Adele happy even if I didn't manage to collect any juicy gossip.

Not wanting to give the appearance of loitering, yet not wanting to leave, I went back outside and helped myself to a cinnamon-sugar coated donut and a cup of hot cider. I talked with people waiting in line. As people exited the store, more entered.

Helen and Lisa came out and chatted with me for a few minutes, both expressing relief that Ham Nelson's death hadn't been tied to any of the others. Helen thanked me again for finding her inheritance. She seemed more relaxed than I'd ever seen her, and I asked if she was still seeing Tim from the bank. Her ready smile answered that question without words.

"Stop by sometime," Lisa invited as we walked toward her car. "We consider you a friend."

There wasn't any good reason for me to hang around longer, except that I couldn't believe Charlie and Cubby were going to be sudden pals. I went back inside, breaking the ten-person rule, and loitered anyway. I bought a new toothbrush. I loitered some more and had another donut. Might as well create a good need for that toothbrush.

Finally Charlie and Cubby emerged from the back. Several shoppers had been waiting for Charlie, and he was suddenly surrounded by people asking questions. Apparently being charged with murder had conferred semi-celebrity status on him.

Almost simultaneously, Valerie Sendak burst into the store,

pointing a finger at Cubby. She must have been waiting and watching through a front window. I recalled the startled woman and her phone call.

"You. You two-bit chiseler. Coming home and not telling me. I suppose you were going to get your share of old Mueller's money and then leave me in the lurch."

Cubby looked behind him as if he hoped she was addressing someone else.

Valerie was dressed to kill. A green silk scarf draped diagonally over a plum wool suit. Gold glittered everywhere. A large brooch held the scarf. Rings sparkled on her fingers, and bracelets and earrings danced as she quivered with anger. Or stage presence. Actually, all she needed was a crown and she could have been one of the Romanovs.

She continued, "Well, daa..rl..ing, you aren't going to have the chance, because we are done as of right now. You killed Milo. My dear Milo."

I thought this accusation was a bit of a stretch. Cubby must have, too, because he looked around again. Maybe he was looking for somewhere to hide. Finally, he pointed a finger at his chest and mouthed the word, Me?

"Oh, I don't think you doctored his pills, but you killed him. He was heartbroken that I preferred you to him, and took his life in grief. Was that ever a mistake on my part!"

My next thought was that Valerie had no idea how much each of Colin Mueller's offspring would inherit. She would have held her tongue and married Cubby in a heartbeat for that. It was a good thing I was busy pondering, or I might have laughed out loud.

Valerie continued her diatribe. "Don't call me or come around. I certainly won't call you. These people are my witnesses."

With that she made a perfect military pivot on one stiletto heel and exited the store.

The woman was high-maintenance, crazy or at least unstable, and she seemed to always be angry. Cubby was one very lucky man to be rid of her without any effort on his part.

54

Adele was the first recipient of the news. I owed her that, so I walked to Volger's and gave her the highlights. She'd heard some things already, because shoppers were coming directly from the drugstore to the grocery. That pleased her immensely.

After I finished my report, what with interruptions to wait on customers, she spent almost forty minutes picking my brain for details. If I didn't know answers to her questions she speculated on three or four possibilities per query.

I walked down Cherry Street to the Caulfield's house, two blocks south of the drugstore. I'd left the car there to avoid getting parked in on Main Street. Jerry must have seen the Jeep and been watching for me.

"Ana, come in here a minute," he called, sticking his head out the front door.

I climbed the steps to the ornate Victorian porch. I'd hardly ever used this formal and official entrance. Jerry had converted what used to be the entryway and parlor into his home office, the room where I'd first learned about the history of the Cherry Hill Herald.

Three walls were painted dark blue and covered with framed copies of historic newspapers and pictures of significant events in Jerry's life. The north wall was floor-to-ceiling bookshelves. A high, off-white tray ceiling, edged with gold, brightened the space.

"Over here." Jerry motioned me toward the large blond desk. "I received quite an interesting email message this morning."

I threaded my way between the creamy leather sofa, and a matching lounge chair and ottoman, which were arranged around a glass-top coffee table.

He swiveled his computer monitor so it faced outward. The

225

header indicated the sender was Julia Hendershot. The name was familiar, but I couldn't place it. The message read:

"There is a rumor going around the building at Accounting Plus that there's a possible embezzlement of approximately $120,000 in township funds from Shashawqua Township. Milo Sendak was supposed to do the audit earlier this fall, but his death made them put it off. Now we've got preliminary findings. There's going to be a full audit. The money has to be verified as missing, with possible suspect(s) identified. It looks like this occurred over several years, and was cleverly accomplished. Maybe this information will help someone. We can't tell the police till we have proof, and don't tell anyone you got this information from me. Julia Adams Hendershot."

Adams... Isabel's sister, who also worked at Accounting Plus.

This message should mean something really big to me, but I couldn't remember what. I closed one eye and realized that side of my face had scrunched. Jerry watched me, smiling.

It hit me. "Faye Dixon," I said.

"Faye Dixon," Jerry echoed.

"Shashawqua Township is here? Cherry Hill?" I've lived in this county a while now, but my brain could hardly process this. I needed verification.

"No, it's not," Jerry said solemnly.

"But, she lives here. How can that be— acting as treasurer somewhere else?"

"That's one of several really good questions. Shashawqua Township includes the Village of Thorpe. It's where Faye's family originates."

"Right, I remember that. She's heir of the Thorpe Metalworks fortune. But don't you have to live in the township where you hold office?"

Jerry rubbed a hand over the top of his head. He winked at me, which seemed odd. "Here's how she's worked that for many years. She sold most of the family property but kept the house. She claims it as her primary residence, gets her personal mail there, pays the utilities from that address."

"You've got to be kidding." Mentally, I added this into all the other rather unpleasant things I knew about Faye Anderson Dixon.

"It's a little on the shady side, but since no one else wants to be treasurer, it's never been called into question."

"Why would she need to steal township money?" I asked. "She got everything from the Thorpe company."

"Maybe that wasn't as much as she wanted people to believe," Jerry suggested. "Maybe she's spent it all. Maybe she just had to have more. Maybe she's not even the one who took it. Julia said it's not verified yet."

"Right." I drew the word out in disbelief.

The corners of Jerry's mouth twitched. "I'm only trying to stick to 'innocent until proven guilty.' Good politics, you know."

"Can we print any of this yet? This is only Monday. Maybe something will break in the next twenty-four hours."

Jerry was quiet for a moment. "We can certainly say that an unscheduled audit is underway for the Shashawqua Township treasury. That could shake the bushes."

We heard the kitchen door open, and a moment later Cora entered the office. "What has you two looking so excited?" she asked, after glancing at Jerry and me. She slipped out of her coat and hung it in the hall closet.

Jerry filled her in, and Cora's face lit up as if inspired by a divine revelation. "Well, there's your motive," she said, lifting her hands as if making an offering. "Faye needed to keep Milo from doing the audit until she could manage to get the cash and herself out of town. She hasn't quite pulled it off yet."

"And she probably doesn't know the audit's finally been started," I said.

Jerry looked thoughtful. "I'm betting she does. As treasurer, she must have received some kind of notice of the accounting firm's timeline."

"So, she'll make her move very soon, I would think," added Cora. "I doubt she's got the nerve to sit tight and play innocent."

"If she's really guilty, that won't work anyway," said Jerry. "They'll easily follow the trail and be able to prove she took the funds."

He turned the monitor back toward the keyboard. "Sit. Write," he said.

And I did. I thought I had a whopper of a story for the Thanksgiving issue of the Herald. But a newspaper is never complete until it's off the press.

55

Although exciting, the day was emotionally exhausting. When I finally got home, I changed to pajamas and stretched out on my bed to rest even though it was barely suppertime. Since Daylight Savings Time had ended, the early darkness made me feel tired in the evening. After easing my muscles, I sat up in bed with a book, trying to read, but I repeatedly dozed off and awoke each time with a stiff neck.

I had no idea what time it was when my cell phone rang. I'd fallen asleep with the novel in my hands again. The strident buzzing startled me, and I jerked, sending the book skittering across the floor.

Even with the bedside lamp on, I groped, searching for the little flip phone. Not many people had that number. It was pure luck the phone was in the room with me instead of tucked in a pocket somewhere. I'd plugged it in to charge and laid it on the nightstand. After about five rings, I managed to open it and push the correct button to answer.

"Hello?" My voice slurred. I'd been asleep, but came fully awake in the next few seconds.

A voice whispered, "Ana? This is Jimmie. I'm at the Cherry Blossom. Can you come over here? I'm a little bit scared."

"Jimmie! What time is it? What on earth are you doing there in the dark?"

"I don't know what time it is. Not too late." He sounded impatient. The time was inconsequential. "But I saw a light inside, moving around, like a flashlight."

"Why are you messing around that old building? Oh, never mind. Where are you exactly?"

"I'm out back, hiding under some old junk. I don't dare talk much. She might hear me."

"She, who?"

"Uh oh. Gotta go. I'll work my way out to the highway, towards town. There's some bushes there. Can you..."

The connection broke.

I flung myself out of bed and hustled into sweatpants and a turtleneck, all drowsiness gone. I added a hoodie with a jacket over top of that. A dark jacket. Would it be good to be less visible? I had no idea.

Was Jimmie hurt? Did the call cut out because someone had found him? I grabbed a blanket from my bed in case of... something. Running down the stairs, I tried to remember the age of the batteries in my flashlight. No clue.

Snatching an additional jacket and gloves from the downstairs closet and rummaging in the junk drawer took more precious seconds, but I found a spare package of batteries, the right size. The flashlight was there, too.

It was at least seven miles to the old restaurant building. I'd never actually clocked it. It would save time if I didn't go through town. Taking Fairgrove would solve that, but exactly how far west was the restaurant? Where should I turn north? I couldn't remember these little-used roads clearly enough. Well, I'd take the first one and then turn west on US 10. That should work.

The dashboard clock read 7:35, so it really wasn't very late, although the night was pitch black. No moonlight aided my fumbling as I threw the extra items in the back seat and started the car.

A light rain fell, making the chilly darkness even more miserable. My road was dirt as far as Cherry Pit Junction, the remains of a hamlet at the dead center of the county. After that, there was pavement as I angled left on Fairgrove, and I could drive faster. I crossed Freetown Road. That would have taken me directly into Cherry Hill and was not what I wanted. Now I needed to watch for the next crossroad. It was difficult; I had to reach Jimmie quickly, but I needed to travel slowly enough to be able to see. I went a mile... nothing. Was the county map in the glove box? I couldn't recall. I'd have to stop to read it anyway... didn't want to take time. A small green road sign glowed high in my headlight arc. Finally!

I couldn't quite read the name, but it didn't matter. It went north and wasn't marked "Dead End." I made the turn, and the highway was only a mile away. The pale dirt road ran straight in front of me. Rolling through the stop at the highway, I turned left with only a quick glance to make sure there were no approaching headlights.

"Dang, drat, damn," I yelled. I couldn't help it. Jimmie was in trouble, and I was too far out of town; I should have turned right. A mailbox loomed in my lights, and I slowed to find the driveway and turn around.

Yes, there was the shape of the long-closed Cherry Blossom Restaurant materializing on my left. What if the person Jimmie saw was still there? Should I turn off my lights? I definitely didn't want to pull into the parking lot and alert someone. Dimly, I saw the line of thick bushes and scrubby trees that Jimmie had mentioned. Now that I was traveling toward town, his hiding place was on the wrong side of the road.

A car closed behind me as I slowed down to assess the surroundings. Hoping the two sets of lights might confuse anyone who might be watching, I veered suddenly left, next to the bushes, without signaling the turn, and snapped off my headlights. The other car laid on the horn. Damn again.

Jimmie ran from beneath the trees, around the front of the car and hopped in the passenger side.

"Hi, Ana," he said, grinning. "She's gone now."

56

"Who's gone? Jimmie, I could wring your neck; you scared me half to death. Are you all right?" Now that the boy was safe, I was angry.

Jimmie was blasé about any danger, and excited at the same time.

"I'm fine. I hid under those old sheets of roofing in the back when I knew she was coming out the door. I had to hang up on you, or she might have heard me."

"Who, Jimmie? Who are we talking about, and what was she doing?"

He shrugged. "Gosh, I don't know her name. Some lady from town. Kinda old but not as old as Nana Cora."

I remembered the things I'd brought. "Are you cold? There's a blanket and extra jacket in the back seat."

"Thanks," Jimmie said, turning and stretching to grab the blanket, which he wrapped around his shoulders. He had on jeans and a sweatshirt, inadequate in my estimation for the chilly November night.

Although he hadn't answered all my questions, I thought of a more important one. "Does your mother know what you're doing?"

"Yeah, she knows I spend time at the restaurant. We're still trying to find proof it's ours, remember?" There was a touch of defensiveness in his voice. "I walked out here because it's too dark to ride my bike. It's not like I was far from home. The Cherry Blossom isn't even a mile from my house. Anyway, I was thinking about leaving and turned off my flashlight because I can see really good in the dark anyway. This car drives through the back gate; there's a side entrance off of Tansy Road for deliveries. No one's got any business being there. So I hid."

"Wait! Don't tell me any more yet. Let's go to Cora and Jerry's house, so they can hear this. You aren't kidding me that your mom knows you're out? Why didn't you call her?"

"No, I'm not kidding," he said defiantly. "But she gets all flustered and isn't very useful when a guy needs help. You're better for that. I'll call her right now and tell her I'm with you and Nana." He slid down in the seat, pulled a cheap mobile phone from his back pocket and pushed buttons.

I listened to Jimmie's end of the conversation, and was convinced he'd told me the truth. At any rate, unless he'd dialed a non-working number and was writing the entire script for his end of the conversation in his head as he went, Dee knew he was with me. It wouldn't do to ask to talk to his mother and rile this headstrong young friend of mine. He'd spent too much of his life fending for himself. His independence was a good thing, but it probably meant he wasn't going to take much direction during his teen years. I decided to trust him. After we'd gotten past our initial encounter two years previous, he'd always been truthful with me.

As Jimmie had pointed out, we weren't far from town, and he broke off the call with his mom as we pulled to the curb behind Caulfield's house. The kitchen lights were on.

We knocked, and Cora opened the door. "Ana, Jimmie. Come in." Her voice took on a note of alarm when she saw the blanket wrapped around the boy's thin shoulders. She hugged him and examined his clothes. "What happened? You're wet. What's going on?"

"I think some hot chocolate would be in order, if possible," I said. "Is Jerry here? Jimmie's got a story, and I think he should hear it with us."

Jerry poked his head around the corner of the door from the hall. "What's up? Jimmie has news?"

"I saw someone, a lady, at the Cherry Blossom. She didn't want anyone to see her. She kept checking to see if there was someone watching, but I don't think she saw me."

"All right," Cora commanded. "Sit down. I'll just get some milk warming and we can all hear what happened."

In a few minutes, Jimmie let the blanket slip off his shoulders as he cradled a hot mug of cocoa in his hands.

"The floor is yours, young man," Jerry prompted.

"OK," Jimmie began. "I was out at the restaurant. I go there lots. My mom thinks we actually still own it, but we're looking for anything that will help us prove that. The offices are a wreck. Stupid little kids have broken in and made a mess, and animals, too. It gets dark so early now I've been taking a flashlight and sorting things for a while after supper most days."

"We understand," Jerry said, man-to-man. "Tell us what happened tonight."

"I'd been there a while, and I saw headlights coming from the back. There's a service drive you can get to that comes off the side road instead of the highway. But whoever it was shut off their lights before coming into the parking lot."

"I know where you mean," Cora said.

"So I hid behind the office door. My light was already off because I was getting ready to leave and I didn't need it just to get out of the building. I wasn't sure what they wanted, but I'm only a kid. Most any adult would yell at me if they caught me. Just for being there. It was a woman; I could tell that much."

"He thought she was middle-aged," I put in.

Jimmie shrugged. "I guess so. She came in through the back door of the restaurant. The locks are all broken, you know, so anyone can get in. She went right to a place near the front windows. She had one of those little tiny lights like you put on a keychain, and she mostly covered it with her fingers so it wouldn't show."

Jerry pressed for the answer I also wanted. "Do you know who this woman is?"

"Nope. I don't think I know her, but it was hard to see her face. All spooky Halloween shadows, like." Jimmie mimed holding a flashlight under his chin and paused to sip hot chocolate.

"Keep going," I said. Then, to Jerry and Cora, "This is all I've heard so far. Pretty much, anyway."

"Then she knelt down and pulled up some of the floor tiles.

They must be loose where the roof leaks in that corner. Underneath was a plastic bag. It was some kind of thick plastic—not like a shopping bag, but I could hear it rattle when she moved it. She either took something out or put something in. Her back was to me, and I thought maybe I could get her license plate number if I went through the office door out to her car."

Jerry interrupted. "Great idea. Did you get it?"

"No, sir. I was trying to be really quiet, you know, and just as I made it outside, I heard the regular restaurant door being opened. I dropped down and slithered underneath those loose sheets of green roofing—that wavy stuff. The place where I found the placemats I gave you." He nodded at Cora. "That's how I got wet. It's all moss and old leaves under there."

"And then you called me?" I asked.

"Yes, but when the lady came outside I was afraid she'd hear me talking, so I hung up. Sorry to scare you." The boy hung his head, but he was grinning.

"Could you see her car at all?" Jerry said.

"I poked my head out a little bit when I heard it start, but all I could tell was that it was small and dark. Not a big SUV or a truck. She left the same way she came and didn't turn her lights on at all. I knew it was safe then and went to the bushes where I told Ana to pick me up."

He took a long drink of cocoa. "That's it," he concluded.

Cora looked at Jerry and said firmly, "We should call the police."

57

"Maybe, maybe not." Jerry said, shaking his head. "We've got a fourteen-year-old boy, sneaking around in a place he doesn't belong..."

"That's not so. We own it." Jimmie turned red and banged his mug on the counter harder than necessary.

"You might, but you, yourself, said you can't prove it yet." Jerry stared hard at the young man.

Jimmie settled down.

"We've got a woman we can't identify, who clearly doesn't belong there, doing something that appears secretive, but we can't tell what it is."

"What do you think we should do?" Cora asked. "You don't plan to ignore this, I hope."

Jerry smiled at his wife and pointed at Jimmie. "I think we should help Jimmie find out what's there and who the sneak is."

Jimmie hopped off the stool and yelled, "Hooray!"

"I think I have just the thing to catch the prowler in action," Jerry said. "I've got a motion activated cam that streams video to my phone. Got it for hunting a few years ago. Never got around to setting it up anywhere after I caught the 'dear' I was really after." He winked and nodded at Cora.

"Oh, you," Cora said, shaking her head and gathering our empty mugs.

"Hot dog!" squeaked Jimmie. "That sounds expensive. Can I see? Can I help set it up?"

"I think so, Jimmie. The biggest problem is that we'll need to do it in the daylight. That's not an issue for the adults here, but you've got school in the morning."

With this disastrous announcement, Jimmie spun around toward me and said, "I can skip a half day. Mom will let me if it will help us save the restaurant. I know she will."

"Not so fast," Cora said to Jimmie. "The sun is lazy in November, but I think it comes up around eight. Even before that there's enough light to see." Turning to Jerry, she added, "How long would this take?"

"Not long. If we mount the camera, then one of us could drive Jimmie to school. What time do classes start?"

"Not till eight-forty. But I can get a note from my mom. Really."

Jerry settled the matter. "All right, son. You've made your point. You get a note just in case this takes a few more minutes than we expect. Can you come here at six o'clock? I'm sure Cora would be glad to feed you breakfast."

"You bet," Jimmie said with a grin.

"Of course I will," Cora said at the same time. "I'll feed us all. Ana?"

"Absolutely, and I'll pick Jimmie up at his house so he can sleep ten minutes longer."

The following morning, the four of us huddled under a tree behind the Cherry Blossom in a thick gray fog.

"Fog is good. It's harder to see us," Jimmie whispered.

"Not so good if we want to capture someone on camera," I said.

We'd come in the back way, in Jerry's car. He'd stopped briefly before leaving Tansy Road and checked the dirt driveway that led to the back of the restaurant parking lot. There were clear tire tracks in the dampened earth, and he took a lot of pictures before driving in.

"This is a pretty good vantage point," Jerry said. "Nice clear sight line, and this fence post won't move in the wind. I'll strap the camera right around it."

"Won't she see it?" Jimmie asked.

"Unlikely," Jerry answered. "The tree branches are sort of in the way from everywhere except the gate, so someone would have to be looking in the exact right spot at the same moment as they entered. Besides, darkness seems to be her preferred time frame."

"What if someone does see it?" Cora asked.

"I don't think most people will bother it. Hunters will know what it is and leave it alone. Besides, with the streaming feed, I'll know the minute anyone or anything trips it, and we can drive right out here. I might even be able to tell who it is, depending on where and how they stand."

"But I'll be in school," Jimmie whined.

"That's possible," I put in, "but we'll have to hope she comes after dark. She might not show up again for days, anyway."

"That'd be awful. I want to know who's in my building," Jimmie insisted.

Jerry laughed and shook his head. "You are a little bit presumptuous, young man. I'll call Ana the minute I see anything, and you, too, if school isn't in session. You have Thursday and Friday off for Thanksgiving, and then it's the weekend. I'd say there's a good chance you'll be in on our little spy mission. Give me that cell phone number."

"OK," Jimmie reluctantly agreed.

I had to admit I sympathized with the boy. It was going to require serious patience to wait for someone to trigger the video feed.

We went inside the building and easily found the loose tiles in the corner. Underneath was a white zippered Tyvek bag. The pull was secured to a ring with a tiny padlock. Anyone could cut the bag open, but obviously that would indicate someone had tampered with it.

"Money, I think," said Jerry after handling the bag.

"Real buried treasure," Jimmie said, his eyes sparkling.

"Possibly, but people do desperate things to protect money," Cora countered. "Let's hope this adventure doesn't turn out to be dangerous."

After delivering Jimmie on time to the consolidated school north of town, I ended up staying at Cora and Jerry's house all day. The fog lifted, and the sun even appeared for a while.

To pass the time, I took occasional walks around town, stopping to chat with Adele on one of them. I helped proofread the pages for the Herald since the paper came out the next day.

Jerry worked late into the night most Tuesdays and always got up early on Wednesdays.

Around three in the afternoon we got a trigger notification. Jerry's phone made an unfamiliar sound, and he poked at it and pulled up the camera feed. Cora and I scrambled over to his desk so we could see who was in the restaurant parking lot.

A deer was moving slowly through the field of vision, unaware she was being filmed. She seemed to like nibbling the grass growing through the cracks in the asphalt. We watched her until she left our view.

Jimmie appeared at the door a little after four. He'd changed since we'd seen him that morning in his school clothes. Now he had on ragged jeans over long johns with a flannel shirt. A winter coat hung from his shoulders. He was out of breath, which made me suspect he'd run all the way from his house.

"Did we catch anyone yet?" he inquired eagerly.

"Just a nice little doe, minding her own business," Cora said. She peeled the lid off a plastic container. "Have some cookies."

While Jimmie inhaled cookies and milk, Jerry's phone sounded the odd tone again. As we adults clustered around Jerry, Jimmie figured it out.

"Wowzer! Is that the camera? Let me see, too." He bounded toward us, wiping milk off his lips.

Jerry turned the small screen so we could all watch. This time, a white plastic bag tumbled across the field of view, catching on weeds as it went, before the breeze carried it out of sight.

Darkness closed in about five o'clock. Cora turned on the kitchen lights and started cutting up vegetables and chicken for stir fry. Jimmie and I sat on the floor to play a game of Rummikub. He won every match.

We ate, Cora joined the game, and Jerry returned to his office to work. The minutes ticked past. Literally. A grandmother clock stood in the front room on the side opposite Jerry's office, and we heard it whenever there was a lull in the game play. I wondered how many days in a row we'd be doing this before our mysterious prowler appeared again.

At exactly 7:17 Jerry's phone notified us of another incident within camera range. We immediately headed for the office, but we had missed the action. Jerry poked things, and the scene replayed. A small dark car crossed in front of the camera with its lights off.

"That's the car!" Jimmie yelled, as if we were in the next room.

"Let's go, troops," Jerry said.

58

We piled into Jerry's car again, and drove toward the abandoned restaurant.

We were still on the highway when Cora ordered, "Here, quick. Turn off your lights and coast to a stop by those bushes. We can get to the door faster than by driving around. Turn off the overhead light."

Jimmie reached up and fiddled with the buttons in the ceiling. "I think I got it. But how can we shut the doors quietly?"

"Do the best you can," Jerry said.

"Is the front door open, Jimmie?" I asked.

"Yup, all the locks are broken—you can just pull it open."

"OK, we'll go in that way," Jerry decided.

Before we had a chance to open any of the doors, a set of headlights appeared behind the building, coming down the service drive.

Cora whispered, "Who's that?"

"How should I know?" Jerry retorted. "But it must be a second car. The first car is parked where I can see a bit of it in the live feed."

Jimmie piped up, "This is our chance to get out. We have to close the doors all together and the person inside will think it's from the car that just drove in."

"Not perfect, but a great idea," Jerry said. "Open on three, and then close on three."

He counted, we slipped out in perfect synchronization, and shut the car doors quietly in near unison. If the person inside was paying attention the sound would be coming from the wrong place, but it was the best we could do.

"Stay low," Jimmie said. "We can follow this line of trees. It goes pretty close to the building, but then we'll have to run for the door."

"If I remember right, there's no entryway. The door just opens into the restaurant, right?" Jerry asked.

"Right," Jimmie said. "I think there were counters for the cash register and stuff on each side, but they got pulled out. You can see the stains on the floor where they were."

"You open the door, Jim," Jerry directed. "You know how it works."

I hoped Jimmie caught that his name had been upgraded by the senior male of our group, but I also hoped he missed that Jerry had adroitly planned things so the adults would enter the unknown inside situation first.

"OK, I can do that. She's probably in that corner again, where the tiles are loose."

Jimmie put himself in the lead, and when he reached the end of the tree line, he dropped to his belly and elbow-crawled to the front of the building. The door was glass, and I knew he was trying to stay as invisible as possible. He peered inside and started to inch backward toward us.

"What's he doing?" Cora whispered.

Jerry motioned her to be quiet, and we all moved back farther into the shelter of the trees until Jimmie was once again part of our group.

Jimmie reported. "The woman is in there, but somebody else is trying to get in the back door. She must have blocked it somehow. And I think there's a board jammed under the front door handle, too, like a two-by-four. If we can sneak around to the other side, there are big windows and we can see what they're doing."

"What's the best way to get there fast?" I asked him.

"We don't have any choice. The other person is out back, so we'll have to go across in front. If we go closer to the road, we can keep low in the ditch till we're past the door at least."

"All right. You lead us," Jerry said.

Jimmie folded himself into a pretzel and sort of squat-thrust himself, like R2D2, toward the road. I knew I couldn't do that, and Cora and Jerry were senior citizens, but somehow we managed to make it to the low ground of the ditch without being detected by the person or people in the building.

My left foot was suddenly engulfed in icy water at the bottom of the trench. I heard a sharp intake of breath beside me, and deduced Cora had also found the low spot.

Despite rough ground, wet feet, and walking in uncomfortable variations on remaining bent over, we slowly made our way past the far wall.

There, we turned and headed for the building. Only Jimmie was willing to drop to his belly, but the rest of us crawled behind him. Thankfully, it was dark, and the bottom of the windows was a good three feet above the surface of the parking lot.

Taking no time to rest, Jimmie positioned himself near a hole in the glass that had been stuffed with rags. He gently tugged them out, cupped a hand behind his ear and motioned for us to hurry. We got the message and hunkered down below the window ledge. Sounds were audible, but we couldn't make out what they were.

Cora tapped Jerry on the chest. I had no idea what she meant, but he did. He pulled his smart phone from an inside jacket pocket, punched at it and raised the instrument to the hole.

We were all seated below window level with our backs to the wall, but what we wanted— no conversation was necessary to know it was primary in all our minds— was to see in the windows. Jimmie was the first to turn and slowly raise his head above the sill. He made a quick circular motion with his lowered hand and then gestured for us to rise. Cautiously, we twisted, knelt and peered through the window.

Inside we saw a woman standing and facing the rear door. Her basic shape was outlined in the glow of the small penlight she carried, but most of what we saw was her back.

"That's her," Jimmie hissed in my ear.

I was all but certain the woman was Faye Dixon.

The rear door was rattling violently, and a length of pipe that had been jammed beneath the handle fell to the floor with a clatter. The door burst open, and Charlie Dixon entered with a gun in his hand. He pointed it at the woman. He might have seen us if he'd looked, but his attention was focused on Faye.

My ear was close to the hole in the window, with Jerry just beyond it, still holding his phone to the gap. I saw the dark scene being recorded. Faye began yelling, so it wasn't necessary to be near that hole. We all heard her.

"Charlie you get out of here. You've got nothing to do with this, and you're not getting involved."

Cora pulled Jimmie down to ground level. I heard her say softly, "Get away from the building, out of earshot. Call 9-1-1. Detective Milford."

Jimmie shook his head and indicated he wanted to stay and watch.

Cora formed her hand into a gun and pointed it at him. For a second I thought she wanted to shoot him, but she clarified. "They have a gun. We don't. Don't be stupid. You're fast. Go!"

59

Jimmie scooted away from the building on hands and feet, his butt in the air, like a dog with too-long hind legs, but it was faster than crawling. He reached the relative safety of the tree we'd stood beneath that morning and pulled something out of his back pocket, which I assumed was his phone. I sent a quick thanks into the universe that the sheriff's office was only a mile west and the village police a mile east of us.

Charlie was yelling now, and my attention was pulled back to the drama inside the building. We all heard him.

"I don't know what you're doing here, but I know you've been sneaking out an awful lot. This is where you come? What for?"

"That's none of your business," Faye snarled.

"I saw an email from Accounting Plus about the upcoming audit. You're the one who killed Milo. He was heading up the team that was looking at the township books, and you thought you could give yourself time to get away with the cash. Good God, Faye, I know you like money but what kind of person have you become?"

Faye laughed. "You're the one standing there with a gun."

"But I haven't killed anyone. Apparently you have. With drugs from my own store. People trust me. How could you do this?"

"So what if I did? I would have gotten away with it if you hadn't knocked off your 'dear father' and made everyone suspicious with all the pills floating around."

"You're crazy! I didn't kill him. We were friends— just not openly. He promised to leave me money; all I had to do was wait."

At this point, I realized it had not yet been released that Colin Mueller had committed suicide. Adele must have kept her mouth shut. At any rate, the news hadn't reached Charlie or Faye.

"Of course you killed him. And I'm going to say you killed Milo as well, to protect me. You won't be around to contradict me." With this pronouncement, Faye pulled a small handgun from her purse.

Charlie and Faye were in a complete standoff. If either one of them lost concentration, the other might fire.

"You won't kill me," Charlie stated, but he didn't sound absolutely positive.

"Just watch me."

"In front of witnesses? How many people do you plan to shoot?" Charlie nodded toward the window where our heads were apparently visible to him like a row of pumpkins in shadow. Or maybe shooting-gallery ducks.

"Get down," Jerry whispered.

Cora and I obeyed.

I wasn't fond of being shot at. I couldn't speak for Cora, but my guess was she hadn't planned on it either.

Jerry stood, pretending to brush off his clothes, but I think he was moving around to cover any motion someone on the inside might see as Cora and I ducked below the sill.

Then he said loudly, "Oh, for Pete's sake, this is ridiculous. I've been hiding out here like we're playing cowboys and Indians because I didn't know who was inside. Let's discuss this like adults."

"You keep your hands in sight, whoever you are," Faye demanded, turning toward us and raising her volume and pitch another notch.

Jerry had managed to prop the phone on the window sill, so it was still recording. How much memory space was on his card? Did it take less memory if it was only voice because the video was so dark? Strange things pass through your mind when stress levels are high. Hadn't there been enough time for a police unit to arrive?

"This is Jerry Caulfield. Mrs. Dixon, I'm going to come in the back door. Then we'll be two against one. I think you should both put down the guns."

He walked toward the rear of the building, but it was all

windows on this side. Despite the darkness, he was in plain view if either of the people inside decided to shoot, but he made it to the rear corner of the building and disappeared from our sight.

Just then, dark shapes emerged from the trees between the parking lot and Tansy Road. They were stooped over and running toward us.

"Don't be fooled, Caulfield," Faye yelled. But she sounded slightly less sure of herself. "I'm holding Charlie for the police. He killed Colin Mueller for his money, and then he killed Milo Sendak to protect me and get even more money. He came here tonight to kill me, too. You'd better take his gun away."

One of the shadowy shapes dropped in front of Cora and me. It separated into two pieces and became sheriff's deputies.

"Ma'am, what's going on right now?" one of them whispered.

"The front door's blocked. The back is open. There are two people inside with guns," I said.

"Charlie and Faye Dixon," Cora added. "But Jerry's going in there anyway. Please stop him."

A shot rang out, and the window beyond us splintered and crashed to the ground. Bits of glass scattered like glitter. I felt a tingling on my cheek. When I put a hand to my face it came away wet. Cora's braided hair was covered with sparkles, but I saw no blood on her.

"Jerry," Cora called anxiously.

Now Faye knew that Jerry wasn't alone.

"Please keep quiet and remain calm," the deputy said. "We'll have this under control in a few minutes." He moved away, and the female officer that accompanied him stayed with us.

A few seconds later, I heard an electronic pop, and a voice distorted by a bullhorn filled the air.

"Faye Dixon, this is Officer Vincent of the sheriff's department. Come out with your hands up. The building is surrounded."

I heard crunching glass and turned my head to see Jerry crouch-walking awkwardly toward us.

"I made them let me come back here to show you I'm all right," he said to Cora.

She pulled him down beside her and gave him a big kiss on the cheek. It was the most overt display of affection toward him I'd ever seen her make except at their wedding. He responded by holding her close, protectively surrounding her tiny frame.

From inside, Faye's voice rose in a shriek. "Charlie's a killer. He came here to shoot me, just like he did away with Milo and his own father. He's crazy, I tell you. I'm just trying to protect myself."

There were several seconds of silence.

The bullhorn blared again. "Mrs. Dixon, Charlie has surrendered his weapon, and we're waiting for you to do the same."

Her answer was another shot. No glass broke this time, but it sounded as if the bullet went through the back wall. I had to give the officers credit. They did not respond with a blaze of gunfire, which probably would have killed her. Instead, I heard a scuffling inside the building. Faye screamed and spouted a string of words I won't repeat.

Milford's gruff voice was heard next, from inside. "We've got her. She's disarmed. We're coming out the front."

The darkness made everything seem dreamlike, even though my eyes had adjusted. I stood up and faced the front door, expecting to see the detective emerge with Faye in restraints, when another disembodied voice yelled, "Yippie." Suddenly Jimmie barreled into me from behind. He hugged me and jumped up and down simultaneously, practically rattling my teeth.

"I told him how to get in through the office! That's how they caught her. I told them Jerry got it all on video! We did it, Ana. We're heroes, and we saved the drugstore, and the druggist, and the township money, and... hey, you're bleeding."

60

Talk about a whopper of a story for the Thanksgiving week issue of the Cherry Hill Herald! The only problem was the paper was scheduled to be printed in just a few hours. Jerry had thought the page layouts were all done and proofed, ready to be sent to the machine that prepares the offset plates for the press.

Instead, Jerry, Cora and I stayed up all night, re-writing the front page stories, and adding a single page insert EXTRA of interviews given by all the major players. All of us except Faye. She was in the county jail. Charlie bought a quarter page ad for the drugstore.

Jimmie was a trooper. He insisted on staying with us until three in the morning, when I delivered him to his house to get a few hours of sleep before school. It turned out that he was a decent proof-reader for a fourteen-year-old. He'd have first rights to telling the story to his classmates. The printed version of our adventure didn't hit the streets until well after the school day started.

We couldn't leave out Adele. She had identified Cubby as the mysterious C. I called her, and she came over to be interviewed. She and Cora kept the coffee flowing and hot buttered biscuits coming while Jerry and I pounded the keyboards. When we ran out of copy, she bought an ad for Volger's Grocery to fill the remaining space. She bowed out around two since the store had to be opened at eight.

I slept almost all of Wednesday and rose early Thursday to drive to Mackinac City to meet Chad for our Thanksgiving meal. I had a whopper of a story to tell him.

As it later turned out, the video portion of Jerry's recording was useless, but the audio was clear, even though it wasn't admissible as evidence. After it was played for Faye Dixon, however, she didn't have much starch left in her claim that Charlie had done all the killings and planned to kill her, too. She confessed.

She'd spent enough time around the pharmacy that it was easy to learn how much oxycodone was required to load up a capsule with a lethal dose. She'd fixed only one and slipped it into Milo's pill bottle after Charlie had filled the prescription and placed the envelope in the bin with other orders. It was random chance that Milo had taken that single pill first thing after opening the new bottle.

Cherry Hill got to keep its drugstore and its favorite druggist, Charlie Dixon. He smiled more than he ever had before. Was it the money, or was it that Faye was no longer around? She was sent to state prison for life. Rumor has it he filed for divorce although I haven't asked him.

Even though the drugstore will never be a huge source of income, Charlie's inheritance from Colin Mueller gives him a financial cushion that allows him to keep the local business open. It seems fitting that money made primarily in Cherry Hill will stay here.

Charlie and Cubby have become close friends as well as accepting that they are half brothers. In fact, Cubby stopped drifting and apparently is finding his niche. He has enrolled in an online college and is working toward a pharmacy degree. He's employed almost full-time at the drugstore, learning the rest of the business. Of course, he also got a sixth of that pile of money Colin Mueller had amassed.

There was cash in the envelope hidden at the old Cherry Blossom Restaurant. Lots of cash. Almost all the money missing from the Shashawqua Township treasury was there. That was really good news. Apparently Faye had planned to leave town with her stash the very night we caught her. A packed suitcase was found in her car and one airline ticket to the Maldives. Nice climate, no extradition treaty.

One Saturday when I was Christmas shopping in Emily City, I saw Helen Bracket and Tim Statler walking down the sidewalk together, pushing Robbie in a stroller. Hamilton Nelson might not have left his little Ellie a huge fortune, but it was looking as if the chain of events it set in motion might bring happiness to her life. She deserves that, I thought.

Lucille moved to Marquette before Christmas. Her house had not yet sold, but its picture appeared on all the real estate flyers in town. Adele said a house of that size wouldn't sell easily, and it looks as if she's probably right. She usually is, as we all well know.

Oh, that blood on my face? A shard of glass punctured a small hole in my cheek and left a permanent dimple. Jimmie says it looks cute. I think he's getting a little fresh. Teenagers!

Notes and Acknowledgements

In any mystery story there are factual details that need to be checked so that savvy readers don't stumble over incorrect procedures or legal steps. Since the Dead Mule Swamp books are never specifically located other than the Upper Midwest near US Highway 10, one could possibly place them in Michigan, Wisconsin or Minnesota. I have purposely chosen to remain ambiguous as to location. My goal has been to make everything familiar, but nothing exactly recognizable.

However, the laws of each state differ on many points. Therefore, I had to choose one state in which to make portions of this plot follow the regulations concerning safe deposit boxes, wills and other minor details. Hopefully, accuracy has been achieved. Many of the regulations and requirements for other civil issues are available on line, which makes research for authors much easier than it used to be.

I would like to thank Nancy J. Sanford, Retail Banking Officer, of West Shore Bank for providing information about how to solve the safe-deposit-box key dilemma.

The names for the village of Shagway and Shashawqua Township are based on a real person of the Ottawa tribe, Henry Shagway. In actual fact, a road was named for him, but never a village or township. He lived from 1872-1953 and is one of the few recorded local Native Americans of the time period. He was the oldest of several children with the last name Sha-shaw-qua, which became Anglicized to Shagway.

Henry bought land, built a log cabin and later a barn and house. That barn is now an historic place restored by Great Lakes Barn Preservation. It served as home to the Shagway Arts Barn, created and operated by Nancy Lynn Miller, to whom this book is dedicated. See shagwayartsbarn.com

Henry Shagway's log cabin, which still stands. (photo by jhy)

Henry Shagway barn and granary, photo probably taken by Eunice Shagway, sister of Henry. Dated around 1940. Provided courtesy of Renee Bailey, great-great niece of Henry.

Henry Shagway Barn as it appears currently, home of the Shagway Arts Barn. Photo by Nancy Lynn Miller.

Many thanks to my Beta Readers: Ester Lamb, Catherine MacKenzie, Dawn Kumm, and Ken Brown. They caught many lingering mistakes, grammar and tense issues. West Side Gang writers' group provided encouragement and early feedback and critique.

As always, any errors in the final text are solely those of the author.

Joan H. Young, December 2017

In *Dead Mule Swamp Mistletoe* there's a ski holiday, a collection of people with strong animosities, a blizzard, and... you know what's going to happen!

1

The shadow separated itself from the black mold speckling the basement wall, creeping forward, a stealthy echo of shoulders, hips, and torso. Its head bulged with cancerous growths and serrations inflicted by the litter of bottles, pots, and a circular saw strewn haphazardly on rusting shelves. Slithering onward, the shape surrendered its bumps and notches with casual ease.

Quietly, quietly. Don't make a sound. It has to be here. Forgotten places. Mustn't forget. Mustn't forget.

2

Silver and blue glitter sprinkled across the black granite kitchen island. Jerry pushed the expensive creamy square of thick, hand-pressed paper toward me, the invitation sparkling with giant embossed snowflakes. "Come with us, Ana," he said.

"Do say yes," Cora agreed.

After all, what else could I say? Jerry and Cora were two of the best friends I'd made since moving to Forest County five years ago. I could hardly believe it had been that long since I'd kissed Roger goodbye. Not literally. I'd felt more like beating in his head with a crowbar when he decided to spend the rest of his life with a bedmate named Brian. I'd held my temper, and instead of a jail sentence ended up with a not-so-small fortune in alimony. Each and every month a sizable amount of cash was added to the assets of the local bank, via my account: in the name of Anastasia Raven. I was surprised to discover I didn't feel the slightest guilt at taking money I hadn't worked for.

Somehow, right after I moved here, I got involved with sorting out the details of several suspicious deaths. Jerry eventually made me the local crime reporter. However, the most serious crime in more than a year was when the Morris boys set fire to their father's boat shed because he pulled up their not-quite-secret-enough marijuana crop. Oh, and Sarah Kellogg sliced her husband Prentice across his beer belly with a steak knife one evening when they'd both had a few too many. He laughed all the way to the hospital, didn't press charges, and rumor has it they're expecting another girl.

It's fine with me that no one seems bent on murdering a neighbor. I'll happily focus on DUIs and poaching in my regular column for the weekly paper.

Thus, unnatural death was the furthest thing from my mind that December. My only child, Chad, was coming to my house for Christmas, his last holiday as a student. In a few months he'd graduate from Michigan Tech, a newly-minted Master of Applied Ecology. Yes, Chad was coming.

"But what about Chad?" I blurted.

"Perfect!" Cora said. "He's welcome too. We've been told to bring two guests." She held up the coffee carafe and raised an eyebrow at me.

I slid my mug in her direction. "What exactly is this party?" I asked, suspecting the glitter might have temporarily dazzled my brain and muddled my thinking.

Jerry explained. "The event is at that big old mansion over at Janes Mill Fork, they call it Janes Mill Bed and Breakfast. You know the place. It's one of the few inholdings remaining within Thousand Lakes State Forest."

"That turret you can just see above the trees from the canoe rental place?" I asked.

Cora nodded, filling Jerry's cup as well. "That's it. Henry Janes cut a mill race in 1867 and built the shingle mill the next year. The big house came later, after he'd made a million. One of the richest men in the state."

"Anyway," Jerry said, cutting off what might possibly become a long exposition by Cora on the history of lumbering in the area, "Frank and Betty Farnsworth own it now. He used to be publisher of the Emily City Ledger; now he's the owner, but he likes to keep a hand in the day-to-day operations. Professionally, I feel somewhat obligated to show up. It would be much more pleasant if you'd come."

I turned over the frosty invitation. "Three days! The party lasts three whole days?"

"Why not?" Jerry tossed back. "They've turned the place into a posh bed and breakfast. At least, it's upper-crust by Forest County standards. I'd guess this is some sort of tax write-off."

"We've saved the best enticement for last," Cora said, a smug smile crossing her face.

"Which is?"

"You'll never guess who's catering the party."

Even Jerry was grinning now. They were right, I couldn't imagine what could make the food service arrangements have any bearing on my decision. Then it hit me... just as Cora said, "Jimmie Mosher."

Jimmie's obsession was to reestablish the Cherry Blossom Restaurant once owned by his deceased father. Details, such as the fact he was only sixteen, were minor annoyances to be overcome or waited out. "How is he able to do this?" I asked.

"His mother registered the business in her name," Jerry explained. "They're renting the old school kitchen at the museum because it's approved by the health department."

"I think we're getting special privileges to bring extra guests because we rescued their plans from disaster when we suggested Jimmie's new Cherry Blossom Cuisine," Jerry added.

"Disaster?" I asked. "That's a strong word."

Cora nodded knowingly, "They opened the B and B so recently they don't have a full staff for the winter yet, and couldn't get anyone to do food over Christmas. I think Betty Farnsworth doesn't like it when she can't get what she wants."

PUBLISHED WORKS BY JOAN H. YOUNG

Non-Fiction:
>North Country Cache: Adventures on a National Scenic Trail (2005 Independent Publishers, third place Regional Non-fiction)
>North Country Quest: Completing my National Scenic Trail Adventure
>Would You Dare?
>Devotions for Hikers
>Get Off the Couch with Joan
>Fall Off the Couch Laughing

Fiction:
Anastasia Raven Mysteries
>News from Dead Mule Swamp
>The Hollow Tree at Dead Mule Swamp
>Paddy Plays in Dead Mule Swamp
>Bury the Hatchet in Dead Mule Swamp
>Dead Mule Swamp Druggist
>Dead Mule Swamp Mistletoe
>Dead Mule Swamp Singer

Dubois Files Mysteries for Children
>The Secret Cellar
>The Hitchhiker
>The ABZ Affair
>The Bigg Boss
>The Lonely Donkey

Other
>Accidentally Yours- a chaotic collection of short works

ABOUT THE AUTHOR

Joan H. Young has enjoyed the out-of-doors her entire life. Highlights of her outdoor adventures include Girl Scouting, which provided yearly training in camp skills, the opportunity to engage in a ten-day canoe trip, and numerous short backpacking excursions. She was selected to attend the 1965 Senior Scout Roundup in Coeur d'Alene, Idaho, an international event to which 10,000 girls were invited. She rode a bicycle from the Pacific to the Atlantic Ocean in 1986, and on August 3, 2010 became the first woman to complete the North Country National Scenic Trail on foot. Her mileage totaled 4395 miles. She often writes and gives media programs about her outdoor experiences.

In 2010 she began writing more fiction, including several award-winning short stories. *Dead Mule Swamp Druggist* is the fifth story in the Anastasia Raven mystery series.

Visit booksleavingfootprints.com for more information.